HER LADY TO LOVE

Visit us at www.boldstrokesbooks.com

HER LADY TO LOVE

by
Jane Walsh

2020

Credits
Editor: Cindy Cresap
Production Design: Susan Ramundo
Cover Design By Tammy Seidick

Acknowledgments

It has been a lifelong dream of mine to write a romance novel. I am thrilled to have the dream come true with Bold Strokes Books and am so grateful to everyone on the team for their warm welcome. I would like to particularly thank my editor, Cindy Cresap, for all of the work that she has done on this book and also for the invaluable help she has given me to develop my skills as a writer.

I couldn't have completed this novel without the support of my wife, Mag. Thank you for showing up at the coffee shop when I struggled with deadlines, for your tireless cheerleading every step of the way, and for offering hugs and kind words whenever I was worried that I should toss all of these pages in the shredder. I owe so much to your keen editorial eye when I was working on those last drafts.

I would also like to thank my friend Anastasia for always supporting my dreams, no matter what they are. The instant that I decided I was serious about finishing a novel, you swooped in with gifts of reference books and buckets of encouragement and it was exactly what I needed.

To the East Coast crew—thank you for helping to make me the person I am today. Your lifelong friendships have meant more to me than words can ever express.

And finally, to my parents—thank you for filling our house with laughter, love, and bookshelves as far as the eye could see.

Dedication

For my own lady to love, Mag

CHAPTER ONE

London, 1813

Miss Jacqueline Lockhart stood at the edge of the ballroom with her dearest friend and only true confidante, Miss Beatrice Everson. At twenty-six years of age, and two weeks after having her heart broken, Jacquie knew to the bottom of her very soul that she had never looked better. She could only hope that everyone else could see it too.

She realized that she was snapping her fan back and forth, faster and faster. Although all she wanted to do was toss her dance card aside and flee the scene for yet another evening of wallowing alone in her bedchambers, she had made a promise to herself when the footman announced her arrival at the ball. This would be the night that she proved to herself that she could move on from love lost.

The woman who had destroyed her happiness was here somewhere tonight.

So although her nerves had her wanting to worry the edge of her lace sleeve and fuss with the pearl combs in her curls, Jacquie refused to fidget and reveal her discomfort. Instead, she relaxed into a careless pose and slowed her fan to a languid flutter. She knew from long experience that the gentlemen found a mix of pertness and affected boredom irresistible. Right now, her bruised ego craved nothing more than to feel adored.

"Oh, Beatrice, is it possible that the dancing is even *worse* here than it is usually at these events?" she sighed dramatically, her voice pitched high enough to be overheard.

Beatrice's laugh tinkled out above the din, and several interested men drifted their way. She waved her fan and smiled at them while she spoke to Jacquie. "You would know, my dear. I vow you haven't sat out for a dance all season. You've had your choice of men around you at every turn."

Their eyes met as they shared a secret smile. Jacquie's heart swelled with gratitude. Bea would always be there for her and would never let her down.

A well-dressed aristocrat wandered over to them and bowed. "Miss Lockhart, I could not help but to overhear your comments on the quality of dancing tonight! It must be my heaven-sent duty to entertain an angel such as yourself and to prove that there is some hope for the evening yet." He twirled her away for a rousing country set.

Jacqueline loved to dance. Her popularity had been assured since her first season by her graceful twirls, teasing demeanor, ready smiles, and wit. The betting books in the gentlemen's clubs were always full of wagers placed on which lucky man would win her heart. In six long London seasons, no man had been lucky enough to win three dances in an evening, a precursor to an engagement, but many men boasted that they were the one, and this was the year.

Jacqueline was not unaware of the gossip, and many times she laughed with her friends about her eager swains, knowing that she did nothing to encourage them toward serious thoughts of matrimony but that they were ever ready to try, try again.

In truth, sometimes it was a little exhausting.

Tonight, it was excruciating.

She hadn't been to a single social event since that terrible night that her lover had told her it was over. Lydia, the widowed Countess of Straund, had sat her down in her charming townhouse with its charming bedroom and revealed with a charming little laugh that it had been merely the thrill of having a widow's freedom that had pushed her into the arms of another woman.

Tonight, she meant to show Lydia—to show *everyone*—that she was in demand, popular as ever. London was still at her feet. She was worth it all. The countess had made a mistake, but the mistake hadn't been their love. It had been giving it up.

Her maid had spent an age making sure that she looked like perfection tonight. But although a beautiful gown and sparkling jewels and inviting smiles could fool everyone around her into thinking that nothing was wrong, it couldn't erase the knowledge that she had spent hours sobbing into her pillows that afternoon. The beginnings of a headache started to throb at her temples.

The dance ended and she took her place again at the edge of the ballroom beside Beatrice, who shook her head.

"If you truly don't want him, Jacquie, you could save him for those of us who do!" she exclaimed, her eyes following the man who was leaving the ballroom for the card room. "Only one set he wanted to dance, and with you. Lucky, lucky you, but unfortunate are the lonely ladies of London!"

Jacqueline sighed, tired of the charade, though they had only arrived at the ball an hour ago.

Bea's face was serious. "I mean it. If you aren't interested in him, you don't need to encourage him."

This was not the reaction that she had expected. Bea was not an uncritical friend, but she had been there every moment for her during the past few weeks, listening to her endless tirades about lost love and heartless harpies, stroking her hair and drying her tears. She had thought that tonight of all nights, Bea would be sympathetic to her.

Stung, Jacqueline snapped, "Oh, the marquis doesn't want me—and you know perfectly well that I have never encouraged a man to anything more than a dance."

Beatrice smiled while her eyelashes fluttered at the nearby men with practiced effort. "Say what you will, my dear, but haven't you the least interest in snaring a husband now? Your future could be settled with the merest snap of your fingers. You could forget all about Lydia."

"You know I don't want to wed," she said, evading her gaze.

"What you want is not always the best thing for you." Beatrice's tone was flat, and her eyes held a warning that Jacqueline had never seen before. Or perhaps she just had never noticed before. "The countess is just the most recent in a long line of heartbreaks. Aren't you tired of it? Maybe it's time to put aside dalliances and flirtations."

Jacqueline's eyes narrowed. "I loved her. And besides, *you* never minded being a dalliance," she said.

Beatrice shook her head. "What we had together was a pleasurable pastime. And I enjoyed every moment of it, as you well know. But it's not the real world, is it? Isn't it time for us both to look to the future? And doesn't that mean marriage?"

She gasped. "If you wish to wed, you are more than free to do so! I have certainly never prevented you nor discouraged you!"

It was true that she never thought much about the future. Why should she, when there were so many amusements and diversions in the present moment? If she ever stopped to consider it, she had thought that neither she nor Beatrice would ever move on to marriage.

She supposed that had been naive.

"If you want the marquis, marry the marquis. He is nothing to me."

"But you are more than nothing to him," Beatrice retorted. "You take up the air in a room, Jacqueline, and you don't even notice it. Men are drawn to you long before they pay me any mind. How do you think you end up with very best looking men every time, when you don't even care for them?"

"That is rubbish, Bea," she said. "You are beautiful, and you never lack for dance partners or escorts to the opera or rides in a gentleman's curricle! If you have decided to marry, then marry you will—and I promise to make sure that you marry *well*."

Jacquie reached out and squeezed her hand, a flash of pure love welling out from her heart. Perhaps they could console each other tonight. Forget about the countess, forget about weddings. They could take comfort in each other's arms, as they had done countless times before.

Beatrice squeezed back, but after the briefest moment withdrew her hand. "You see? These dalliances must end, and I must turn my eyes to others. I will never find a man to marry if I am distracted by what has always been between us."

For the first time, Jacqueline was struck with astonishment. They had been youthful lovers, kissing during stolen moments at their finishing school, then in a burst of excitement and passion during their first season. Every moment seemed so intense, so overwhelming, so very grown up—and their love had sizzled and burned bright. But after the first year or so, they had turned to being only occasional lovers while maintaining a close friendship.

Jacqueline had never imagined a time where they were not casually interested in each other. A pang of loss ran through her, a loss that she had never anticipated and thus it hurt all the more.

Beatrice smiled. "Don't look so forlorn, Jacquie! I said I wanted to marry, not move to the Americas and never see you again!"

The moment broke and they laughed together.

They were still laughing when Sir Phineas Snow sauntered up to them. Jacqueline beamed at him, her spirits brightened. He had an air of fashion that had young men forever aping his cravats and older men taking note of the height of his heels, which made him just the sort of friend she wanted most to see tonight. Surely he could entertain her with gossip and distract her from heartache.

"What's the news, fair ladies?" he drawled in greeting. "Please tell me anything and everything. I am laid low with ennui and need to borrow your good cheer."

Jacquie tapped his arm with her feathered fan. "Sir Phineas! We were just laughing about the odds of us ever visiting the colonies. Beatrice says she thinks it will never happen, but I say, bring on the adventure!"

He smiled. Jacquie had never once met a man who sparked her interest, either romantic or carnal, but she could understand the masculine appeal every time he smiled like that. Even though it had been out of fashion for decades, he was fond of affixing a beauty mark below his left eye, and when he smiled it drew attention to his beautiful eyes. He had a way of looking at someone like they were the only two in the room.

"Sir Phineas! Lud, what is this? Darling, you know I've told you to call me Phin almost since the very day that we met. So formal you are tonight!"

He drew his hand up above his eyes, pretending to scan the ballroom. "Where is my lighthearted Jacquie who can down a bottle of champagne and challenge a man to cards?"

She bit her lip and cast her eyes down, feeling the weight of her failed relationship press down on her again.

"Our dear Jacquie is mourning love lost," Bea said.

Jacqueline shot her an annoyed look. She smiled, and Jacquie knew her well enough to understand that this was retribution for their argument over the marquess. Beatrice was loyal, but Jacquie was well acquainted with her selfish streak. She always wanted to win a point, whether or not they agreed that they were playing a game.

Phin idly unlooped the handle of her ivory fan from her slack wrist and started fanning himself. "A love affair gone wrong! I knew I had not seen you in recent weeks, my dear. I was pining for your presence. Were you holed up in your chambers all this time, wailing and rending your frocks? Do tell all."

"There is not much to say, Phin. I was involved with someone. And now that person has moved on to someone else."

Jacqueline made a move to grab her fan, but Phin scowled at her. "It's bloody warm in here. Let a man cool down, my dear."

"It was the Countess of Straund," Bea piped up. "I think she was rather a bore."

Jacquie fumed. Bea had stroked her hair just the other evening and had agreed that the countess was quite the most intelligent woman in London.

Phin snapped her fan closed and tapped her on the hand. "You shall find yourself another lover soon enough."

"I don't want another lover," she said, hating the petulance in her tone. "I am done with love."

He twinkled down at her. "My dear, those are the very magic words that will guarantee that love is not yet done with you. Love can present itself to you whether you are looking or not. In fact…look before you! A potential lover awaits." He wiggled his brows.

Jacquie laughed. "It matters not how many times you make the same offer. Many apologies, my dear friend, but my reply is never going to change." She patted him on the arm.

Beatrice rolled her eyes and tossed her brown curls over her shoulder. "Phin, if you're going to bother us, then make yourself useful, please! Bring me a suitor—I wish to marry this season."

He bowed again. "My dearest Bea, your wish is my heart's desire. I present…myself."

"Phin, I am *serious*! Are you never so?" Bea tittered as Phin spun her around and then kissed her hand.

He looked down his nose at her. "I am serious, dear Bea. I make no frequent offers of my hand in matrimony. In some circles, I assure you that my name has value enough to be sought after. But the offer is on the table only for the duration of tonight's ball, so are you quite sure that neither of you want to become Mrs. Phineas Snow of Sudbury?"

Wrinkling her nose at him, Beatrice replied, "I assure you, I do not want to become your wife! Honestly, Phin. You've slept your way through half of the *ton*—and you make your money at the gambling tables."

"You wound me, Bea," he said, pressing his hand to his heart and shaking his head. "Only *half* the *ton*? You have not been paying attention to my exploits at all, have you?"

She ignored him and tapped her finger against her chin. "I think I am looking for someone younger than you. Certainly richer. And titled."

He pulled a face in mock outrage. "And when did you become such a snob? Just because I am not of the peerage doesn't mean that I don't have impressive attributes to offer." He winked. "And I do mean impressive."

Jacqueline gave him a push. "We have established many times that you are not the man for either of us, you shameless flirt. Now—do you have any leads for Beatrice? Any lord would do, I would think."

"Now *you* aren't paying attention, Jacquie!" Bea scowled at her. "Not just 'any lord' will do for me. You are quite forgetting *rich*. I have had enough of saving my pin money for dresses and would very much like to move on to larger coffers to suit my spending habits."

Beatrice smoothed her mint green silk dress over her hips and twisted to admire the way it clung to her. Jacqueline felt the old familiar tug of desire deep inside her. Sighing, she reminded herself to focus. She needed to remember that Bea no longer wanted to go down that same path with her.

"You would look all the rage in rags," Phin told her with every appearance of sincerity. "But I can understand the need for money." He readjusted his diamond encrusted cravat pin with a smirk.

He frowned down at them. "In fact, both of you should be looking for the best possible match. Jacquie, my love, have you set your cap for anyone this season? It would be just the thing to distract you from your romantic entanglements. Nothing kills the idea of romance quicker than sitting across from a gentleman every morning eating kippers and speaking of nothing but hunting pheasants and fixing the tenant's broken fence."

She pursed her lips. Her parents were forever urging her to wed, but she was far from ready to settle down with some tedious lord and raise a brood of tedious children and get together with a group of tedious matrons for tea and commiseration every week. Surely her parents would understand and grant her one more season to enjoy herself, wouldn't they?

Her parents had been content for years of waiting in vain for a nobleman to offer his hand in matrimony to their only daughter. But this season, Jacquie sensed their patience was wearing thin. A mere mister would have never been considered worthy of her hand in previous seasons, but her mother's flights of fancy could change that notion at any moment, as it did with most things.

From across the room, Jacqueline could see her mother gossiping with her gaggle of friends. She gave her a little wave. Her mother either didn't see her or didn't care to pause her conversation to acknowledge the greeting, and she straightened her spine.

"No, this will not be the year that I marry," she said. "We shall busy ourselves making Bea's dreams come true. I will have to make do with the society of friendship."

Phin raised a brow. "If you won't consider marriage, then a dalliance must be what you need, darling. You need a woman in your bed to get over the countess."

Dear man, she thought. He was the only one besides Beatrice who knew of her amorous exploits with other women. Jacqueline enjoyed flirting with men though they held no romantic interest for her, and she had a certain reputation among society matrons for being fast— she did like to sit at the gaming tables and laugh too much and drink too many glasses of wine. She suspected it was why she was never invited to the highest of highbrow events, and why many women in society ignored her at the events that she did choose to attend.

The opinions of the sticklers of society never bothered her. London was large enough to find plenty of other women who were happy to pay a great deal of attention to her. Cautious about whom she invited to her bed, she took great care with her secret and was proud that no one in society seemed to guess at her proclivity for a beautiful woman.

Beatrice snapped at a passing footman and took a glass of wine for herself and for Jacquie. "Here you are, dear," she said as she pressed the glass into her hand. "Of course you can get over Lady Straund, and you don't need another lover to mend your heart. Just let time heal your wounds." Her dark brown eyes shone with concern.

Again, Jacqueline felt the pull between them. It would be so easy to be drawn into Bea's embrace tonight. It was always easy between them. So unlike the wild passion she had shared with Lydia. Her hateful words rang through her ears.

She willed herself to forget about Lydia and tossed the contents of the wine down in one unladylike swallow. She could hear a group of debutantes behind them titter at her, but she refused to blush. Let them think what they would and judge her!

She took Bea's wine and gulped it down as well, feeling a delicious warmth spread through her. "I have no thoughts of love, my dears, whether it's some old lord warming my bank account or a lovely lass warming…other things."

Phin gave her a doubtful look.

"There will be another woman out there for you one day, if you don't wish to turn your focus on marriage now," Bea said.

"Perhaps I don't want anyone, ever again." Narrowing her eyes, she reached out for Phin's wine glass, but he moved it away.

"Now, now, my little pullet," he cooed. "Keep your wits about you. Bea is right. Another woman is what you need right now to distract you."

She sighed. "I am telling you, I don't want *anyone*. Please do let me enjoy the season alone. I want to picnic with the Anderson twins on a warm day like we did last year, and I want Mr. Monteroy to take me out in a rowboat again at his estate where he always throws the very best parties with the wittiest people, and I want to play endless rounds of cards with my pin money. Is it so very much to ask?"

"Yes," they replied in unison.

Phin took Jacquie's arm. "This is nothing that can't be fixed by dancing," he declared, and in what felt like the blink of an eye, he whisked her away to join the other couples on the dance floor.

"You're going rather fast," she gasped, half breathless with laughter and exertion. "Phin, do be careful! I value my feet, even if you don't seem to!"

He grinned and continued to maneuver her with purpose among the dancers, sweeping them from one corner of the ballroom to the other. After the first set, Jacquie saw why he had been so careful in their destination.

Heartless, faithless Lydia was on the dance floor with a middle-aged man, laughing up at him, clutching his arm like a lifeline.

Jacquie had known that she was engaged again—this was the real reason that Lydia had broken off their affair. But it was one dreadful thing to know of the engagement, and quite another and much more appalling thing to see the pairing in the flesh. Lush beauty dancing with an old moneyed beast.

"Phin, I am not ready to see her again," she whispered, plucking at his arm with nerveless fingers. "We need to leave the dance floor. Now."

His hand clamped down on her own. "If you don't want a new lover, then what you need is closure with your old lover. Look at her and remember why she is not good enough for you."

"She was the one who parted ways with me," she pointed out.

"But that does not mean that she is in the right, or that you should have stayed with her."

The second set started up again, and Jacquie felt dizzy as she tried to keep her eye on the countess as she whirled around in Phin's arms. Lydia looked radiant tonight. She wore that silky champagne-hued dress that Jacquie had last seen draped over the chair in her sitting room. Jacquie remembered when that smile had been directed at her, when that laugh had rung in her own ears. Now they were aimed at some man who didn't deserve her. Had he seen that dress strewn on the furniture yet? Consumed by jealousy, she was on fire to know.

Lydia caught sight of Jacquie, and her smile faded. She looked away.

Jacquie could bear it no longer. She pressed her hand hard against Phineas's shoulder, but the dratted man was as immovable as a rock. "Please, let us leave the dancing!"

Panicked, she pushed again with as much force as she could muster, but then they were off balance, their limbs twisting against each other, falling. It was no surprise at all when they crashed into another person.

Jacqueline stumbled and, flailing, reached out to try to secure her balance. She connected with a smooth arm and fell against a beautifully endowed bosom. Her eyes flew from lace-covered breasts mere inches from her face up to a cool pair of gray eyes and a long narrow face. Her blond hair fell in gentle curls to her shoulders.

Jacqueline straightened but kept her hand on the other woman's arm. It was so soft and inviting. She couldn't quite bring herself to relinquish it just yet.

Phin exclaimed, "My lady, I do apologize for falling into you! I misjudged where I was swinging this enchanting armful and I put us right in your path, where you ought to have been safe." He bowed to her. "Please tell me you are unhurt?"

"It is such a crush tonight," she said, her voice soft and cultured and captivating. "I was pushed as someone made their way past me, and I ended up quite in your laps." She inclined her head at them. "As you can see, I am fine."

Jacquie realized that she was still clasping the woman's arm, and she let go with a pang of regret. "I am so glad that you are not harmed by our clumsiness. Please forgive me for intruding upon your person in such a way!"

The woman wasn't familiar to her, and she wondered if she was new to society. One thing she knew was that wherever she was from, if she had known what it would feel like to be thrust up against her, she would have sought her out much earlier.

"Your apology is accepted," the woman said. Jacquie hung on her words, mesmerized by her voice. "I am certain I am to blame. I should not have been so close to the dancing." She nodded to Phin after a moment.

Jacqueline hastily introduced herself and Phin.

The woman curtsied. "I am Lady Honora Banfield. It is a pleasure to meet you both."

She perused them in silence. Jacqueline thrilled under her eyes, feeling awareness in every nerve. Her gaze felt like a lover's touch, sweet and heated. She took a deep breath and exhaled only when she moved a step back. The teasing scent of roses lingered in the air. Her perfume? Her soap? She ached to know more.

"I don't think there is any lasting damage to you," Lady Honora murmured. "You look well enough. Your hem is untorn." A faint smile touched her lips. "I can see just the faintest smudge of dirt on your shoes from where I must have tread on them, Miss Lockhart."

Jacquie looked down. Her white satin slippers were a little gray around the toe, but they would not have lasted beyond the evening anyway, with all of the dancing she tended to put her shoes through every chance she got.

"I shall leave you to the dancing. I do hope you enjoy the rest of your evening." She nodded at them again and walked away, leaving Jacqueline with stars in her eyes and the faint scent of summer roses lingering in her nose.

As soon as she was out of earshot, Phin grinned at her and crowed, "What a success! That could not have gone better. A new woman to set your sights on already. Don't you think Lady Honora had plenty of space to avoid us, though? Our hostess would be *lucky* to have the gossip columns calling her ball the barest squeeze! I wonder if she may have even let me push her into you on purpose."

Jacqueline shook her head and tried to clear the image of the perfect woman away. "I won't pretend that it was a hardship to be against her, but I told you, I want nothing more to do with women right now! I am quite off the market for even a single heated look, let alone a kiss or more," she said.

Phin said nothing but gave her a knowing smile.

She shook her head again and took his arm. "Now Phin, let's focus and arrange Bea's hand in marriage to some eligible bloke. That shall be a task to keep us all occupied, and away from wayward thoughts of pretty women."

Chapter Two

L ady Honora Banfield sipped watered down wine from a crystal glass and watched Miss Lockhart and Miss Everson across the ballroom, entertaining their bevy of gentlemen admirers. She wasn't a creature of impulse, but she was coming to the conclusion that drastic measures would need to be taken in order to steal away a suitor.

Nora had been overcome by a rare reckless fancy when she had stumbled into Miss Lockhart. If only she had the nerve to have parlayed the chance encounter into a dance with Sir Phineas. He didn't have the title that she was looking for, but this was the third ball she had attended since her arrival in London, and she was tired of sitting out for most of the dancing.

In most situations, she would have considered it the height of mortification to bump into someone at a ball. But there was something so intriguing about Miss Jacqueline Lockhart that had glued her feet to the floor, instead of propelling her to scurry away after a muttered apology. She radiated warmth and welcome, and something cold and locked inside her had felt a little ease in her presence.

Lingering against Miss Lockhart's supple form had felt shockingly immodest. She took another sip of her wine and tried to calm her agitated nerves. She hoped it had appeared to be an innocent encounter, no matter how she had felt while pressed against her. Nothing could have prepared her for the warmth of that hand on her arm, and the sparkle in those emerald green eyes from such close quarters. She shook her head to try to clear the memory away. After all, the odds of Miss Lockhart being interested in her were slim, and she wasn't in London to indulge herself. She couldn't let herself be distracted by a winsome smile.

Aunt Mildred swept by and swooped away her glass of half-finished wine. All too accustomed to her aunt's managing ways to bother protesting, Nora merely quirked a brow. Then she saw the answer to her unasked question appear in the form of a very eligible gentleman indeed.

In fact, the handsome Earl of Sinclair was the answer to many a woman's earnest prayers. He was a commanding presence, broad shouldered and dark eyed and blond haired. The earl was considered to be the chief prize of the Marriage Mart, with debutantes in every corner gossiping about his wealth and health. And, of course, his above average dancing skills.

"Honora, good fortune is smiling on you if the earl wants to ask for a dance," her aunt declared. "Sinclair inherited the title and the fortune a few months ago. Tragic story. He was the younger son and a determined military man but had to sell his commission and return to England once his older brother died from a fever."

The earl reached her side and bowed over her hand. "Lady Honora," he greeted her. "I do hope you have been enjoying the evening."

Aunt Mildred replied, "We have been very much enjoying the ball, Lord Sinclair. The musicians are faultless, the company exceptional." She gave an imperious nod which was meant to include him in the category of exceptional company. "Now that you have deigned to grace my niece with your presence, the evening is perfect."

Nora wondered if it was possible to melt with embarrassment. Her composure did not slip, but she couldn't help but glance at Lord Sinclair to gauge his reaction.

The earl wasn't smiling, but he did bow again to her aunt in acknowledgement of her effusive compliments. "What would be perfect is if your niece would grant me a dance tonight," he said. "Dare I hope that you have an unclaimed set, my lady?"

In fact she had many unclaimed sets, and she suspected that he already knew it. She had been in London society for only two weeks and was far from the toast of the season. There were many women younger and wealthier than she, and who did not have her serious demeanor. Those were the ladies who were getting the most attention on the dance floor, as well as ladies like Miss Lockhart. Feisty, bright, teasing women who seemed easy to dance with and easy to talk to.

Doubtlessly also easy to flirt with. Nora pushed away the thought of flirting with Miss Lockhart.

She admitted to the earl with a lack of artifice that she was free for the next set, and he led her out to the dance floor.

"London air must agree with you, my lady," Sinclair told her as the violins started the dance.

If she was looking well tonight, she thought, it was because she was still recovering from being pressed against the incomparable Miss Lockhart.

"I have been enjoying tonight's ball, Lord Sinclair," she said. Sighing to herself, she thought of Aunt Mildred and her boundless ambition and added, "And of course, I am considering myself lucky to have such a skilled partner on the dance floor."

Sinclair smiled. "I am the lucky one to have a graceful partner such as you to dance with."

Nora knew that her role as a prospective bride was to be encouraging, flattering, warm, and receptive. All things that she was not by nature. But though she was not good at flirting with men, surely she could come up with something to say? She searched her mind for a topic. "My aunt tells me that you were in the army," she said. "Thank you for your efforts against Napoleon. We are all relieved to have brave men such as you fighting against the French."

Lord Sinclair smiled. "I regret to reveal that I never fought against the Corsican. I have been stationed in the East Indies for the past decade."

Nora blushed. "Oh! But my thanks remain the same, no matter where you served on behalf of our country."

"It was a sad day indeed for me to return to England," he admitted. "I had wished nothing more than a happy and long life for my brother. And to be truthful, I would have liked a longer career overseas with my brothers in arms, instead of settling into an earl's responsibilities."

"I am sorry to hear of your brother's passing," she said. "There is nothing more important than family."

He nodded. "Thank you, my lady. I appreciate your kind comments."

They danced in silence for several minutes. Despite her nerves, Nora was surprised at how fast the half hour passed. It had been her sole dance of the entire evening, and she didn't think she would gain another one as the ball was almost over. He brought her back to her aunt and she felt a pang of regret.

"Thank you for such a graceful turn about the dance floor, Lady Hannah," he said as he kissed her hand and departed.

Oh. Nora watched him nod to their hostess, and then turn and bow over the hand of another wallflower.

Aunt Mildred noticed as well. "The Earl of Sinclair is a man who understands his duty, Honora," she declared. "A certain lack of attention to detail doesn't mean that he is not interested in you. He is just doing his part to make sure that the young ladies have a dance partner, which is to his credit as he is in such popular demand. A kind man makes an excellent husband."

But her voice lacked conviction.

"He is not so very interested in me that he bothered to remember my name," Nora said. But her voice was quiet, and Aunt Mildred either didn't hear her or was choosing to ignore any criticism of a potential suitor.

It would be rather nice if this marriage business could be arranged with expediency, Nora thought. She yearned already to be back in the country. Perhaps the earl was always so obliging with wallflowers, and she could seek him out at other balls where he might feel compelled to dance with her again. Then maybe he would become a dedicated suitor.

As far as plans went, it was not very convincing.

Aunt Mildred was studying her. "You need to face facts, Honora. You are older than other debutantes and will need to work extra hard to attract a husband. You have spent long enough in the country."

"Mourning is a suitable reason to delay a season of entertainment," she replied.

"Of course it is," Aunt Mildred agreed. "But you mourned for years, far longer than is customary." Her tone softened. "I understand why you stayed so long in Wiltshire. Do not think me heartless, with no memory of your parents. I think of your mother, my dearest younger sister, every day. But you need to think of your future and not dwell in the past. You are already twenty-five years of age. Your parents would have wanted you to be well settled by now, and I am determined to see to their wishes about this. I owe that much to my sister. Now is the time to make sure that their hopes for you come true."

Nora sucked in a shallow breath. Yes, her parents would have wanted her to be happy and successful, and for most women, that meant marriage.

For herself, she wasn't so sure.

Her aunt continued to lecture her, but she stopped paying attention.

The future she had always envisioned was marriage to a nobleman, raising their children, in an idyllic country estate. But a grand passion was never part of the dream. She feared she was incapable of it.

She felt the stirrings of something interesting indeed when she spied a pretty face and a pleasing figure. Nora had never once been physically intrigued by a man's presence, but many times she had felt her heart leap or her belly tingle when she was in the company of other women.

Several times, she had even known the pleasure of that company in the bedchamber, alone with another woman who had the same feelings. Nora wasn't embarrassed to think of those passionate nights, though she wasn't fool enough to bring it up in conversation. She knew that it wasn't a common thing. But if she could find companionship like that in the countryside of Wiltshire, then it must be available to find everywhere. Especially in the country's capital.

She frowned as she watched the whirling couples in the ballroom, beautiful women dancing in gorgeous flowing gowns. It didn't matter what she thought of the ladies in London. She needed to concentrate on snaring a husband instead of wasting her time thinking of women like Miss Lockhart. Her dowry was large, but she needed to wed or it did her no good. Aside from the dowry, her personal inheritance was the small country manor in Wiltshire, and although she managed it well enough, it had not yielded a very comfortable living in recent years. Still, she had been lucky that her beloved country home was not entailed with the rest of the properties that had gone to her cousin with the title five years ago. It might be a living of genteel poverty, but at least she had a home. She was grateful for her aunt's help in bringing her out into society, as she could never have afforded the expense by herself.

"Honora, sometimes I despair of you. One would think that it wouldn't matter a jot to you whether or not you are invited to the Countess of Marchfield's ball next week! As if these events didn't hold the key to your very future." Aunt Mildred shook her head and gave her a gentle push. "Now, go make yourself useful and fetch me a glass of negus."

Nora made her way to the refreshment table, trying to convince herself that moving at a glacial pace wasn't quite the same as dawdling. She refused to admit to herself that perhaps she might be trying to avoid returning to the oppressive steel will of her aunt, or the depressing reality of her unpopularity on the dance floor.

She was concentrating on the grace of her walk. That was a valid enough excuse, wasn't it? One foot in front of the other, gliding, no hint of a wiggle at the hip. It was the same as she had practiced with her governess, with Homer's *Iliad* on her head. Sometimes she thought she would like to wiggle, just a little. There were any number of fashionable London ladies she had watched over the past two weeks who seemed born with a delightfully attractive step, their nipped in waists and curving hips speaking a silent language that she had never quite learned despite years of very dedicated study.

The *Iliad* on her head had not been dusty from disuse. She had been well schooled by her governess. But the classics were not all that she pursued in the wilds of Wiltshire.

No, she wasn't wasting time by being the slowest woman to ever fetch refreshment at a ball, which despite her hostess's best efforts, could not at all be determined a crush. She smiled as she recalled her lie to Sir Phineas about the crowd pushing her into their path.

A lady was meant to be admired, and after all, a suitor could be watching her graceful progress and thinking of paying court to such an elegant creature. Amused at herself, she glanced around to see if any gentlemen had appeared.

No suitor was watching. Of course not.

She reached the refreshment table and busied herself by nibbling on a sliver of dry cake. Nora frowned at the assortment of wine while she waited for a footman to fetch a glass of negus for her aunt. She would want it very well heated, she explained tiredly to the servant, who had nodded and disappeared. She hoped he wouldn't be efficient so she could prolong the errand. Though given the rest of the cold collation, she could understand if poor service was a contributing factor to the lack of a crowd beating down the door for entry to the evening's entertainment.

She accepted half a glass of white wine as she waited and was pleased to find that unlike her earlier glass, this wine was full strength.

"I say, I very much like your dress," a kind voice said behind her right shoulder.

Nora turned her head to see a willowy vision of a woman in an ivory frock. Thin blue silk ribbons crisscrossed her bodice in a frilly mess of delicate fabric and seed pearls. Auburn hair fell in bouncy waves well past her shoulders, and a smattering of freckles danced across her pale face.

She held out her right hand and firmly shook Nora's in greeting. "I do not believe we have met," she said, "but I am quite taken with your gown."

Nora looked at their joined hands. Was a handshake a common greeting in London? It was more familiar than she was accustomed to in the country, more suitable for men of business than ladies in the ballroom.

She glanced down at herself. Her aunt had a firm opinion in what was becoming for a debutante, even one as long in the tooth as she was. On the other hand, her aunt also believed in excellent tailoring, so although the cut of the gown was rather higher on the bosom than she would have preferred, and the style wasn't in the first stare of fashion, the dress was a perfect fit and showed her figure off to advantage.

"I much prefer your dress," Nora said, "though I haven't your height to make it look as fetching on me."

The woman introduced herself as Lady Georgina Smith. She smiled at Nora. "I hope you don't mind me intruding on you, but I was looking for a quiet moment away from the dancing. I find it a trifle warm in the ballroom."

"You are not intruding in the least. This is a whole table meant for refreshments, so please do refresh yourself," Nora murmured. She stepped back from the table.

"You have recently arrived in London, haven't you?" Lady Georgina asked with a little laugh. "You don't have that look of ennui that so many of us have when we have been here in the capital for too long. It is…refreshing."

"I don't intend on staying here beyond the season," she replied. "I have a rather unoriginal ambition toward matrimony, with a prompt return to the country."

Lady Georgina laughed again. "Which part of England do you hail from?"

"Wiltshire. It is lovely there at this time of year," Nora said with a pang of longing.

"Well, London offers a great deal of entertainment that you can't find in the country. And not just entertainment, but education as well. There are many women here who don't think that marriage is the sole ambition that we all need to be working toward."

Nora went very still and her mind blanked. Had this woman seen her watching any of the ladies with a closer eye than was common? Had she witnessed Nora falling against Miss Lockhart's generous bosom earlier? Had she lingered too long in admiring Lady Georgina's dress just now?

"Marriage will suit me very well indeed," she managed to reply.

Lady Georgina nodded. "I am sure it will. But I know many ladies for whom it is an anathema. They are a remarkable group. They spend their time writing pamphlets and discussing politics, and it is all very eye-opening, especially if you have not spent much time in such circles before."

The footman reappeared with Aunt Mildred's negus. In a moment of desperation, Nora wished she had asked for one for herself. She despised the drink, but right now a hot strong glass of port sounded like it might solve a lot of problems. In particular, the issue of her sudden onslaught of nerves.

She took the glass with unsteady hands. "It was a pleasure to meet you, Lady Georgina," she said as cordially as she could.

She leaned in close, so near that Nora's pulse quickened and she started to calculate the odds that she was coming close for a kiss. She stopped a mere inch shy of her cheek. "It was lovely to meet you as well. And please—call me Gina."

Nora nodded again and hurried back to Aunt Mildred as fast as she could manage without spilling the negus.

Chapter Three

Nora slowly fanned herself during an endless afternoon of shopping with Aunt Mildred. The shoemaker presented yet another silk dancing slipper to her, bowing again as if she hadn't already endured enough of his toadying in the hour that she had been in his establishment.

"The blue silk is all the rage, my lady," he murmured. "And the embroidery—divine!"

The low-heeled shoe with its delicate silk embroidered cornflowers was pretty, suitable for a debutante, and in exquisite taste. To her, it looked identical to all the other pairs they had seen.

"They're perfect," Aunt Mildred said. "So original. We'll take the blue silk, the daffodil yellow, and the pale green."

Pastels. Perfect for Aunt Mildred, thought Nora. But of course her aunt didn't ask her for her opinion, so she merely snapped her fan shut and laid it on the padded bench beside her. Aunt Mildred had reviewed Nora's failures of the past few events—the last to be asked to dance, the last to be offered an arm into the dining room—and decided that her wardrobe must be at fault.

"You already have good breeding and a good name," Aunt Mildred had announced at the breakfast table. "And we have the connections through your father's relations. Why, your cousin is an earl, and you are related to the Duke of Hawthorne, even though he has a terrible reputation these days and has been living in Paris for a decade or more."

She had tapped at the soft-boiled egg on her plate. "You have an enticing enough dowry, and heaven knows there should be enough gentlemen to jump at it. It must be your attire. It seems as though fashion never stops evolving despite all of the upheaval in France. We shall make sure that you don't look too common in your dress, not like those vulgar girls who are falling out of their gowns and rouging their lips to gain attraction! Proper attire will gain you all the courtship that your name deserves."

It was always about their name, their legacy. It was never about Nora's wishes, her desires. Her needs. But it was kind of her aunt to be so diligent in trying to make Nora a success, so she said nothing but frowned down at her own breakfast and hoped that she wouldn't end up looking *excessively* antiquated.

Mr. Addington's Ladies Emporium was a busy shop filled with women looking at shoes and gloves, but Mr. Addington himself was assisting the Banfields today. He hadn't spared a glance at his many other customers this afternoon, which Nora thought was a shame but Aunt Mildred thought was their birthright.

At any moment a younger woman with a larger dowry could come sailing through the doors and claim all of the owner's attention for herself.

It would be rather a relief.

One of the assistants slid the shoes from her feet and had her bundled back into her half boots in a trice. Mr. Addington bowed yet again. "May I interest you in gloves?" he asked. "We have all of the latest fashions, in every length you would require."

"Of course we are interested in gloves," Aunt Mildred declared.

Nora reminded herself that patience was a virtue, though she was hard-pressed at the moment to remember why.

She peeled back her cotton day gloves so the assistant could take the measurements of her hands and let her gaze wander again about the establishment that her aunt proclaimed was the *only* place in all of London to go for such all-important items as shoes, gloves, and umbrellas.

The shop was spacious and opened into several rooms, so there were plenty of women to look at and plenty of time to do so while the shop owner murmured in exaltation over the gloves that he had to offer.

In a corner of the shop, she spied the most beautiful woman in her field of very tenuous acquaintanceships.

Miss Jacqueline Lockhart. Her raven black hair fell in perfect waves over her shoulders as she leaned forward to look at her shoes. Nora recalled how those midnight locks had caressed Miss Lockhart's bosom when she danced. Even from a distance, Nora fancied she could see the sparkling green in her eyes.

Miss Lockhart hiked her skirts up higher than necessary when the shop assistant attending to her slid the dancing slippers onto her feet. Nora took in the way her head dipped low to whisper something in her friend's ear.

Not only was she the most beautiful woman Nora had seen in London, but she also had the loveliest and trimmest ankles that had ever been seen anywhere.

Her pulse quickened. She relived the delightful press of Miss Lockhart against her. Her rosy lips had seemed to promise wonder, and her large expressive eyes under her straight brows had been full of humor. Humor, and possibly something a little more interesting. Such as flirtation.

Nora had a surprising urge to go over to the pair and join them, to shake their hands as Lady Georgina had at last night's ball. She would give anything to borrow some of Miss Lockhart's warmth, to pretend that she belonged with them as they sat and gossiped and shopped as if they were friends, without a care in the world.

It would be so nice to have a friend in town.

But she couldn't go over to them. She wouldn't.

If she went over and joined them, she knew the laughter would stop, and she wouldn't be able to think of anything to say. She would stand there, hesitant and shy, because she didn't know how to act in front of popular women. Such an action would spoil Miss Lockhart's afternoon. That was the last thing that Nora wished to do.

They hadn't seen her yet, and Nora slid over closer to the wall until she was certain that she would be blocked from their view if they chanced to glance this way.

Nora snapped her fan open again.

"Are you quite all right, my dear?" Aunt Mildred's imperious tones interrupted her thoughts.

"Of course, Aunt," Nora said. "Simply a little tired."

Aunt Mildred nodded in satisfaction. "We'll leave soon enough and then we can begin to plan our week. There was a nice pile of invitations on my desk when we left home this afternoon."

While her aunt issued a series of instructions to the shopkeep to finish up their transaction, Nora wandered over to the elaborate displays of shoes. Every fashion imaginable was arrayed on the shelves, in styles more daring and more enticing than the ones her aunt had ordered for her. There were rows of shoes that she loved but could never have.

Stifling a sigh, she trailed a finger around the fine stitching on the beautiful leather, dyed in rich blues, forest greens, and bold reds. London seemed full of lovely things that had no place in her life, if she wanted to be sure of achieving her goals of matrimony.

Her eyes were drawn again to Miss Lockhart and her friend, who were giggling together in the corner. Her heart panged with yearning for female friendship. She bit her lip and turned her attention back to the shoes.

Then she saw them. The most perfect pair of dancing slippers that she had ever seen in her life.

They were the pale color of the newest rosebuds of early summer, a sweet pink that reminded her of the lush gardens of Rosedale Manor where she had grown up. Beautiful satin rosettes were arranged in a gorgeous cluster at the toes of the shoes. Satin ribbons trailed from the side, meant to lace around an ankle with perfect elegance. The glossy slippers gleamed at her.

Nora looked again at Miss Lockhart, and then at the shoes. Couldn't she have something of her own now, while she prepared for her future? Was it so wrong to think of sending a gift and extending a hand of friendship?

She swept the pink shoes into her arms and hurried over to the shopkeep, careful to avoid Aunt Mildred's attention.

"Excuse me," she said to the man. "Would you happen to know that woman over there—Miss Jacqueline Lockhart?"

"Of course, my lady. Miss Lockhart is a frequent patron of our shop," he replied.

"She is a—well, a friend of mine," Nora lied, "and I wish to make these shoes a gift for her. Could you please send these to her address and put them on my aunt's account?"

"Yes, my lady. Would you wish to include a note?"

She accepted a pencil and a scrap of paper and, thinking briefly, scribbled a note to include with the shoes.

"Honora, are you quite ready to leave?" her aunt called out to her from the doorway.

With a grateful smile at the shopkeep, Nora whirled around and followed Aunt Mildred out the door and into their waiting carriage. Relieved that they had left the establishment without Miss Lockhart noticing her, Nora sank into the comfortable carriage seat next to her aunt and listened with half an ear to the upcoming plans that her aunt had for the season.

In the late afternoon, Nora sat in the sunshine in the drawing room, skimming a book of poetry that she had borrowed from the circulating library. A half full cup of tea rested on the side table next to the narrow sofa, and she nibbled at a biscuit as she flipped the pages in her lap.

Her mind was only half on the words in front of her. The other half was fixated on Miss Jacqueline Lockhart. Nora suspected that it would be unwise to pursue a friendship that would result in her pining for something more. All she wanted was to find someone to marry, and then to return to the country.

Longing lay heavy in her heart as she thought of Rosedale Manor. The estate's wide hallways and sunny rooms were empty now. The furniture had been wrapped in white cloths in most of the rooms even while she had lived there. Partly due to the fact that she was the only inhabitant of the house except for the few servants that the estate employed, and partly due to the strained circumstances in which she had been forced to live. Since her parents had passed from their illness half a decade ago, Nora had entertained no one.

Aunt Mildred had been the only visitor to the estate. She had been widowed some ten years earlier and lived in a nearby county. When

Aunt Mildred hadn't been with her at the manor, she had remained a most frequent and dedicated correspondent.

On her last visit, her aunt's patience had worn thin. "This is how you honor your parents' memory?" she had snapped. "By fading away, by failing to contribute to their legacy? You are coming to London with me, my girl, and you will fill this old house with life again."

Within the month, she had been whisked away to London, and all Nora had to show for herself so far was an inappropriate blaze of desire for a certain black-haired miss.

She flipped another page of her book without taking in any of the words printed on it. She didn't like the idea of disappointing her aunt after all she had done for her, and she knew that she should be more focused on her marriage goals. Friendship with Miss Lockhart would be a dangerous path to follow, and it would be the height of folly to engage herself further. It was a mistake to have sent her the dancing shoes, particularly when they were the barest of acquaintances.

It was a most regrettable action.

With any luck, Nora thought, she could be gone from London soon and could forget all about her inconvenient passion. As long as he was kind and polite and approved by Aunt Mildred, she planned to accept any man who made her a respectable offer. She could be away from town as soon as the banns were cried and the ceremony over. They would go to her husband's home upon their marriage, but she hoped that they could visit Rosedale Manor often enough to maintain the small estate and honor the memory of her parents.

Memories still burned bright in her mind—her father's grin as he chucked her under the chin and called her his princess, her mother's warm hug and her whispered *I love you.* Years had passed, but she was still learning to live without them, trying to understand how to live a full life of her own instead of suffocating under the weight of her loss.

Well. She was here now in London, wasn't she? Wasn't this proof enough to Aunt Mildred that she was ready to see what was out there for her? She wouldn't find the great love that her parents had been lucky enough to share, but she was willing to settle for far less. Anything would be better than returning to the country accompanied by nothing but her loneliness. She had lived that life for too long.

Whatever London held for her, she would always be grateful for her aunt for shaking her out of her grief and solitude.

Friendship could ease her loneliness, she thought, tantalized by the thought of having Miss Lockhart as a friend. She imagined them walking arm in arm, shopping on Bond Street, strolling in Hyde Park, greeting each other at a ball. But then her traitorous mind went to thoughts of Miss Lockhart's soft lips, of leaning in for a slow passionate kiss.

No. This wouldn't do at all. She reminded herself that she needed to concentrate on marriage and not friendship. Especially not the sort of romantic friendship that she had enjoyed with one or two other ladies back in Wiltshire. That path would lead only to distraction, or worse. She settled down with her book in hand and banished all thoughts of Miss Lockhart from her mind.

CHAPTER FOUR

Jacqueline and Beatrice clambered out of the carriage and into the Lockharts' townhouse, with a manservant trailing behind them carrying the packages from their excursion to Bond Street.

"Do bring everything into the drawing room, Thomas," Jacquie said cheerfully, "and please bring us some tea."

She stood in the middle of the room, hands on her hips, and looked at the small mountain of fripperies with happiness. "I think I have quite everything I could wish for. There is nothing like starting a new season with all of the latest fashions, is there? And nothing so guaranteed to throw off heartbreak like a new wardrobe, unblemished with memories."

"Nothing in the world," Beatrice agreed, and then busied herself with her hair after catching sight of the mirror above the mantel.

Jacqueline picked up a package and unwrapped a jaunty velvet cap, joining Bea at the mirror to try it on. "I shall be all the rage," she declared with a little laugh, but Beatrice didn't reply. She frowned. Beatrice had suggested an afternoon of shopping to take her mind from Lady Straund, declaring that she had an urgent need for fabrics, accessories, and people to gossip about—and yet Jacquie had done most of the shopping. "You didn't purchase much of anything today, did you?" she asked in surprise.

"I saw nothing worthy of spending my guineas on," Bea said, raising a brow and turning to the tea tray as soon as Thomas brought it round.

Jacqueline took the cap from her head and tossed it onto the table. Now that she paused to think about it, Bea had not seemed herself these past few days. She added a spoon of sugar to her tea and stirred it. "Tell me about your plans for husband hunting," she said. Perhaps that was the reason why she seemed distracted.

Beatrice settled back into an elegant armchair and sipped her tea. "I could see myself on the arm of many a man in England," she declared. "It is such a pity that I must choose only one."

Jacqueline laughed. "The law would not be on your side if you chose more than one, my dear," she said. "But truly—you know all of the men who are available. The crowd is much the same as it was last year when you turned your nose up at them all! So why would you choose one of them now?"

Beatrice rose and examined the bright array of hothouse flowers that had arrived this afternoon for Jacqueline after last night's ball. Jacquie couldn't think who it was who had sent them over, nestled among a half dozen other similar bouquets. Bea plucked a white chrysanthemum from the vase and twirled it in her hand.

"Ignoring the question?" Jacqueline asked. "Does your heart indeed beat faster for one of the men who you have previously disdained?"

"I am in dire straits," Beatrice announced.

Jacquie was at her side in a heartbeat. "Oh, darling, this is nothing we cannot handle," she said, but inside she fought to stay calm. This was much worse than she had thought. "We can find you somewhere to go until the baby arrives. I have seen advertisements in the papers—it can be so very discreet these days!"

Bea blinked. She pulled away. "No. Not those kinds of straits. Honestly, Jacquie, whatever do you think I have been doing since you and I have kept company in that way?"

Jacquie paused in the midst of a sympathetic back rub. "What other kind of straits could you be up to, if not for bedroom matters?"

"My *family*," she snapped. "My foolish father is in over his head in debts. Again. Only this time, our cousin is refusing to front him the funds. If word gets out, we are sure to be ruined, so I need to choose one of these blockheaded bachelors now and get his fortune to pay off our debts. Within the very month, if I can manage it."

Jacqueline breathed a sigh of relief. This she could help with. "We can find you a wealthy man. London is rife with them. Who is the richest man you can think of?"

"The Earl of Sinclair. He just inherited a few months ago and all I've heard about these days is how wealthy he is now. I am sure my family's problems would be a drop in the bucket to him."

"I think the Viscount of Amherst is wealthier," Jacqueline said.

Bea scowled down at the flower in her hand. "I am willing to do my part for my parents, but I am not a *martyr*! Amherst is a wizened old man. Sinclair is handsome and young. And rich enough for me." She stuck the chrysanthemum back into its vase.

"The viscount is but forty years old," Jacquie pointed out. "And he dances quite well."

"Positively wizened," Beatrice declared with narrowed eyes. "It will need to be the earl." She hesitated, and muttered, "He seems kind enough to overlook my family's troubles."

Jacqueline's heart ached. Bea's parents were forever disinterested in her. It was mercenary of them to turn now to their daughter and insist on her marriage for their own purposes. It was much the same as her own family, except her own mother's obsession was with the nobility instead of wealth.

Bea and Jacquie had been family enough for each other since they were in school. How often had they been the only girls left at the school during holidays? How many times had they sat together with nothing as other girls received letters and parcels from home? Jacquie had been lucky to receive a scrawled line or two from her mother every once in a long while, but Beatrice had never received even that token of affection.

Jacquie leaned her head on Bea's shoulder and slipped an arm around her waist. "Oh, Bea, I am sorry that I haven't noticed. You've been beside me this whole time as I've been wrapped up in my own problems."

Beatrice sniffed. "Yes, you have," she said. "It's been beastly."

"You are too good for me."

"You have never spoken truer words." But she grinned at Jacquie as she said it and gave her hand a little squeeze. "Now I must take my leave of you, Jacquie dear. It's almost time to dress for dinner."

"It's hardly four o'clock in the afternoon."

"And I have more need than ever to look exquisite every time I leave the house," she replied.

"If you have need of me, let me know. You know I would do anything for you," Jacquie said.

"You know I despise such tedious displays of affection." Bea rolled her eyes and flounced off but gave her a little wink as she left, which Jacquie knew from long history meant that she understood and appreciated the sincerity anyway.

❖

Jacqueline was playing the pianoforte with more verve than talent, trying to distract herself from heartbreak. Thanks to Bea's impromptu shopping trip, she hadn't shed a single tear over the Countess of Straund today, but the pain of seeing her a few nights ago at the ball in her fiancé's arms was still fresh. Memories crowded her mind as she pounded on the keys. Lydia's red-lipped smile from across a room, the warmth of her kisses on her lips.

Perhaps Phin was right. She did need a distraction from the countess. The pianoforte was the sad recipient of her passion right now and it wasn't doing her any good. Her playing wasn't becoming any better from her careless practice.

A footman appeared at the door to the music room and discreetly coughed above the noise from the pianoforte. He presented her with a parcel wrapped in paper and left the room.

Had Thomas left one of the packages in the carriage when she and Bea had come in from the shops earlier today? She hadn't noticed anything missing, but then again it had been a significant amount of accessories that she had purchased today. It was no surprise that something had been left behind. Jacqueline's mouth fell open when she tore the paper away to reveal a beautiful pair of pale pink satin dancing slippers, with the most gorgeous little satin rosettes on the toes. These had not been part of her shopping today.

She gazed at them, turning them over and over in her hands and studying the buttery soft kid leather soles and the tiny perfect stitches and the glossy satin fabric, before seeing the crisp white note peeking out from inside the right shoe.

Miss Lockhart,
I hope this missive finds you well. I could not think of my clumsiness the other evening without some chagrin, and I do fear that I may have caused some damage to your dancing slippers.
Please allow me to present you with this replacement, and consider forgiving me for my intrusion upon your person.
Your friend and servant,
Lady Honora Banfield

Jacqueline blinked. A gift? From Lady Honora? How very unusual! She snatched the note again to read it twice over. Surprise gave way to delight. She kicked off her shoes, slid the dancing slippers on her feet, and laced the silky satin ribbon around her ankles, tying a neat little bow at the back of her heel. She admired them, turning her ankles this way and that for the sheer pleasure of looking at her gift.

As she looked at the shoes, a warmth spread all over her. She felt quite deliciously aware of her body from her toes all the way up to her heart. When was the last time she had received a gift for no particular reason?

It was the sort of thing that the countess had never been wont to do. Jacquie's happiness dimmed. Lydia had been so beautiful, so sensual. Jacquie had been in a fever to be with her, to hold her hand when no one was looking, to steal hungry kisses in the garden. But for all the adoration that Jacqueline had poured out, she had received far less than she had given. She was the one always in pursuit, and the countess had been content to be chased and adored.

Lydia had said all of the right words. That she wanted to be with her, that she loved her. But in the end, they turned out to be just words. No heart behind them. No action to prove that her love was real. When she looked back, Jacqueline could remember how willing Lydia had been—but only when it was convenient for her.

How many notes had she received from Lydia urging her to visit, and how many more had arrived within the quarter hour to cancel plans in lieu of other social engagements? How many times had Lydia achieved her own pleasure, then found an excuse to end the time they spent together?

Looking at the rose slippers again, she felt a well of tears at her eyes. But this time it was not about the countess. Instead, it was a curious mix of gratitude and wonder that Lady Honora had been so thoughtful. Her steadiness of character was refreshing, her manner so calm and undemanding. She was simply *different* from everyone else that Jacqueline knew.

Her mother came into the room, bringing as always a constant stream of laughter and chatter that seemed to start from before she entered the room. "And I do declare, I have never seen so many dogs in all my life as I have this season in the parks! Everywhere one looks, one sees a lady with a little yapping snapping pup, and the leash studded with jewels twice as expensive as my best necklace. However do the wealthiest among us think of such ways to spend their money, I shall never know. But perhaps my dear Mr. Lockhart could indulge my fancy with a dog. I shall ask him this very day."

She paused to peek at herself in the mirror above the mantel before she sat on the edge of the chair in the music room. "Have you been out all afternoon with Beatrice again, Jacqueline?" she asked. "I thought for sure you said you would be at Mrs. Rutledge's musicale— but when I popped in to make an appearance, I saw neither hide nor hair of you. How many times do I need to remind you that you should be thinking of *husbands*, not shopping? Your wardrobe is full enough."

"Mama, you always said that I could marry for love," Jacquie said softly.

She sighed and leaned back in the chair. "That was during your first season, and your second—and yes, even your third. Goodness knows how we ever survived your third, as I remember you moping about the corners of ballrooms with the most sullen of looks on your face. Crossed in love that year, I have no doubt. But this is your *sixth* season, Jacquie darling. I know of no other daughters still on the market for a *sixth* time. My friends quite despair of the situation and

I am becoming most aggrieved by their pointed comments. It is all anyone will speak of to me this year and it is ever so dull. People are starting to wonder if there is something *wrong* with you."

She peered at her. "I see nothing wrong. You are as beautiful as ever, thank goodness. Not even the hint of a line on your face— you could pass for much younger than twenty-six, you know. If you pinched your cheeks more like I keep *telling* you, I declare you could look twenty at the utmost."

"I have no interest in looking younger than I am, Mama," Jacquie said. "I have told you—I want to wait for love. No matter how long it takes." It was a lie that she had stuck to for years, and it had always met her mother's romantic sensibilities with success.

"Jacquie, if you haven't found anyone to love in all this time, you will have to settle for the best of the bunch who will doubtless pester your father this year for your hand. Of course it would be much, much better if he were noble. It would be an absolute travesty to waste a face like yours on a mere mister when you could have so much more."

Wariness crept through her. Mama paid great attention to gossip in her eternal quest to pander to the nobility.

"There are perfectly good gentlemen without titles!" she exclaimed. If her mother insisted on seeing Jacqueline with a suitor this season, then maybe she could persuade Phin to pretend to pursue her. Oh, if only her parents would accept a sir!

"If one must marry, it is just as well to wed a peer than not," her mother said.

Jacquie was aware, on the rare occasion when she chose to admit it to herself, that this was the real reason why they had allowed her six seasons. Not out of love, or the wish to indulge their only daughter. But because Jacqueline alone had the power to increase the Lockhart family's standing in society.

With a nobleman's patronage, her family would benefit. She had many in her family tree who worked in trades—respectable trades of course, doctors and lawyers and the occasional entrepreneurial soul who owned a smattering of factories or mines. They would all be affected by her good fortune through the patronage of the nobility, if only she would reach out her hand and grab it for them.

She vowed to never admit to her parents that she could have wed as high as an earl in her second season, or a wealthy baron in her fifth. The men who were foolish enough to disregard her dissuasions and beg her father for her hand had been the lowest born. Her father had felt safe to reject them, so positive he was that Jacqueline's beauty would win the prize for them all in the end.

There was no real scandal in her behavior, but she knew that it all depended on how high ranking and influential were her severest critics. Snide talk and persistent rumors could fell a woman in an instant, and she didn't move high enough in the upper echelons of society to dispel any such rumors.

Her mother broke off her narrative when she saw Jacqueline looking at her feet.

"For all that you should be focusing more on husband hunting, those are exquisite dancing shoes," she said with approval, moving closer to examine them. "Did you purchase them today with Beatrice?"

"No, they were a gift."

Her mother recoiled as if the satin ribbons were snakes. "Jacqueline Lockhart, are you accepting *inappropriate gifts* from gentlemen? How many times have I told you—no matter how besotted they are, a tome of sonnets is as personal a gift as you can allow. Already we are not invited to as many society events as one might hope. This will blacken your name!"

"No, Mama, of course they were not from a man. They are from Lady Honora Banfield—she quite ran me over at Lady Markham's ball the other evening, and feared that she had ruined my slippers in the encounter."

She tilted her head and pursed her lips. Her knowledge of the nobility was encyclopedic, and it took her only a moment to retrieve the information from her troves of meticulously acquired gossip. "Lady Honora Banfield? Of the Wiltshire Banfields, the niece of Lady Mildred, Dowager Countess of Rosedale? Why, I didn't realize that you were friends with them. They just arrived in town for the season, and it would be a wise friendship to cultivate. The family is a small one but has excellent connections, you know."

"We aren't friends. I met her once."

Her mother tapped a finger against her chin. "I should call on Lady Mildred. She and my mother were friends, though this was a long time ago now. I have never met her, except perhaps as young girl, but I think she would remember our family well. They are connected to some of the highest in the land—it would be wise to take advantage of them if you can. She is a cousin to the Duke of Hawthorne, which is still a very grand thing despite the scandals of the current duke. With friends in higher places, who knows who you could attract!" Her eyes were shining with glee. "I cannot wait to tell all of my friends the good news. That will put them in their place."

Jacqueline sighed, annoyed with her mother's eagerness to further the connection. How she wished she had sisters who could share the burden of being marriageable. Or a brother who could save the family by wedding an heiress. It was difficult to be an only child and the focus of all familial ambition.

"You needn't bother Lady Mildred," she said. "I can attract my own suitors, Mama."

"We aren't invited to the best events, and you have never been granted access to Almack's. With Lady Mildred and Lady Honora helping you, you could gain the notice of someone *worthy* of you at last, my dear."

Jacqueline felt the compliment warm her. Her parents were fond of her, she knew, but they tended not to say as much to her. She let the words linger in her heart with joy, wanting so much to please them.

Her mother's tone softened and turned dreamy. "That is what I want for you, Jacquie. Someone worthy of your beauty. With a face like yours, you deserve the best. Someone to rise us up and bring us to better things."

The words turned to acid and curdled her heart. Of course her mama was thinking again of her ambition, and not about her. Her mood came crashing down and resentment welled at being seen as the only cipher to break the code of the upper echelons, instead of a person worthy of good things because just maybe she was a good *person.*

"I am going to invite the Banfields to the opera," her mother declared. "I am sure they would appreciate an old family friend calling on them and bringing them to an evening of such culture. London has a great deal to offer that the country doesn't, after all. I wonder if Lady Honora will enjoy the opera."

"Well, I know that I do not," Jacqueline said briskly. "If you wish to attend the opera with the Banfields, I wish you well and happy of your evening. But I don't want to sit in a dull opera house listening to a warbling soprano all night."

The look in her mother's eye was pure steel. "I am doing this to secure our futures, Jacqueline Lockhart, and you will do your duty to this family. You will be at the opera. And at any other event that we can squeeze from this acquaintanceship. Our hopes depend on it."

She studied the slippers on Jacquie's feet. "Lady Honora has good taste—you could do well by spending more time with the Banfield girl."

Her mother bustled out the door, and Jacquie sat in silence on the piano bench. She might need to go where her mother dictated, but all she had to do was make her appearance. If only there was a way that would stop her mother from her insistence on using every social outing and every potential social contact as the basis of a plot for marriage!

How could she continue to enjoy the pleasures of London if her mother decided that it was high time to watch her like a hawk and pull her hither and yon to preen in front of eligible gentlemen? Her mother's habit as a chaperone was lax, as she preferred to spend time at social events with her own friends with a glance now and then at Jacquie to watch that she didn't get into mischief. Jacquie excelled at getting into as much mischief as she ever wished to, but it would be more difficult if not impossible if she was going to be in the constant presence of her mother.

With a pang, she thought of all the opportunities she had stolen so that she could sneak into a garden to share a cheroot with Phin, or to encourage the young bucks at a party to set off fireworks, or to primp and giggle with Bea in any nook they could find. If her mother insisted on a closer friendship with Lady Mildred, then she would expect Jacqueline to entertain both her and her niece. And despite how attractive Lady Honora was, and how thoughtful the gift from the shoe emporium was, Jacquie rather doubted that Lady Honora was the type of woman to sneak around a ballroom in search of fun.

Jacquie pulled the dance shoes from her feet and wrapped them carelessly in the paper that they had arrived in, her mother's machinations dampening her excitement over the gift. There must be a way out of this, she thought. She straightened her spine. And she would just have to depend on her mind, and not her pretty face, to think of how to solve the problem.

Chapter Five

When Aunt Mildred told her that their next outing would be a musical afternoon, Nora was relieved. At an event such as this, there would be no dancing, and her lack of popularity could go unremarked. After three weeks in London, she was attending an event for the purpose of enjoying herself.

Aunt Mildred's friend Lady Florentia had a very grand house in Mayfair and excellent taste in music. Three rooms had been opened up to accommodate the guests, the wide double doors of the music room folding back to allow fifty or more people to gather together. Nora gazed around the large series of rooms with pleasure. Splendid artwork adorned the walls, and she thought that she could sit here for hours in quiet contemplation.

She hadn't realized how tense she had become by attending so many overcrowded society functions with the single-minded purpose of finding a suitor, until the first notes of the pianoforte and harp blended together in marvelous harmony and she felt herself relax.

The musical performance featured a quartet of violinists, a harp, and a pianist. Nora had been to different musical events in the country, but the level of talent in this London troupe was impressive. Her joy in the music meant that she would have been happy for the afternoon to stretch on for hours, but when it was over she realized she was glad to stand up and stretch her legs again. Her aunt's friends clustered around them, and Nora was reminded of a group of hens clucking over their errant chicks.

Then she realized that *she* was the errant chick.

Lady Mary smiled at her. "Lady Honora, what are your thoughts on town life? Are you happy here in London? Lady Mildred has been telling me that you have been whiling your time away in the country."

Her innermost thoughts on town life were that it was inordinately stressful here in the capital, but Nora supposed that was not what anyone would wish to hear at a social gathering. "Afternoons in London such as this one are very fine," she said. "The musical talent gathered here is exceptional."

Lady Mary nodded. "Exactly as it should be. London is at the heart of everything, after all. The country air is good for the soul, but London is the center of education, good society, entertainment, knowledge."

"And what knowledge should I be gaining here in town?" Nora asked with interest.

"Knowledge is for the *men*, dear," she snapped. "To wed a man who is knowledgeable would be to your endless benefit. He can teach you whatever you need to know."

Nora nodded, frustration mounting inside her although she didn't dare express it in front of her aunt. In Wiltshire, she had managed the goings-on of the estate during the past few years. She had a very competent steward and accountant, but she was responsible for many of the decisions, and she thought she had done a good job despite the meager income that it provided her. The tenants were fed and taken care of, and the quarterly town fairs were always well attended with people in good cheer. The events in Rosedale were nowhere near London standards, but she did try to encourage entertainment for the village, even if it was a simple arrangement of a fiddle and a lute in one of the barns for the occasional dance.

Lady Sarah nodded. "You just need to know how to best spend your coin, and how to bear an heir," she said with a broad grin. "It was a great comfort to me that my dear husband had everything else well under control. It gave me plenty of time for dancing, you know."

"Of course you can also join charitable pursuits," Lady Jane, a dowager baroness, broke in. "I have long been on several boards providing necessities for the poor here in London. One should use money and influence for some good in this world, if one can."

Aunt Mildred agreed. "There is much that a woman can do after marriage to make a difference in the world. But the key thing is to find a man to make it all possible. Otherwise you are right back where you started, Honora—alone in the wilderness with naught but a half dozen families to socialize with. With a husband by your side, you could have many more options for your life."

She turned to one of the women. "Now, it has been some time since I have brought a young lady into society," she confided.

"This one is not so young," the dowager murmured.

"Exactly so," Aunt Mildred agreed. "I have done what I could, but I shall need your help to make her a success."

Five pairs of eyes turned to Nora.

"She has a lovely face," one of them said finally.

"A trifle long."

"Yes, but only a trifle. And lovely eyes. It's a shame they are gray and not a more fashionable blue, but they are a lovely shape."

"Beautiful golden hair. Not cut in the modern style, but a beautiful color nevertheless."

Nora found the fortitude deep inside her to smile. "Thank you for your compliments," she said, though they seemed tepid at best.

"I think there is potential here for at least a baron," Lady Sarah announced with satisfaction. "I know Baron Montford is on the market this season. Recently widowed. No heir yet, just a pair of young girls running about the estate. Has a good parcel of land up north, I believe near Kent."

"The Viscount of Amherst is available," another suggested. "He's a little older, but a seasoned man can be such a good match for a woman these days. They know what they want, and they don't have such high expectations of a wife."

"A man closer in age would be a better bet," Aunt Mildred said thoughtfully. "Amherst must be in his late forties by now and his heir is already a grown man. Although he would do for Honora, I had hoped her to be the mother of a nobleman's heir instead of only bearing younger sons."

"The Earl of Sinclair is without a doubt the man to bet on this year. Young, handsome. Moneyed."

They all fell silent for a moment.

"The Earl of Sinclair! Every woman's dream," Lady Mary sighed. "Those military men carry themselves so well. Is there anything so dashing as a man in a red coat? But I think my own grand-niece will have him all trussed up by the end of the season. Beautiful young lady, just out for her debut this season."

"Or perhaps my granddaughter," the dowager sniffed. "Only her second season and already described as an Incomparable at Almack's."

"My cousin's daughter will be the one to nab the earl," huffed the viscountess. "Now *she* is an accomplished woman. Speaks French as nicely as you please, and is a fine hand with the embroidery needle."

"Honora could manage to obtain Sinclair's attention," Aunt Mildred said, but her tone was doubtful.

"He did dance with me last week," Nora reminded her, but then remembered that it had been an act of kindness to their hostess. She winced. It still stung to remember how he had forgotten her name.

Lady Jane thumped her cane on the floor. "If you need help with bringing Lady Honora to the gentlemen's attention, have you tried reaching out to your family?"

Aunt Mildred frowned. "The highest connection we have is the Duke of Hawthorne, but of course he has been out of the country for years and it would not do to mention his name in good circles right now, touched as he is by scandal. We have never had much to do with his duchess, though I don't think it would do much good. I do not believe she has been to the capital in some time."

"Actually, the Duchess of Hawthorne has arrived here in London last week," Lady Mary said with interest. "Perhaps she will do some entertaining this year."

"Well, even without the duchess's help, I think Honora will take quite well as soon as she is a little more settled in society. I have ordered her a new wardrobe," Aunt Mildred said with satisfaction. "This will help make her noticeable to the gentlemen."

Nora gritted her teeth and looked down at her new day dress. It was a sober gray, covered in deep satin flounces that did nothing but weigh her down. Very distinguished. Entirely dispiriting. She was tired of being talked at and talked about. And it was beyond frustrating that no one would ever tell her what the duke had done that was so very dreadful. He was her own cousin, after all.

She scanned the grand room, looking to see if there was any possibility of escaping her aunt's circle of friends. She spied someone that she recognized, deep in conversation with the musicians. It was Lady Georgina, in a graceful flowing white gown, embellished at the hem with tiny bows and pleats, looking like a sweet confection. Nora suppressed a sigh. She would never be as fashionable as Lady Georgina.

Lady Georgina looked up from her conversation and beamed at Nora, who felt gratitude well up inside her heart. She must be the friendliest woman in London, she thought. Her aunt was still deep in an argument with her friends about the marriageability of various bachelors, and Nora fought off her shyness and forced her feet to drift across the room toward the musicians.

"Lady Honora, it is a pure delight to be in your presence again." Lady Georgina shook her hand, as she had done when they had first met, which surprised Nora anew.

"Oh, I have no claims to being delightful," she said.

"*Au contraire*, I would consider you to be entirely delightful," she replied, and sent her a searing look that had Nora reeling. Did Lady Georgina mean what she suspected she did?

Nora swallowed hard. "Thank you," she murmured, every sense on high alert.

"I had very much hoped to see you again, and am so pleased to see you here at this musical gathering." Lady Georgina gestured to the woman beside her. "Anyway, to the matter at hand. Doesn't Mrs. Bathurst play the piano gorgeously?"

"Your skills are very impressive," Nora complimented the pianist, a handsome woman some years older than herself. "The Mozart piece was wonderful."

She nodded modestly. "Thank you, my lady. It is very kind of you to say so."

"Do you play often for parties such as this?" Nora inquired.

"Quite often. We have been playing together for some time as a group, and I am happy to say that we have experienced some modest success."

"Only modest success?" Nora said in surprise. "I would think you should be very successful, given your talents."

"It would be a different situation if they were a troupe of men, isn't that right?" Lady Georgina said. Her face darkened into a scowl.

Mrs. Bathurst glanced around before confiding, "We would indeed be most successful if we were men. Begging your pardon for mentioning something so crass as finances in such a genteel gathering, but female performers are not compensated the same as men, even if the level of proficiency is the same or higher."

Nora frowned. "But that is unfair."

"Unfair, and too common," Lady Georgina announced. "It is a travesty that women and men are treated so vastly different in so many ways."

"Men and women are very different," Nora said thoughtfully. "But I never considered that it would make such a difference in art such as this. I don't think I have heard finer playing than I have this afternoon, from either another woman or a man. You should surely be paid the same."

Mrs. Bathurst shrugged. "I wasn't even able to play for most of the winter due to the arthritis that has begun to settle in my hands. If women were permitted membership to the Royal Society of Musicians, we might be in a better situation."

"The Royal Society?"

"It's a charitable organization that helps musicians survive when they are unable to work. If women were allowed to join, we would be in a better position to make a more sustainable living with our music." She shook her head. "I don't mean to complain, my lady. My friends and I are lucky to have such patronage among London society, and we are grateful for the chance to play our music for you."

Nora smiled at her. "You are all exceptional musicians, and I would be delighted if I get the chance to hear you again this season. Thank you for sharing your talents with us."

Lady Georgina leaned in closer to both of them. "If you would like to discuss the situation more in depth, with like-minded women, might I suggest that you join myself and my friends on Tuesdays in my salon?" Lady Georgina asked. "We are a group who are most interested in discussing these sorts of issues, and in trying to make changes. I am intrigued by this idea of the Royal Society. There must be a way for you to petition for women to join. Let us discuss further together."

Mrs. Bathurst hesitated, then nodded with hope in her eyes. "I would like that very much, my lady." She gave a little curtsy. "Now if you will excuse me, I must join my friends. I see them in a discussion with our hostess, and it would not do for me not to thank her for the opportunity of playing for you all." She walked away.

"A salon?" Nora's curiosity was sparked. "Do you mean like a group of—well, forgive me, but are you a group of bluestockings?"

"Yes," Lady Georgina said in a tone that brooked no arguments. "Haven't you ever wished for a space where you could express yourself as you wanted to, without the annoyance of a man telling you how you ought to think about things?"

Nora smiled. "Yes. But I admit that I also have an aunt who does much the same thing. These days, she is most fond of telling me how to think about marriage."

Lady Georgine laughed. "You would always be welcome to join us at my salon if you wish to learn about your options besides holy matrimony. Remember—every Tuesday afternoon at my home in Mayfair."

Aunt Mildred glided up to her. "Honora, do come with me," she announced. "There are many people here with whom you should be speaking. Many connections can be made at an event such as this, though I admit there are not as many eligible gentlemen here as I would have liked to have seen."

Nora managed to give Lady Georgina a smile over her shoulder as Aunt Mildred pulled her away.

"Perhaps I am making my own connections," she murmured.

"Connections with whom? The musicians? Honora, have you no sense? Although it is polite of you to thank those who provide a service, you cannot go about cultivating them as *friends*. What value will they give to your life here?"

Nora considered the excellent music that they had enjoyed this afternoon, and wistfully thought of having friends with whom she could discuss music and art. She thought she would have more to say to the musicians than to Aunt Mildred's friends. Perhaps they would even listen to her, which would be a welcome change.

Maybe she could accept Lady Georgina's invitation to her Tuesday salon and meet those types of women. The thought filled her with as much unease as it did excitement. Something about the idea seemed almost dangerous. A new world might lie ahead of her, if she were brave enough to grasp at it. She had never considered herself a brave or dangerous sort of woman. With a feeling of uncertain pleasure, she wondered what else she could discover about herself that she had not known before.

"We have no end of entertainments ahead of us for the next several weeks," Aunt Mildred said with satisfaction. "Two private balls, three suppers, and an old family friend has invited us to the opera. We shall marry you off almost before you know it."

Nora managed a smile at her aunt as a reply. But inside she sighed at the thought of more evenings with her aunt's friends, all of whom seemed to take great delight in judging her inferior to their own debutante relatives. The entertainments themselves were wonderful to experience—if only she could have the luxury of relaxing and enjoying the moment, and not be always on the watch for a moneyed gentleman to cross her path.

Chapter Six

One week later, Nora slipped into her seat at the Covent Garden theater and wondered if she was more thrilled at the prospect of hearing the opera for the very first time, or at the idea of sitting beside Miss Lockhart for hours on end. When Aunt Mildred had told her that they had been invited to the opera by an old family friend, Nora hadn't thought to enquire the name of the family. Her shock was palpable when she realized that her aunt was familiar with the Lockharts.

Nora had murmured a confused greeting and took care not to look at Miss Lockhart after they sat down, passing her comments only to her parents or to Aunt Mildred. Miss Lockhart's presence unraveled her composure.

Frowning, she stared at the stage. She desperately wanted to know if Miss Lockhart enjoyed the gift of the slippers. Nora was far too embarrassed to mention it, however. The more she thought of it, the more convinced she was that it had been the act of utmost stupidity. What if Miss Lockhart had laughed about it with her friends? She struggled not to squirm.

The opera was glorious, and a welcome distraction from the woman beside her, but even the talent on stage couldn't fully capture her attention tonight. Nora ran her fingers over the clasp of the reticule that she held in her lap, up and down the smooth metal hinge, and she considered how much to risk. Could she spare a sidelong glance at Miss Lockhart? If Miss Lockhart seemed relaxed and friendly in her company, she could be assured that the gift had not been unkindly received. But if she took her eyes from the stage, would the Lockharts think that she wasn't appreciating the opera? Should she wait until the intermission?

Risking a glance seemed the most practical way to ease her mind. With care, Nora moved only her eyes so that she could just see beside her.

Miss Lockhart was looking straight at her.

Shocked, she forced herself to look at the stage again. Her heartbeat picked up and she tried to control the rise and fall of her chest, unwilling to appear affected by her gaze.

After a few long minutes had passed, she dared to peek again. Miss Lockhart was still looking at her, a smile playing on her lips, but it was not the mocking smile that Nora had feared. Her heart slowed to normal, and she turned her head to look at her and return her smile.

Intermission arrived. Aunt Mildred demanded her customary drink of negus from Mr. Lockhart, and graciously thought to include Nora in her request.

"I am your servant," Mr. Lockhart said, an amused and indulgent look on his face. He seemed a dear man, rather short and portly with a smile for everyone.

Miss Lockhart stood. "Come, Lady Honora, will you stretch your legs with me in the aisle?"

Nora hesitated. She wanted nothing more than to go with Miss Lockhart, but at the same time realized that to linger in her presence was to risk temptation. Already she knew that her sleep tonight would be restless, wild with the memory of that green-eyed gaze.

"Go." Mrs. Lockhart shooed them away. "It will be a long second act."

Nora slipped into the aisle beside Miss Lockhart. "It is indeed nice to stand again," she said politely. "It was considerate of you to think of it."

Miss Lockhart tossed those gorgeous locks of hair so that they fell against her bosom. Several interested pairs of male eyes looked their way.

"The opera is always a bore," she pronounced. "I would do most anything to forget that we are at such a tedious event."

Nora narrowed her eyes. "I think it is exhilarating." The words flew out of her mouth, surprising her.

"Aren't you fresh from the country?" Miss Lockhart asked. "I expect most things are entertaining when you have so little to compare them to."

A pair of gentlemen came to their side, attracted by the lodestone that was Miss Jacqueline Lockhart. Nora watched, fascinated, as they bowed and laughed and teased, all smiles and warm affections, promises of dances and offers of carriage rides falling from their lips. Miss Lockhart handled them all effortlessly, laughing and beaming back at them with a careless wave at one and a beckoning smile at another.

Nora stood beside her, her nerves increasing as she realized that none of the men paid her any heed. It was a disappointing repeat of every event she had been to thus far, except she had not realized how much worse it felt to stand beside such dazzling triumph at the same time that she recognized her failures.

Mr. Lockhart returned and handed round the drinks that he had been so kind to fetch.

Relieved, Nora relaxed in his warm presence. She grasped her glass too fast, eager for the courage that the wine might lend to her, and spilled the entire cup of hot negus on her dress.

With a horrified gasp, she watched the red wine soak into the white satin like blood. The opera could not have provided more drama than she felt in that moment. Faintly, she stammered an excuse and hurried away, cheeks flushed, before her aunt could chaperone her to the retiring room.

Nora was almost never clumsy, and she hated to appear gauche or ill-mannered in company. It was agonizing to have done so in front of Miss Lockhart and her flock of admirers. Of course, she was of so little consequence to them that perhaps the spill was overlooked and her hurried flight unremarked. For once she thought of her lack of popularity with gratitude.

The retiring room was down a flight of carpeted stairs and hidden to the side, but she found it quickly enough. It was well appointed with velvet upholstered chairs, ornate mirrors, and enough space for a dozen or more ladies. It was near the end of intermission, and she was relieved to see that the room was deserted.

Nora sat on a low stool and examined the damage to her dress, a feeling of helplessness stealing over her. A red wine stain was impossible to deal with. However, she had fled to the retiring room with as much intent to compose herself as fix the stain, so she sat still, took a deep breath, and tried not to crumple her satin skirts in pure frustration. How embarrassed she felt, on an evening that had promised so much.

"Lady Honora, are you quite all right?"

Nora sucked in a sharp breath. There was Miss Lockhart stepping through the door, looking like a vision in a pale blue gown that floated around her curves.

Her stomach dropped. She had not had a single drop of wine to drink from her spilled glass, but her head spun as if she were half a bottle in.

"Miss Lockhart, thank you for your kind attention," she replied. "But it is a stain, nothing more. You needn't have left your admirers."

Miss Lockhart looked at her dress and Nora winced, flustered.

"Wine is the very devil to remove, isn't it?" she said.

"Quite so. There's nothing more for me to do here to fix it," Nora said, and stood on wobbling legs. "We should return. The second act should be starting soon."

"There is no reason to hurry," Miss Lockhart replied with a grin, and flung herself into an elegant thin-legged chair. "I can hear the music starting up again so you've already missed part of it. Personally, I plan to stay here as long as I can. Maybe even for the duration of the entire next act. That soprano is dreadful."

"She is a beautiful performer." Nora could hear the stiffness in her voice, and she struggled to regain her usual composure. "But if you wish to return, I am sure the gentlemen can distract you from the stage."

"Oh, them," she said dismissively. "Gentlemen are as common as grapes on the vine. That lot was nothing special." Miss Lockhart's face brightened, and Nora felt several degrees warmer by the light in her eyes. "By the by, thank you ever so much for the slippers, Lady Honora! I received them last week and they are quite the prettiest pair in my wardrobe."

Nora was flustered. Oh no. The rose slippers. The *note*. Panicked, she tried to remember what she had scribbled that afternoon at the shoe emporium. Nothing personal, nothing intimate, she recalled with relief.

Nothing had been put into writing that she truly wanted to say when she looked at Miss Lockhart.

This was not how she had wanted to talk about the gift. Not when she felt so tongue-tied. Not when they had come upon each other like this by mistake, without any forethought or planning.

Confronted face to face about it, she worried that she might faint from the sudden lack of air in the retiring room.

Nora swallowed and said, "I simply wanted to express my regret at having damaged your own pair."

"It was unnecessary," Miss Lockhart assured her, "but I think that's the hallmark of the very best kind of gift! Those slippers deserve to have an exquisite dress made for them, which will give me an excellent reason to visit my modiste again—so I really must thank you."

Nora smiled, some of her tension easing away. "Your dresses are always beautiful, Miss Lockhart, so I am sure that this one will be no exception. The slippers will pale in comparison."

"Never," she said with a look so full of sincerity that it took Nora's breath away.

This was only friendship, Nora reminded herself, though she was uncertain even of that. She was in danger of forgetting herself in Miss Lockhart's presence, captivated by her charm.

A heartbeat passed, and Nora spoke again. "I should return. My aunt will be wondering where I am."

"Lady Mildred must know that you are here in the retiring room examining the damage to your dress. Where else would you be? No one should wonder anything at all. Besides, the longer that wine settles into the fabric, the less chance you have to remove it. Come, let's try to fix it together!"

Nora looked at her in alarm. "No, please do not trouble yourself."

But Miss Lockhart was already applying herself to her supple leather gloves. She worked the pearl buttons free of their looped buttonholes and peeled the gloves from her hands, freeing finger by finger.

Nora's mouth went dry at the sight of those beautiful hands, narrow and slender with perfect white tipped fingernails. Her arms were now bare, and Nora wished for nothing more than to trace a finger down one elegant arm.

There was a basin of water on a low shelf for washing up. Miss Lockhart reached out her bare hand to clasp Nora's gloved one and pulled her to her feet. She tugged her over to the basin, as if her touch didn't crack through Nora with a thunderclap of physical awareness.

"I think we shall get the stain out in a trice," she said, and she dipped the fabric in the basin and rubbed at it, bending low over the skirt with industrious effort.

Nora looked down at her glossy raven hair in its elegant array of curls and was close enough to smell her perfume. Orange blossom. She inhaled, savoring the scent.

After a moment, Miss Lockhart looked up with a rueful smile on her face. "I should have confessed something," she said. "I've never done this before, and I don't think I'm helping."

Nora blinked after a startled moment. "Well, it's no worse off for trying," she assured her.

They looked at the white satin, which now sported a large water stain. Instead of fading, the red wine spread slowly but surely.

They looked at the fabric, and then at each other, and all of a sudden both of them were laughing and laughing.

Nora clutched the back of a chair with one hand, the other low on her belly as she tried to stop her whoops of laughter. When had she last laughed like this? When had anything been so funny?

When had she had a friend like this?

Could she count Miss Lockhart as a friend?

Miss Lockhart wiped tears from her eyes and took a deep, steadying breath. "Well. Your maid can spend tomorrow morning soaking your dress, providing that I haven't done irreparable damage. We are not our maids, after all, and we are simply not up to the challenges that they excel at."

Nora considered this. "Yes, my maid does have a knack for fixing this sort of issue."

"Good! Then I won't feel too badly about this," she replied with a mischievous smile.

"We should go now. We've been here long enough, and my aunt will be on edge if I am unchaperoned."

Miss Lockhart rolled her eyes. "I am sure your aunt doesn't expect you to be up to no good in the ladies *retiring room*, of all places. We don't need a chaperone here!"

But the crackle of awareness remained, and they locked eyes. Nora remembered her gaze earlier when they were sitting together during the first act of the opera, and was quite, quite sure that she was not the only one who felt the pull between them.

"Besides, I need to enlist your help. As soon as I saw you leave, I knew I had to follow so we could speak in private."

Nora felt a twinge of chagrin, and her mood fell as she realized that Miss Lockhart had not come to the retiring room with the intention to help her with her dress.

"What do we need to talk about?" she asked.

Miss Lockhart sighed. "My interfering mother. As soon as she saw those gorgeous shoes, she interrogated me as to their origin. And once she realized your standing in society, she encouraged me to befriend you and to take advantage of your connections."

Nora blinked at her frankness. "I do have connections, but they have barely helped me in my own quest for matrimony thus far. You desire *my* help to land a husband? I have been a wallflower at every event I have attended."

Miss Lockhart waved a hand. "I do not care about anyone's connections—it is my mother who wants me to marry well, so she is pushing me toward any opportunity that she can scramble at, all in order to wed me to a nobleman."

This was much worse than standing beside Miss Lockhart as she flirted with the gentlemen who ignored Nora. This whole evening was a sham, a mere pretense of friendliness from the Lockharts. Her pleasure in the opera was fast fading.

"You will need to explain to your mother that I cannot help you," Nora said quietly.

Miss Lockhart leaned closer. "But I do not wish to wed," she confessed. "I have no intention of accepting anyone's hand in marriage this season, whether or not you can improve my standing in society."

"Then what is it you want?"

As soon as she said it, Nora regretted it. Those green eyes sparkled with desire, and the very air seemed thick with tension. If she had really followed her to the retiring room to help with her skirt, or to flirt, then Nora would be leaning in right now, touching those ebony curls, pressing her lips to hers and throwing caution to the wind.

But Miss Lockhart's mercenary goals soured her desire.

"I want my mother to stop bothering me about marriage. If she sees that we are friends, she will think I am trying to advance myself and she will leave me alone. Otherwise, she is going to increase her chaperonage and I shall never have a moment's peace or have any opportunity to enjoy myself. I do *not* consider hanging about for a husband an enjoyable use of my time."

Nora considered. "So you would pretend to have a friendship with me until your mother ceases her agenda?"

Miss Lockhart hesitated. "I don't know if I would call it a pretense," she said slowly. "All I am suggesting is that we spend more time together. It shouldn't be such a hardship, I promise you. My friends say that I am a most entertaining companion."

"I am sure you are," Nora murmured. "So I am to gain a most entertaining companion, for as long as you need me?"

"Well, what is that you want in return?" she asked.

You, she thought. But instead she said, "I do want to marry. I am not accustomed to London and would much prefer to return to the country. But I am not popular and no man has paid me suit thus far."

Miss Lockhart nodded. "This I can arrange. I know a great many gentlemen."

"I must marry a title. My aunt is like your mother and will not hear of me marrying into anything less than a baronetcy."

"Well then. I am not invited to all of the best places—the Lockhart name is not so illustrious as all that, and although I do know a baronet or two, I suspect your aunt would prefer as high a title as you can reach." She paused, lips pursed. "But if you could obtain access for me at all the best places, I could help charm the noblemen for you. I assure you I have no desire for them for myself. My mother will think me most industrious in my search, but the benefit there will be all yours."

Nora considered. "This seems a fair bargain. I will gain a husband, and you will gain respite from your mother."

"So we have an agreement?"

"We do."

They shook hands. Miss Lockhart's hand was still ungloved, and Nora fought the impulse to hold it longer than necessary.

Miss Lockhart took a deep breath and stepped back. "Well, I am glad that it is settled," she said, and took a seat in front of a gilt mirror. "Look at that, my hair is not behaving itself anymore. I shall have to miss the second act after all to rearrange myself." She peered at herself in the mirror as she tugged her kidskin gloves back on.

Nora went over to her. Her hair was beautifully arranged, but some of her curls were working their way out of the thin gold combs holding them back.

"It doesn't look too bad," Nora said.

Miss Lockhart kept her eyes locked on Nora's. She ran her hands through her hair and dislodged her pins. "Oops," she said, and her lips quirked upward. "Dear me."

Nora looked at her. Friendship, she thought again. They had an agreement to help each other, didn't they?

"Unlike my skirt, this I can fix," Nora declared.

She stepped behind her, and keeping her eyes fixed on the mirror, she swiftly slipped the combs out of the black tresses. She took her time to arrange the curls one by one, and gently, slowly slid the combs back into the coiffure. She wished she wasn't wearing gloves, so that she could feel that silken hair against her skin.

She stared into Miss Lockhart's eyes in the mirror. Nora swept an errant curl off of Miss Lockhart's shoulder, brushing a gloved finger against her collarbone and against her elegant neck, pausing before lifting her touch away, longing for it to remain longer.

"Now we should go," Nora said, her voice just above a whisper.

Her skirts swishing as she turned, Nora headed out the door to the retiring room, straight up the wide carpeted stairs with Miss Lockhart following behind, and they eased back into their seats halfway through the second act quite as if nothing exceptional had happened at all.

Chapter Seven

When the morning light slanted into her room through the open curtains and her maid Mary clattered a cup of chocolate and a biscuit on the table beside her bed, Nora wanted nothing more than to pull the thin wool blanket over her head and drift right back to sleep where the image of Miss Lockhart beckoned to her in memory.

But it wouldn't do to be lazy. She most assuredly did not want her maid carrying tales to the downstairs staff, where they would find their way to the ears of Aunt Mildred. Enjoying a few more moments in bed might feel like a triviality, but her aunt was a rigorous follower of routine. If she didn't wish to be interrogated, Nora would need to be prepared to break her fast at the usual hour regardless of how late their evening had been last night.

Punctuality was the unwritten eighth heavenly virtue, according to Aunt Mildred.

Nora drew the blankets off and rose from the bed, taking the chocolate with her. Oh, last night! The aria from the opera was still soaring through her mind, and she continued to relive the glorious performance during her morning toilette as Mary brushed her hair.

Her thoughts were preoccupied not only with the music from the opera, but with the music of Miss Lockhart's teasing laughter. She had never met anyone quite like her, so exuberant and witty and vibrant. She had approached the stain on her dress and the conundrum of her mother's interference with the same cheerful determination, prepared to throw herself into finding a solution.

Had she been in earnest about working together to find Nora a husband? In the morning light, away from the romance of the evening, she felt doubts creep in. They hardly knew each other. Yet Nora wanted to discover her favorite poetry and whether she cared for novels, to learn if she liked a quiet stroll in the park during springtime, or a cozy chat by the fireplace on a winter's afternoon.

But those were thoughts of romance.

Nora stared into the oval mirror as Mary arranged her hair into a braided pile and slid pins into her locks. Her back was ramrod straight in its delicate stays, and her ankles were crossed neatly under the stool in front of her dressing table.

Even in her state of undress, she looked like the perfect lady. She thought she must appear the same as every other young woman in London at this very moment, getting ready for society life, dressing herself to fit into place next to everyone else. Cloaking herself with the same wishes and dreams that all young ladies claimed they desired for themselves. Marriage. Money. Men.

Deep inside, she was starting to feel the build of something more. Something different. Nora looked into her own eyes in the mirror and realized with an uncomfortable start that she didn't just wish to know more about Miss Lockhart's needs and wants. She wanted to learn more about her *own*. Unease shivered the hairs on her forearms.

Nora smoothed the thin fabric of her chemise over her knees as if she could brush all errant thoughts away from her, willing to bottle them up and throw them into the River Thames. Her heart was beating in triple time with nerves as Mary helped her into her day dress.

At the breakfast table, Nora kissed her aunt's cheek before settling down to her usual repast of eggs and toast. Everything was just as it should be. Everything was arranging itself in her life as she had always expected it to. Exactly as it would have been if her parents were across from her now, instead of her aunt.

She waited to feel reassured.

Instead, the ripple of unease inside of her was growing into a rising wave.

Frowning down at her eggs, she pushed the plate aside and picked up the newspaper that her aunt had already finished.

"I remember looking forward to reading the papers every morning when I was your age," Aunt Mildred said. "I too didn't have many suitors, and it was such a thrill to see my name written there, blanked out beside the title of the man who would later marry me."

She placed her wrinkled hand on top of Nora's. Her eyes were warm, her face serious. "I wanted you to come to London to find your future, and I wanted to help you find it. I am determined that you will be successful." She lifted her hand from Nora's and picked up her teacup. "I have been thinking that we should pay a social call to the Duchess of Hawthorne. We haven't been in contact since the duke left England so many years ago, but she nevertheless is still family through her marriage. She may be able to help you get settled with the right sort of people, now that you are growing more accustomed to London. After all, I could see how the gentlemen at the end of the evening last night were becoming interested in you, even after you spilled that wine all over your dress."

The lecturing side of Aunt Mildred was the side that she was most familiar with, and Nora took a deep breath of relief, reassured by the routine.

"Perhaps the gentlemen were more attentive because of my new friendship with Miss Lockhart," she said, watching her aunt's reaction. She wasn't sure what her aunt thought of Miss Lockhart, as her flirtatious behavior had not been strictly proper with the gentlemen. Part of her hoped that she would forbid the association, which would remove the choice of friendship. Then Nora could forget about their agreement to help each other, and could forget the pull of attraction between them.

But Aunt Mildred nodded. "Miss Lockhart does have spirit, and was among the most popular last night with the young men. Her mother tells me it is only a matter of time before she settles down this season with one of them. Now, put that paper away and go practice your pianoforte. You never know when it will be useful to show your talents."

Nora cast one last longing look at the paper. She had never been much interested in the news of the day, but being in London was awakening all sorts of thoughts and feelings inside her that she had never realized that she had. She rather fancied that she wanted to read the political section today. As she rose from the table, her eye caught the date at the top of the paper.

It was Tuesday.

For a moment, she couldn't recall the significance. Nora slowly walked down the narrow hallway toward the drawing room, trying to remember, when it occurred to her. Lady Georgina hosted her salons on Tuesdays.

She hadn't given a second thought to the invitation, dismissing it as bluestocking falderal. But the invitation seemed more intriguing to her today. Lady Georgina had seemed so interesting, and friendly. It might be no bad thing to visit her salon.

Nora sat on the hard bench in front of the pianoforte and rested her fingers for a moment on the ivory keys. She played a Scottish air that she knew her aunt would enjoy, and then a hymn.

Her uneasiness growled inside her like a hunger that she didn't know how to satisfy. She was tired of forever trying to please her aunt and to present herself as marriageable to the men of the *ton*. More and more, it seemed to her like a good deal of work for uncertain gains. And yet, what other option did she have?

It was very kind of her aunt to sponsor her season. She couldn't imagine Aunt Mildred wanting to go to all of the events that she had been whisking her off to attend, but there she was at every one of them without complaint, overseeing her charge. Nora owed her a debt that could never be repaid, and it went far beyond the exorbitant cost that Aunt Mildred had invested in her wardrobe alone. The sole way she could make sure that her aunt's efforts were not in vain was if she could scare up a proposal.

By ear, she played a few bars of last night's aria, swept away again by the opera's story. Before long, Aunt Mildred glided into the room. "Another Scotch air would be nice, instead of this modern nonsense," she suggested, and Nora understood it for the command that it was.

She abandoned the whimsical aria, earning a sharp satisfied nod.

It wasn't that she didn't want to please her aunt. It was just that sometimes she wanted to be the one who was pleased, who issued a command. Who was served, instead of forever serving.

She thought of the fashionable London men she had met, gentlemen who had the politeness to dance with wallflowers such as herself. Considerate though they were in doing their duty by their hostesses, she wondered what they might be like as a husband. Probably they would be no different from most gentlemen, wanting everything their own way.

Marriage had sounded like an ideal bargain when she was in Wiltshire. She would gain a diffident partner who would leave her to her own devices, and in return she would demand enough children so that she wouldn't feel so alone. Here in London, those same thoughts seemed depressing and selfish.

The memory of Miss Lockhart's cheery smile blossomed in her mind's eye. They had an agreement now to help each other. It might be a tenuous and temporary friendship, but Nora felt its warmth regardless. Even if it was the pretense of friendship that she was offered, it would go a long way to ease her lonely spirit.

But how long would Miss Lockhart even pretend to be friends with her? As soon as she obtained the invitations that she desired, would she really stay and help Nora to attract a suitor? Was she trustworthy?

It was time to take control of her own life. To do what she wished, even for only a few weeks of freedom. Then if Miss Lockhart did renege on their deal, she would have gained the courage to handle the rest of the season on her own.

In the end, it wasn't difficult to find her way to Lady Georgina's house. Her townhouse was two streets away from Nora's, so it was simple enough to tell her aunt that she was going with her maid to purchase ribbons for a new hat and visit the library, and instead took her maid to Lady Georgina's.

Nora walked quickly, her feet light and her heart happy. She wasn't sure what she would find at the salon, but the power of making the choice to attend invigorated her. The walk was short, but along the way Nora looked at every green blade of grass, every passerby, every lazy cloud in the bright blue sky, curious about everything as if seeing it for the first time. She felt calm and confident, up to the moment where she was knocking on the door. Then she felt her stomach dip and her spirits flee.

The ornate door opened to reveal an elderly butler, blinking at her. He seemed kindly, instead of forbidding.

"You would be here for Lady Georgina, I suppose. Pray come in, come in." He waved her forward with a trembling hand.

Nora's nerves almost failed her as she followed him down a wide hallway and into a drawing room filled with women.

Lady Georgina rose from the sofa to greet her. The light silk of her white dress wafted behind her as she moved to her side. "Lady Honora, I am so very glad you came!" she said warmly.

She shook her hand again, as she had done every time they had met. Just like Nora had seen men do on occasion. Like Nora had done with Miss Lockhart after they had agreed to their alliance. Rather than surprising her, now she felt it was rather in the spirit that she expected, and she smiled.

"It was kind of you to invite me, Lady Georgina," she said.

"Please, didn't I tell you to call me Gina when we first met? I absolutely insist. At least when we are in more private conditions, that is. And might I call you Honora? We do not all agree with titles and pomp and circumstance within these rooms. I do hope you understand."

Nora raised her brows at the familiar address. "Then I prefer if you call me Nora."

Gina beamed at her. "Good! Now, please meet my friends."

There were a group of eight women in the salon, of various ethnicities and social classes. Some were dressed as finely as Gina and Nora. Others wore practical sensible dresses. There was a journalist for one of the papers, a governess, the head seamstress of a fashionable atelier, and two Quakers who shook Nora's hand as firmly as Gina had and addressed her as Friend. She was very pleased to see Mrs. Bathurst as well, the pianist from the musical afternoon that she had attended the previous week.

The room was full of bright chatter and movement. Nora could hear a heady debate about coal mining from one corner of the room, and a sympathetic discourse about the plight of working class women in another.

The journalist sat at an open escritoire, scribbling so fast that ink was flicking onto her dress from her nib. She didn't seem to notice, though Nora thought that judging from the state of her dress that perhaps she didn't care.

Gina drew Nora to a quiet sofa near the fireplace. "Isn't it wonderful?" she breathed. "To be in the presence of such free spirits?

Nothing said here is dismissed as too trivial or too difficult for a lady to understand. We are a society of equals within these four walls every week, no matter what the outside world thinks of us."

"I am enjoying myself immensely," Nora admitted. "But why did you invite me here? I am no writer, I have no political connections. I feel like all these other women are contributing their viewpoint or their skills to further these causes."

Gina laughed. "All women are welcome here. I invite anyone who I think could be a good fit for our little society and could provide good conversation. You looked so serious and so thoughtful at the ball the other night when we first met. Maybe I wanted to know what it was that you were thinking about."

Nora wondered if she was flirting.

Gina leaned closer. She had a very slight bosom and it was covered in ruffles and bows and trims, but Nora suspected that she was trying to give her an eyeful.

Definitely flirting.

Nora was charmed. But although Gina was beautiful, she didn't have the same reaction that she felt in the presence of Miss Lockhart.

"My thoughts are not so very interesting," she said lightly.

Gina pulled back. A shadow passed across her face, but then her sunny smile returned. "I'm sure you have many interesting thoughts," she said, and stood up. "Come share them with Madhavi. She is organizing a letter writing campaign protesting the working conditions of tea plantations in India."

The next hour saw Nora engaged in conversations with several interesting women. As the afternoon drew to a close and the women began to depart from the salon, Nora took a deep breath. This had been one of the best days that she had spent in London thus far. Perhaps friendships outside of her aunt's set could be found after all. The unease that had been building in her all day had quieted, and a sense of satisfaction spread through her.

If today was about satisfying her own desires, then Nora knew where she needed to go next.

CHAPTER EIGHT

Jacqueline and Beatrice watched another gentleman depart from the Lockharts' sitting room. "There, my dear," Jacquie said with satisfaction, "you have made so many conquests already that they are spilling over into my home to seek you out for a visit."

Beatrice laughed. "They are doing no such thing!" she cried. "Really, Jacquie, you are too much." But she smiled as she said it, and Jacqueline knew that she was pleased by the attention.

"You will be a bride by season's end, and your troubles will be over," she said, and reached out to squeeze her hand.

Her mother frowned at them. "You shall *both* be brides," she declared. "Well, I must go back to my letter writing. My sister needs all the latest news from the city as she isn't planning to come to visit for another few months. If another gentleman comes to call, do have Mullens fetch me at once."

Jacqueline and Beatrice shared a fond look, and then Jacqueline turned her attention to the embroidery hoop that she kept in the drawing room for afternoons such as this. She was working on a reticule and fancied that it was turning out well. One could hardly see the skipped stitches.

"My mother may wish to marry me off this year, but her behavior might do the work of discouraging the gentlemen for me," Jacquie said. "I daresay none of the gentlemen that she would wish for me would desire her as a mother-in-law."

Bea grinned. "Although this may be true, would you wish to spend all of your time at a ball with your mother by your side, carrying on as she does?"

Jacquie sighed. "I know, I shall have no peace at all."

They sat in companionable silence as Jacqueline painstakingly embellished a leaf with shiny silk thread, and Beatrice flipped the pages of a novel.

The butler reappeared, and she was getting ready to tell Mullens that enough was enough and she could not be considered to be "at home" to any more visitors, when he held out the calling card. She saw the name written in bold black ink on the thick cream card—*Lady Honora Banfield.*

"We are at home," Jacquie told the butler, her breath catching in her throat. "Please escort her to us."

Mullens bowed. "Very good, Miss Lockhart," he said, and glided to the door.

"Oh—and one more thing. Please turn away any other visitors after this."

Beatrice frowned. "No more visitors?" she said.

Jacqueline waved a hand airily. "I am growing tired. After this, I think I will need a rest before dinner." This was a blatant lie—she always had energy to spare, and Beatrice knew it.

Lady Honora entered the room and the day brightened. She was buttoned up to the chin in a satin day dress with a lace bonnet hiding her blond curls, and Jacqueline was struck by her elegance.

"How delightful to see you again," Jacquie greeted her. "Please do sit down. May I offer you refreshment? Have you met my friend Miss Everson?"

Jacqueline poured and handed her a delicate china teacup perched on a saucer. As she took the cup, Lady Honora's fingers brushed her own, and she felt a pulse of awareness. She was just as captivated as she had been in the opera house.

"Thank you," Lady Honora murmured, and their eyes met for a brief moment.

"Lady Honora, it is a pleasure," Beatrice said. "How do you like London so far?"

"London is a very fine city. There are so many people here. One never knows who one might encounter at a ball, or under which circumstances that one might meet a new friend." She looked at Jacqueline, who realized that she must be remembering their first encounter when Phin had swung her into her path.

"London society offers so many opportunities for—friendship."
Jacquie beamed at Lady Honora, who returned the smile a little shyly.
"Please, can I offer you anything further? Lemon cake? Or a biscuit?"

"I am quite content as we are in this very moment," she said, and
her words seemed heavy with meaning.

Bea sipped her tea, her eyes focused on Lady Honora. "Have you
had any excitement? Have you many beaux?"

"Not anyone in particular," Lady Honora admitted. "I did dance
once with the Earl of Sinclair, who was a perfect gentleman."

"The Earl of Sinclair! He is considered quite the catch. I trust
you enjoyed yourself?"

Jacqueline gave her a sharp look. Bea was determined to catch
Sinclair and selfish enough to wrest the prize from any other contender.

Lady Honora looked nonplussed. "I suppose I did enjoy myself,"
she said. "If I recall, it was a cotillion. An invigorating dance."

Bea made a show of admiring of her hands. "An engagement
ring from the earl would look quite, quite charming on my finger, do
you not agree?"

Jacquie groaned inwardly. Even for her, this was laying it on thick.

"Has Lord Sinclair shown you any partiality?" Lady Honora
inquired. "If congratulations are soon to be in order, pray allow me to
be among the first to give them to you."

"Well, there is no such understanding…as yet. In fact, I am not
even sure if the earl should be my first choice, should he ask. There
is such a wealth of opportunity out there in society!" She simpered at
Jacqueline. "And my dear, dear friend Jacquie has agreed to help me
to land any gentleman that I so desire. *Friendship* is so very important
to a girl these days. With darling Jacquie's help, all of London shall
be at my feet."

Lady Honora set her cup on her saucer with an audible clink and
looked sharply at Jacquie and Beatrice.

"I would do the same for any friend," Jacqueline said, but it
sounded weak even to her ears.

"How selfless you are," Lady Honora replied. Her voice was icy
enough to chill the remainder of Jacqueline's tea.

Beatrice tittered. "'Selfless' may not be quite the word. Though
Jacquie is a very *giving* friend."

She drew out her words, and Jacqueline clenched her teeth, wishing that Bea could at least be less obvious in her jealousy. She drew her embroidery hoop onto her lap again. And stabbed the embroidery needle into the fabric with frustrated fervor.

"Your embroidery is beautiful," Lady Honora said to Jacqueline, clearly eager to turn the conversation away from talk of beaux. "Is it your own design?"

"You flatter me," she said. "No, I took it from a lady's magazine some time ago. I'm slow with the needle—my mother despairs of my efforts."

"I think your efforts are beautiful," Lady Honora said with a smile. "Is it a fruit motif?"

Jacqueline looked down at the fabric. "They're supposed to be leaves and flowers. I thought it was coming along nicely." She held it out in front of her and looked at it again. "It does look rather like a fruit basket, now that you mention it! I should change the design."

"I am glad to be of service," Lady Honora murmured with a smile.

Jacquie laughed. "I welcome any and all offers of service from friends."

Bea sniffed. "You should continue embroidering flowers on your reticule, Jacquie," she broke in. "Much more refined."

"Oh, it is meant to be a reticule?" Lady Honora inquired gently. "Forgive me, I had thought it would be a scarf."

She met her eyes and they both broke into laughter. Jacquie felt deliciously happy to be teased, sharing the moment together, and doubled over her work, her shoulders shaking with laughter. It reminded her of the retiring room at the opera, when they had laughed so hard together that she had to wipe tears from her eyes. She felt Bea's hand on her forearm and was irritated at the disruption.

"It's clear that country standards are very different from the city, if you think that *that* fabric would be meant for a scarf," Beatrice said with disdain.

Jacqueline's mother arrived in the room. "I've just finished my letter to your dear aunt," she announced. "She shall be well entertained when she receives it, though it might be a miracle if she can read it at all. I had to cross the page to fit in all of the latest talk of the town, and even still it was a squeeze to include all the choicest news."

She beamed at Lady Honora. "How kind of you to come to call on us, Lady Honora. I do hope you and your aunt enjoyed the opera last night."

"The opera?" Beatrice said with a question in her voice, her eyes narrowed.

"Yes, Lady Honora and Lady Mildred were our guests at the opera last night. It was such a fine evening. So many people in attendance! I swear I saw some gentlemen in the boxes with ladies who were *not* their wives. You can be sure I named who they were in the letter to my sister! She will be most intrigued."

"We enjoyed it very much," Lady Honora replied. "My aunt passes along her regards and thanks you again for the invitation."

"I wanted to mention that I saw those beautiful slippers that you sent to my daughter—she told me about your little encounter at the ball. So very amusing! Quite generous of you to send over a new pair of dancing shoes, and ever such pretty ones. You are a thoughtful young woman—your aunt must be proud of you."

Lady Honora gestured at Jacqueline. "Your daughter deserves better than being trampled by my gracelessness, and it was a pleasure to send over a pair of shoes that will suit her so well."

"They are exquisite—from Mr. Addington's Ladies Emporium, aren't they? Jacqueline and Beatrice, weren't you there quite recently? Did you notice them on the shelves?"

Lady Honora said nothing.

Beatrice looked at her with thunder on her face.

Jacqueline replied, "No, Mama, I don't think I noticed them there. They really are beautiful. Thank you again, Lady Honora."

Lady Honora rose. "I should be on my way home before my aunt starts to wonder where I am."

"Oh, do you keep country hours even here in the city?" Beatrice drawled. "How quaint of you."

"Did you come in your carriage?" Mrs. Lockhart inquired. "I shall call for it to be brought around at once."

"I will walk with you to the door," Jacqueline said quickly. It was an unusual thing to say, and both her mother and Bea looked at her with almost comical expressions of surprise.

She hurried out the drawing room door just behind Lady Honora but stopped her before they could reach the front hallway, pulling her into an empty room.

"Lady Honora, do forgive my friend," she said, wincing at the thought of Bea's pointed words.

She raised an eyebrow. "Miss Everson has done nothing that needs forgiveness. I gather you and she are very…close."

Jacqueline wasn't sure what she meant by that—was it possible that she could have guessed by so few words that she and Bea had once been lovers?

"You do not see that she means nothing by her words."

"I think that it is quite clear, Miss Lockhart." An expression of sadness flitted over her face. "You would help find a husband for Miss Everson out of loyalty, love, and friendship. But at the opera, you offered to help *me* to find a husband for the sole purpose to thwart your mother's plans for you." She took a deep breath. "I had thought you sincere, but after seeing you with your true friend, I find myself not up to the task of being a second fiddle to Miss Everson."

Jacquie bit her lip. "I said that I would help you, and I will."

Lady Honora looked skeptical. "But meanwhile you would push Miss Everson at the biggest prizes in the Marriage Mart? Perhaps we should call off this agreement now, Miss Lockhart. It may be of no benefit to either of us."

"I understand how this must seem," Jacqueline said slowly. "But I promised Beatrice that I would help her before I even met you. I can help both of you—there are single wealthy aristocrats all over London, and each of you needs only one."

"Do you have a multitude of such friends, all of whom you give the same offer, in order to take what favors you can from them?" she snapped, her eyes bright with emotion, and then clapped a hand to her mouth. Visibly upset, she stammered, "I apologize, Miss Lockhart. That was uncalled for."

Jacquie was startled. Lady Honora always seemed so restrained, and this sudden burst of emotion shocked her. "I can assure you that I don't make such promises lightly," she said. "And I don't take any favors that I haven't earned."

Lady Honora considered her words. "I believe you," she said, but uncertainty still showed on her face. She fidgeted with her reticule. "And our agreement still stands, if you wish it to—but only *if* you promise me that you will help me win the hand of the Earl of Sinclair. Everyone has been telling me that he is considered to be the most eligible of unmarried gentlemen."

Jacqueline winced. Beatrice would not rest until she was on her honeymoon with Sinclair, and heaven help anyone in her way. "Would you consider settling for a rather nice baron?" she suggested.

"If you do not help me win over the earl, at the expense of your friend Miss Everson, then I will know that you are not sincere in our arrangement." She stood there defiantly, but there was something vulnerable in her eyes that tugged at Jacqueline's heart. Lady Honora, for all of her quiet grace and elegance, did not look like someone who was used to standing up for herself, and Jacquie found herself wanting to help her. She looked in sore need of a friend

Jacqueline's hesitation was brief. "I agree," she said, hoping that she could find a way to hide her agenda from Bea.

"Good," she said, and with a triumphant smile, reached into her reticule to withdraw a crisp white paper. "Here is your first invitation. The Countess of Marchfield is hosting a soiree on Friday. My aunt tells me that there should be plenty of noblemen in attendance, and the earl is certain to be there."

Jacqueline's blood sang though her veins. Lady Honora was jealous, and she was willing to bet that she wasn't just jealous of the earl's attention to Beatrice. She was jealous of Beatrice's attention to Jacquie. This was very interesting indeed.

Staring at the invitation with its elegant black script, she was impressed. "The Countess of Marchfield," she repeated. "This is a high honor for the first invitation."

Lady Honora smiled coolly at her. "And there is more to come… if you can deliver the earl."

As an exit line, it was as good as they came. She swirled around, her day dress whipping around her ankles, and strode down the hall and out the front door.

When Jacqueline returned to the drawing room, she found her mother beaming after her and Beatrice tapping her knee with her fingers.

"What a sweet young lady," her mother exclaimed. "I am so pleased that you are cultivating some friendships with ladies who don't put on such airs as some of them do! If she has friends with whom you can rub shoulders, you must do so posthaste—this is a circle that you should be thrilled to have the chance to gain entry to."

"Oh, she hasn't been in London for very long," Bea said with a quick shake of her head, "and I haven't seen her in any company of note. She may have a grand dowry and nice manners, but I wouldn't say yet if it's a friendship that will gain us any particular notice in the upper echelons."

Jacquie sat down and picked up her embroidery hoop, frowning down at her stitching. "That's not quite true. She has relations who are quite high in the instep. And the Earl of Sinclair did dance with her once."

"There is another who may gain the attention of the earl's favor yet," Bea sniffed.

"Very true," her mother said. "Why, you have set your cap at the earl, haven't you, Beatrice? I daresay he could choose any girl he wants. He's rich enough to marry a pretty face instead of a pretty dowry. Lady Honora is not the sole contender."

She looked at Jacquie. "You could also put out a few lures in that direction."

Jacquie pricked her finger with the embroidery needle, startled. She couldn't mean—oh. The earl. "Mama, I would never set out to snare any man that my friend has her eyes on," she said, and was rewarded when Bea beamed at her.

She sighed. "Commendable is the friendship of young ladies these days. In my day, we would not have hesitated to snatch what we could from the men who were available! If there was no ring on their finger, then they were fair game, no matter who they were courting. Well, there will be a man for you yet, my Jacquie." She sashayed out the door.

Beatrice poked her in the arm as soon as her mother had gone. "Jacquie, what is it that you aren't telling me? What shoes did Lady Honora purchase for you? And why on earth would she do such an odd thing?"

"She was being friendly. She sent me the dancing slippers last week—remember when Phin and I fell into her at the ball? She said she trod on my feet and wanted to replace my shoe, that's all."

"You have more dancing slippers than anyone I know," Bea said, her voice flat. "And you wear them out so often that they would have been finished by the end of the ball anyway."

"Well, Lady Honora couldn't know that. We barely know each other. My aunt invited her to the opera with us, but I haven't seen her otherwise."

With an unladylike shriek, Beatrice flung herself back against the sofa cushions. "Jacqueline Lockhart! You despise the opera. Almost *nothing* would compel you to go to a theater. Are you falling in love again?"

"Of course not! I told you, I don't even know her!"

Bea sat up and counted off her fingers. "She sent you a gift. You attended the opera together. Something happened there, I saw the way you looked at each other when you said you had both been there! And then here she was, visiting you the very next day, late enough in the afternoon to be quite sure that no other visitor would be here, in the hopes that she could see you alone." She held up her three fingers and wiggled them in Jacquie's face. "She is certainly interested in you, even if you are not interested in her!"

Jacqueline fidgeted with the embroidery hoop and then set it aside on the table. "There might be some interest," she admitted.

Bea shrieked again and threw a small pillow at her. "Why did you not say anything? You have kept everything from me!"

"There isn't much to reveal. She is here in London to find a husband, and I don't want to get involved with anyone right now—especially not someone who will be here for a few months at most." She paused, then said, "I do think it's possible that the Earl of Sinclair might be interested in courting her." She hoped she could make the lie come true soon enough with Bea none the wiser. Guilt nibbled at her. But she could find suitors for them both, she was sure of it.

"Who is to say she won't be here for longer? Lord Sinclair has been making eyes at me and I have danced with him at every event in the past two weeks. Sometimes these courtships take a long time to develop." Bea shook her curls over her shoulder and preened in the reflection of the silver salver on the table. "After all, I am prettier. She has a long face and looks so serious. Men must find her country manners deadly dull. No, it's quite decided. The earl shall choose me as his countess, and then Lady Honora would have to remain in London waiting for another suitor. Or if she can't find one, she will return to town again next year. Isn't that just as you would wish? More time to pursue her. Honestly, I would be doing you both a *favor* if I married the earl."

"Her face isn't long," Jacqueline protested. "She looks... distinguished."

Bea's mood darkened. "I don't see how that woman could attract Sinclair. I would make a much better wife for him."

"I'm sure you're right," she soothed her. When Bea was wound up, it took a long time for the dramatics to fade. She consoled her in the best way she knew—flattery. "You would make a wonderful countess."

"A better countess than that soulless witch you were with earlier this season!" Bea said.

It was true, but the wound of Lydia's betrayal was still fresh enough to hurt. Jacquie busied herself by pouring a cup of tea that she didn't want. Stirring in the sugar, she said, "She was not always a witch. But I see your point."

Beatrice was at her side in an instant and threw her arm over Jacqueline's shoulders for a quick squeeze. "I am sorry for bringing up her name. It was not well done of me."

Jacqueline managed to smile. "Think no more about it. Now— let's talk about what gown you should wear at the next ball to entice the earl."

CHAPTER NINE

Beatrice lounged in Jacqueline's dressing room, as she had hundreds of times over their years of love and friendship. She was a fixture in the room, much the same as the cherrywood armoire or the pale blue wallpaper. Ready for the countess's ball, she was ensconced in a low-backed chair in the corner of the room, studying her perfect manicure and idly tapping her slipper against the chair leg.

"However did you get this invitation again from the Countess of Marchfield?" she asked, picking up a mirror and checking her makeup, which looked as perfect as always. Her maid was an expert at darkening lashes and brightening lips. "She invited *me* only because she is desperate for her daughter to marry my cousin. God only knows why. Cousin Wilfrid is a dead bore, even though he is in line for a title. Though I suppose he's rich enough for her horrid daughter."

Jacqueline's maid Sally was dressing her hair into an elaborate upsweep. She was itching for her toilette to be completed and for them to sail out the door and get the entire evening over with. She felt that they were spending far too much time on her appearance tonight, but it was her mother's special instruction that no pains must be spared.

Her mother was beside herself with excitement at the invitation. Jacqueline had already been the unhappy recipient of no less than three lectures on proper comportment today.

"Lady Honora arranged it," she said. She knew she had told Bea this multiple times already, but Beatrice tended to be selective in choosing which conversations she remembered. "And her daughter isn't horrid. You just don't like her because she snubbed you that one time at Vauxhall. With good reason, too—you oughtn't have flirted so outrageously with all of her beaux right in front of her."

Bea stretched like a cat in her chair, and her thin muslin gown rippled over her curves. "One simply can't live in the past," she proclaimed. "If she wants to snub me with her wretched little nose in the air for something that I don't even remember doing, then it is her issue. Not mine." She considered. "I think I ought to warn Wilfrid tonight about her wiles. On further reflection, he does deserve better than that chit."

Jacquie shook her head, causing Sally to redo some of the curls that she had been fixing to the top of her hair. "Then she will dislike you all the more, and at her own mother's ball. You could at least wait for another opportunity."

"You know I can't," she sighed. "I cannot bear to be wronged."

"You will make things more difficult for yourself," Jacquie said. "Spite isn't going to win you an engagement."

Beatrice played with the edge of her lace sleeve and ignored her. "By the by, I cannot believe that you are befriending Lady Honora," she said with a tiny yawn. "There is nothing duller than a country mouse scurrying in the corners of a ballroom when one is trying to enjoy an event. Wallflowers are the epitome of boredom."

Jacquie stared straight ahead at her reflection in the mirror, determined not to be bothered by Bea's barbs. "If we help her to attract more attention, then she won't be a wallflower any longer, and you wouldn't find her so tedious."

Bea snorted. "I don't see that happening."

"For my sake, don't ostracize her," Jacquie said. "I will be spending some time with her. She's the reason I was invited to this event, and I will show her common courtesy."

"Well, I suppose then that you will need to be spending all your time with your wallflower and not in more interesting pursuit," she said languidly.

"She's not *my* wallflower!" Jacquie snapped.

Beatrice gave her a silky smile, and Jacquie knew she had been goaded on purpose. She seethed as Sally continued arranging jeweled pins in her hair.

"Begging your pardon, miss, but both of you are so beautifully put together that you will have suitors to spare," Sally said. "And it will do you good to show to your best appearance next to a wallflower."

Beatrice beamed. "Sally dearest, you are a treasure. Do tell me how much the Lockharts pay you, so I can offer you double and take you into my own employ."

Sally smiled cheekily. "Oh, miss, you know for sure and good that I would never leave my mistress, no matter how often you make the same offer!"

Jacqueline shook her head. "As if your maid didn't do exceptional work herself, Bea. You know you look beautiful."

"Knowing is never the same delight as hearing it repeated often," she replied, eyes bright with merriment. "So do continue to flatter me, Jacquie dear. And, Sally, you could do with a few more compliments to me as well."

They all laughed, having been in the same room doing the same evening preparations together for many years. The fact was a comfort to Jacqueline.

Her mother bustled into the room. "Oh good, you're almost ready, Jacquie. You look wonderful—excellent work, Sally. And, darling Beatrice, you look a treat as always." She beamed at them.

"You're so very kind, Mrs. Lockhart!" Bea cried. "We are ever so excited for the evening, aren't we? So many interesting people to see at a ball." She fluttered her lashes at Jacquie.

Jacqueline smiled past gritted teeth. "Of course we are excited. It will be…memorable."

Her mother looked down at her. "Now remember what we discussed. Be on your best behavior, especially in front of the countess! At long last, we are invited somewhere where you can rub shoulders with those worthy of your looks. It has been an age since we have been invited to hobnob with the upper crust. Of course this is nothing new to you, dear Beatrice—you have always been invited out due to your cousin Wilfrid."

"Yes, dear Wilfrid," she said. "One can be an utter ass when one is the heir to a viscountcy and still be invited to all of the very best places."

Mrs. Lockhart tittered. "Young Wilfried has his good qualities," she insisted. "I admit, I had hoped that our Jacquie would catch his fancy, but alas, they never did seem to suit."

"Wilfrid is the sort of man who pinches the maids and dismisses them as soon as they are in the family way," Jacqueline said with a frown. "*His* family way, of course. I would never had considered marrying him."

"You are not to mention that sort of worldly knowledge tonight," Mrs. Lockhart snapped. "Honestly, Jacquie. You should be so lucky for such a man to ask for your hand in marriage. Noblemen all have their little peccadillos."

Then it was all the better for her that she didn't plan to marry, Jacquie thought, but knew better than to argue yet again. If a man had a title, her mother refused to see any flaw.

"Now, there is one more thing that you both must remember. The Duke of Hawthorne is rumored to have finally returned to England. He has a dreadful reputation but no one is quite sure if he will be invited anywhere yet. Or if he would have any interest in attending any society events. I wouldn't put it past the Marchfields to have issued a last-minute invitation to him in order to make their ball the talk of the town, so I am warning you both to keep your distance from scandal and from him."

Beatrice perked up. "The mysterious duke has returned? How very intriguing."

"A married duke," Jacquie pointed out. "Not so interesting after all."

"A *scandalous* duke," Mrs. Lockhart said, eyes narrowed. "If either of you see him, do not approach! One likes to hear the gossip, not become the gossip."

"We don't even know what he's done to earn the rumors," Jacquie complained.

"Earned or unearned, it doesn't matter," her mother retorted. "Words spread quicker than fire and are twice as hard to dampen. It is well and good to be friends with his cousin, Lady Honora, but that is as close as you should get to Hawthorne. She has all the benefits of relation, with the blessings of it being distant."

Bea rolled her eyes at the mention of Lady Honora.

Her mother continued her usual lecture. "You need to be very correct in your behavior tonight, and bright and happy with the gentlemen. A glum girl never got a proposal, remember that. Neither would a bashful belle, nor a forward filly."

"Nor even a daring debutante, or a woeful woman," Beatrice said, her face serious but her eyes twinkling at Jacquie.

"This is a wonderful opportunity for you," her mother continued, too accustomed to their flippancy to pause in her lecture. "Do not embarrass the Lockhart name in front of the Earl and Countess of Marchfield when they have been so good as to extend an invitation to us tonight."

Jacquie rather wished the evening would be over already. This was becoming unbearable. "I will behave as you wish, Mama. You have nothing to worry about."

And for the first half hour of the ball, she was true to her word. She saw some surprised glances passed her way at her presence, and some mild snubs from some ladies who clearly considered her to be reaching above her station. Although embarrassed at how much her mother was toadying to the nobility, she had to admit that this was the happiest that her mother had looked all season.

Lady Honora and her aunt arrived, and Jacqueline saw how the peers greeted them with far more warmth. She tucked away that tiny hurt and took another glass of wine from a passing footman, despite her mother's sharp glance.

Lady Mildred inclined her head regally as she approached them, and they exchanged greetings. Jacqueline had not spent much time in the older woman's presence and was impressed with her demeanor. It was like being around a weathered general who had never known defeat but always stayed primed for battle.

"Why don't you girls spend some time getting to know each other while Mrs. Lockhart and I catch up," Lady Mildred said, dismissing them with a quick wave.

Lady Honora nodded and walked away without hesitation. Jacqueline followed, and after being the recipient of an impatient look from Lady Mildred, Beatrice sighed and went along as well.

Jacqueline touched Lady Honora's shoulder. "You can have an opinion of your own," she said quietly. "You don't need your aunt to make all of your decisions for you. You can answer back."

She gave her a tight smile. "That is much easier for you to say than for me to do," she replied.

Bea sniffed. "If Lady Honora wishes to continue to play act as the country mouse, then by all means allow her to do so. Let us go in search of the gentlemen, if you do please. I am on a mission to marry."

Lady Honora looked at her but said nothing. Jacqueline felt her temper rise. "Bea, behave," she muttered.

Beatrice flipped open her carved ivory fan and started preening. "There are ever so many men here tonight," she cooed. "I am sure they don't wish either of us to behave."

Lady Honora's composure slipped. "Perhaps I am *de trop*," she said.

"Beatrice loves to be outrageous, but she doesn't mean anything by it," Jacqueline lied through her teeth.

The three of them stood together in an uneasy alliance. Beatrice simpered, Jacqueline simmered, and Lady Honora was silent.

"Oh, the Earl of Sinclair is here!" Beatrice said brightly. "Look at that powerful chest and that handsome face." She fanned herself. "Wouldn't I look striking in those strong arms of his?"

With a sinking heart, Jacqueline realized that this was not going to be easy—both Beatrice and Lady Honora were expecting her to prioritize their cause with the earl.

She supposed she could see the appeal. The Earl of Sinclair had the sort of chin that could inspire a generation of boys to join the army, Jacqueline thought as she watched him bow over the hand of a debutante across the room, and move on to nod to a matron. That chin was strong and heroic, with the gentlest of clefts. It went with a chiseled face that could make a sculptor weep. Even in civilian clothes, he cut a dashing figure.

Sinclair approached them. He greeted them with impeccable politeness, dropping into a bow.

Jacquie's eyes darted between Beatrice and Lady Honora. Who would he choose?

Well. The first step was to make sure that she could entice him to stay with them so that he could make a choice at all, instead of greeting them and moving past to the next group, which he had been doing thus far. Jacquie found it in herself to beam at him. "It is ever a pleasure to have an earl in one's midst," she said, infusing as much cheer into her voice as she could. "I am quite properly in awe, I assure you."

She wasn't in the least awestruck, but her mother would be if she spied Jacquie speaking to the earl. Jacquie glanced around and saw her, not too far away. Somehow she had grabbed hold of a pince-nez and was on her tiptoes peering at them, jabbering away to her friends. Jacquie's smile turned real and her heart welled with happiness. She could recognize the signs. Those were indeed palpitations at the sight of an earl.

At long last, her mama must be proud of her. Working with Lady Honora might be worth it for this moment alone.

Sinclair smiled, and Jacquie thought that there must be many debutantes present who were swooning at such a smile. "I am not so high in the instep to insist upon awe, Miss Lockhart."

"Of course one ought not insist, but do be assured that the awe is quite free for the taking," Beatrice all but purred at him.

Jacqueline's mouth dropped open at the blatant boldness, and she flicked her fan in front of her face to hide her shock. The Earl of Sinclair also looked taken aback. Before either of them could speak further, Bea took matters into her own hands.

"My my, you must have read my mind from afar," Beatrice said throatily to the earl. "I was just thinking how perfect it would be to be swept into a dance in the very next minute, and here you have appeared."

He blinked, but bowed again. "Then this is fate, Miss Everson, for I was thinking I would be glad to have a beautiful woman on my arm. What better way to secure such a thing but with dancing?"

She grinned at him and they swooped off to join the dancing, leaving Jacqueline and Lady Honora staring after them.

"If only it were that easy for all of us," Lady Honora said with a little sigh.

Jacqueline raised a brow. "Found your voice now, did you?" she said.

Pink covered her cheeks. "Lady Beatrice is an intimidating figure," she said. After a brief hesitation, she added with more vigor, "I thought you had promised to help me win Sinclair's hand! Isn't that why I secured this invitation for you?"

"Well, Beatrice does have a habit of making things go her way. Anyway, she is dancing now, and the earl is unavailable, so let's find other prospects," Jacquie said briskly, wishing the entire evening behind them. She was embarrassed by Beatrice's actions, and even more so because Lady Honora had witnessed her own failure to handle the situation.

She scanned the ballroom. There must be someone she knew who she could persuade to come over for a dance. But every time she met the eyes of a nobleman, he averted his. Jacqueline felt her frustration rise. It might have been a long time since she was invited to a gathering with so many high ranking gentlemen, but it was not as if she was *never* in their presence. Why, she had flirted with barons and earls and even a marquess earlier in the season. Why were they avoiding her now? Her reputation was not in tatters, after all. It might be a little dusty and spotted, but not torn outright.

Finally, she spied Baron Rowe. He could be convinced to enter into a dance with Lady Honora. He wasn't quite the sharpest mind in the *ton*, but he was a nice enough man with a title and a modest fortune. She mustered all her charm and tried to convey it in her smile, fluttering her fan and beckoning with her eyes.

He trotted over to them and made an amiable bow. "Miss Lockhart, how charming you look tonight! And who is your pretty companion?"

"Lord Rowe, may I introduce you to Lady Honora Banfield? She is new to London, from Wiltshire."

Lady Honora's curtsy was elegant enough but lacked any charisma whatsoever, Jacquie noticed with dismay.

"Ah, Wiltshire," he said. "Quite a nice cheese industry up in those parts, though I wouldn't expect you would be so inclined to discuss industry on such a fine evening at a ball!"

She dipped her head in assent. "Yes, my lord," she replied.

"Yes, quite as I thought. Such a refined lady has more on her mind than cheese at an event like this!" he chortled.

Jacqueline watched with disappointment as Baron Rowe's cheerful face acquired a quizzical look as Lady Honora continued to smile at him without speaking. She was beautiful as a porcelain doll, but that wasn't going to help her win any suitors.

Jacquie tried to think of a conversation for them but realized that she didn't in truth know much about Lady Honora. "Lady Honora is very accomplished at dancing," she blurted out. "You have never seen such a graceful sight in your life as her during a reel." It was inane, and she wasn't even sure if it was true, but she hoped it would be enough. All she had promised were dances, after all—not scintillating conversation.

"Such a beautiful woman must of course be an excellent dancer," he said. "I wish I had not promised all of my dances away this evening! Another time we shall spin across the floor, my lady."

He swept them a bow. They watched in silence as he left the ballroom in the direction of the card room.

Jacquie fixed Lady Honora with a steely eye. "This is going to be very difficult if you cannot find your voice in the presence of gentlemen," she said, exasperated. "I had thought you were too shy to speak against your aunt or Beatrice, but you seem to have no conversation for anyone."

Those alabaster cheeks that Jacquie so admired were showing a faint blush. "I have a voice," she said with dignity. "But I didn't have much in common with Lord Rowe."

"How would you know if you had anything in common with him? You didn't even speak to him! How could you have found any common ground in silence?"

Lady Honora stiffened her spine. "I know who I want to wed—the Earl of Sinclair. What a shame that he is already occupied with your friend," she said coldly.

Jacquie wondered why she had agreed to help her at all. She hadn't expected Lady Honora to be a social disaster. She had assumed that once she made some introductions, things would fall more or less into place.

"Besides, I don't see so many gentlemen looking our way. I had quite depended on us being in a crowd. Is there some reason why they aren't around us now?" Her face was solemn.

"They will be," Jacquie retorted, blinking in surprise. "I am always surrounded. Everyone loves me."

She scowled, then caught a glimpse of her mother laughing with Lady Mildred and some other matrons in the corner. Her expression eased. Her mother was in her element, and except for today had not bothered her for days on the subject of marriage. Finding dances with the unsociable Lady Honora would be well worth a season of better balls with more dance partners and less parental pressure.

With more invitations to events such as this one, her own popularity among the nobility would grow and she would start gaining invites on her own merit. She let herself think of the opportunities that could await her. Picnics lazing about on the grassy shores of a grand estate. Men swirling her around a lavish dance floor. Maybe she would even dance with the wild Duke of Hawthorne, if she ever had the opportunity to meet him. Or with a foreign prince! She smiled dreamily as she thought of the higher echelon of society. Marriage might not be on her mind, but there was a great deal of fun to be had.

"Jacquie dearest, that was ever so delightful," Bea's gushing voice snapped her out of her fantasy.

"I'm so pleased for you, darling," she said, old habit coloring her voice with the warmth and enthusiasm that occasions with Beatrice often demanded.

Then she recalled that Bea had been dancing with the Earl of Sinclair. Where was he? She needed to convince him to dance with Lady Honora. But he had slipped away while she was lost in thought, and now Lady Honora was looking at her with reproof.

"Oh, were neither of you invited to dance?" Bea said with exaggerated surprise. "It could not be on *your* account, Jacquie dear." She assessed Lady Honora. "It must be the company you keep."

Jacqueline rolled her eyes and rapped Bea's hand with her fan. "Do stop your teasing, please. Go find your other beaux."

Beatrice laughed. "That is what you are supposed to help with! However can one hope to stand out in this crowd without the help of friendship." She grabbed her hand, shining eyes burning into her own. "Do come with me, and let's fill up our dance cards. I want your help to find me the very best of men."

Jacquie tugged her hand free, but not without a pang of longing. "Go," she said, with a lack of conviction. "We shall stay here."

Beatrice fluffed her hair. "Fine, I will go find my own partners," she said sulkily. As she walked off, she threw a parting shot over her shoulder. "Enjoy your evening with the wallflowers."

"What a charming individual," Lady Honora said.

Jacquie forced a smile. "Lady Beatrice is a very old friend, and as such, she takes certain liberties. She means nothing by her teasing," she lied, knowing full well that although Bea had been a steadfast companion to her that she was not above being spiteful. She was also starting to wonder if Bea was jealous of her attraction to Nora.

"I am sure she doesn't," Lady Honora agreed without an ounce of conviction.

"Here are two ladies before me, shamefully neglected by my fellow men," a baritone voice boomed behind them.

Jacquie grinned. "Phin!" she cried. "Never have I been so happy to see you."

"And you are with the charming Lady Honora," he said, at once grasping her hand and bringing it to his lips for a quick press of his lips. "How are you, my lady?"

"I am very well, Sir Phineas. How are you?"

"Never better for having spied your fair locks and pretty eyes," he replied.

Jacquie sighed. "You needn't waste your flattery on us. Lady Honora is on the hunt for a title, just as Beatrice is."

Phin's lack of a title might allow Lady Honora to speak to him, she thought, if she didn't see him as a romantic prospect.

He shook his head at them. "Such snobbery from such pretty women. Please grant me the pleasure of a dance, Lady Honora. If not for love, then as penance. I did almost knock you over on our first meeting, after all. I owe you a show of grace and elegance that will convince you that such a happenstance could never again befall any lady in my path. Please take my apology, and my arm."

He bowed and offered his arm to her in an exaggerated stance.

"He never takes no for an answer when it comes to dancing," Jacqueline confided. "You are better off agreeing now, or he shall pester you all evening."

Nora hesitated, but put her hand on Sir Phineas's arm and he clasped his hand on top of hers. "Worry not, fair lady! I shall protect you from dragons and demons and poor dancers for the next half hour that you are in my care."

He was a ridiculous flirt, and Nora was reluctantly charmed by him. She felt herself relax for the first time that she had entered the ballroom. In truth, she was regretting her agreement with Miss Lockhart. She had not considered that she would be at the mercy of Miss Everson's pointed words all night.

Sir Phineas was a welcome break from her position at the edge of the ballroom, even though he did not possess a title and would not be considered at all acceptable by Aunt Mildred.

"You are a quiet little thing," he commented after they had gone through several turns of the dance.

She struggled not to blush but knew she was fighting a losing battle as she felt the embarrassing warmth spread over her cheeks. "I suppose I am," she said. "Do you require a witty companion on your arm?"

"A country mouse will do as well as a dashing debutante when she is as pretty as you are," he said to her, grinning.

"Beauty is your only requirement?" she asked.

"Not the only one," he replied. "I am not quite so shallow as all that. I require...hmm, do let me see. Besides beauty, I would look for...warmth. Oh, and stamina. One must endure all the dancing, of course."

"So it could be a lady, or it could be a horse?" she said skeptically. She knew she would not have this ease of conversation with anyone that she could consider to be a romantic prospect, but Sir Phineas was so very irreverent that it was difficult to be serious with him.

He grinned. "I quite like you, country mouse."

Her blush returned in full force. "I do ask that you refrain from comparing me to a rodent," she said with as much dignity as she could muster.

"You may ask until those charming pink cheeks of yours turn blue, country mouse," Sir Phineas drawled. "Think of it less as a comparison and more as an endearment."

"I am not sure that my aunt would be pleased to think of me as your *endearment*."

"Is your aunt some dreadful dragon that I need fear?" He cast a glance around the ballroom. "I did swear to protect you against dragons whilst you are in my tender care."

Nora shook her head up at him and realized that she was hiding a smile. Somewhere without her noticing, she had started to enjoy herself at this ball. Even if Miss Lockhart couldn't secure eligible dance partners for her, it was nice to be in the company of people who were not her aunt or her aunt's friends.

He returned her to the edge of the ballroom, where Nora was pleased to see Miss Lockhart and Miss Everson preening together in the midst of a small crowd of men. Pasting a smile on her face, she snapped her fan open. When Miss Lockhart or Miss Everson plied their fan, it seemed to draw the immediate attention of men toward them. She fanned more vigorously. But none of the men even glanced her way. Neither did Miss Lockhart.

Annoyed, she realized that there were few things less entertaining than watching other people's success at something she wanted for herself with such desperation. This was even worse than the evening at the opera, when Miss Lockhart entertained her admirers during intermission. The effect of both Miss Lockhart and Miss Everson together was staggering. Nora admitted that Miss Everson was beautiful, but her viper's heart lessened the appeal for her.

Aunt Mildred arrived by her side and smiled at her. "I knew it, my dear," she said to her, sotto voice. "All you needed was a little town bronze and you would be in the midst of their admiration."

She snapped at one of the men at the edge of the throng, "Young Lord Langford! How do you do, my boy? How is your father these days?"

Jumping back from the crowd, the young man stammered a greeting. "Lady, er, Lady Mildred, good evening. My father is well, thank you."

"I would like to introduce you to my dear niece, Lady Honora," she said.

He bowed quite nicely. "Lady Honora, ever so charmed." Under Aunt Mildred's eagle eye, he added, "May I ask you to dance, my lady?"

She forced a smile and nodded, allowing herself to be led back onto the dance floor. Lord Langford was not as smooth of a dancer as Sir Phineas. Nora guessed that he was just out of university, as he looked considerably younger than herself.

"Are you friends with Miss Lockhart?" he asked without preamble, adoration shining from his eyes. He looked longingly at his friends gathered around Miss Lockhart and Miss Everson.

"Yes," she said without hesitating to stretch the truth. She would happily take any social credibility that came her way.

"She is a shining star," he breathed.

Nora didn't reply to that. Although she agreed, it was not the polite thing to express while dancing with another lady.

"She is so clever and so beautiful!" he continued. "I say, as her friend, could you persuade her to dance with me? I would be ever so grateful."

She sighed. "I will do my best," she murmured, and endured the remainder of the dance while he extolled the many virtues of Miss Lockhart's beauty. It was unnecessary, she thought, as she was already very well versed indeed about Miss Lockhart's raven hair and alabaster skin and cherry lips. If she were a writer, she could fill a tome with rhapsodies for her beauty.

By the end of her dance with Lord Langford, Miss Lockhart and Miss Everson had already been caught up by their own partners for the next set, and Nora saw with dismay that the throng of gentlemen had dispersed.

The rest of the evening was tedious, as she did not cross paths again with Miss Lockhart and gained but one more dance from a very kind man who was unfortunately already married.

Frustrated by the end of the night, Nora managed to find Miss Lockhart again. She was sipping a glass of red wine and giggling with Miss Everson and Sir Phineas. Nora's mouth parted in shock as she realized that Miss Lockhart had certainly imbibed too much.

"Lady Honora!" she cried, as if they were the very best of friends. "Do join us. Have you a glass of wine? If you haven't, would you mind hunting down one for yourself and another one for me?" She fluttered her lashes, her smile full of mischief.

Nora frowned. "No, I haven't any wine," she said.

"You might have better luck with the gentlemen if you did have some," Miss Everson said with a smirk.

Sir Phineas smiled at her. "Worry not about them, country mouse. They are funning, they are not serious."

"Country mouse!" Miss Everson cried. "Did you know, Phin, that is exactly what I said of her? A dreary little country mousy wallflower."

Nora forced herself to fix her smile on her face. There would be time enough to cry into her pillow later, she told herself, though she could feel the threat of angry tears already burning behind her eyes. These people were not worth a display of temper or embarrassment.

Miss Lockhart glared at her friends. "Bea, you are a torment. Do stop taunting my friend at once," she said crossly. Her smile at Nora was tentative but seemed more genuine than her earlier one.

"Miss Lockhart, may I speak to you?" she asked. "In private?"

Miss Lockhart handed her wine to Miss Everson and followed Nora to a more secluded corner of the room.

"Miss Lockhart, I am not sure our agreement is working," Nora said, surprised at how easily the words came to her. She hated confrontation, but outrage had stiffened her spine. "I obtained an invitation for you and you are spending it getting drunk with your friends? Why ever would you want to be here if you are just spending your time in the same way that you would at any other event? All you accomplished was introducing me to Baron Rowe, who didn't even dance with me!"

Miss Lockhart blinked. "You danced with Sir Phineas," she pointed out. "And I saw you with Lord Langford."

"Which doesn't even count," Nora debated. "My aunt introduced Langford to me. And all he wanted to talk about was *you*."

"But he was only around to be introduced to you because he was hanging about myself and Bea! That counts as one dance from me. And I don't want him as a suitor, so it matters not that he was focused on me. What you do with the dances is up to *you*. All I can do is provide the circumstances."

Nora fumed. "If this is how you would consider your word to be met, then our agreement is well and finished. Why should I try to obtain more invitations for you if there is no benefit to me?"

The expression on Miss Lockhart's face softened. "Don't be angry," she pleaded. "Let's not argue. You don't even care about the other gentlemen, do you? You have eyes for the earl. I can guarantee a dance with Sinclair for you. Just give me time. We are friends now, aren't we?"

She leaned in, her eyes sparkling, and Nora tried to fight the attraction that she felt deep within her soul when she looked into those eyes. "I refuse to see a repeat of this evening if I am able to give you another invitation," she warned. "I have higher requirements for friendship."

Miss Lockhart grinned at her and swayed closer. "I promise you can trust me," she breathed, and Nora helplessly looked at those ruby lips and knew she would promise her anything.

Chapter Ten

Nora peered out the carriage window with interest. They were still in Mayfair, and not very far from their own townhouse. But in terms of wealth and power, they were in a part of the neighborhood that felt as far removed as the Continent. Grosvenor Square was lined with imposing estates built for the likes of royalty, which was befitting as they were on their way to pay a call on a duke.

Aunt Mildred sat in the opposite seat in the carriage, her back ramrod straight as usual. Despite the rocking motion of the carriage, she remained immobile. She stared ahead with grim determination. "I would not encourage such a visit under ordinary circumstances, were he any other individual," she snapped at Nora, as if it had been *her* idea to visit the duke. "But the Duke of Hawthorne is terribly well connected despite the scandals, and the duchess has always been above reproach. If you can manage to talk to her while avoiding him, it would go better for you. Yes, that's the way to manage this reunion. Do not speak to him directly."

Nora nodded. She wasn't sure if she would be able to manage to speak at all to either the duke or the duchess, so it shouldn't be too difficult to follow her aunt's edict.

Her lips thinned. "I never thought to see him return to London. But if he is here, then it is best for decent people to make use of the situation. The duke is a close enough relation that it will cast favor on you, but distant enough that no one could tar you with the same brush from his scandalous behavior."

She paused, and several moments of silence passed.

"It is a gamble to pay him a visit, but he is the highest ranking relation that we have, so it's no use bemoaning the fact." She looked at Nora, an intense look in her eyes. "We must do everything we can to promote you in society, Honora. Sometimes success means doing uncomfortable things. I promise you, it shall be worth it if you will be wed to a man worthy of the Banfields."

Nora thought of her own uncomfortable agreement with Miss Lockhart for the same ends and nodded her understanding.

This was becoming more and more fascinating. Nora had read enough of the papers to know that the duke had been embroiled in scandal after scandal since he left London, but she couldn't seem to find the actual reason why he was considered so shocking. She supposed leaving the duchess for such a long time was outrageous enough.

Not for the first time, she wished her maid Mary knew all the gossip about these sorts of things. But maybe when she saw her next, Lady Georgina would be able to fill her in on the news. She seemed well informed about everything. The thought of Gina's kindness to her brought a smile to her lips.

They descended from the carriage onto a cobblestone path and were ushered into the great house and whisked into a sitting room far grander than any that Nora had ever been in.

The house was perfectly quiet. Nora marveled that she could not even hear a bird chirping through the French doors that opened onto a lush garden, and she wondered if it was possible to accomplish such silence by design, or if it was a coincidence.

The sharp click of heeled shoes on the waxed floor announced the presence of company. An elegant woman entered the room, and Nora and Aunt Mildred went into deep curtsies. The duchess was a tall woman with pale blond hair and intense dark blue eyes, and Nora shrank away from her imposing presence.

"Welcome," the Duchess of Hawthorne said, though her tone seemed to imply that her guests would be much more welcome to leave than to stay. "To what do I owe this pleasure?"

Although Nora felt uneasy, Aunt Mildred looked relieved to be in the presence of the duchess instead of the duke. "Your Grace, we heard of the duke's return and wish to pass on our well wishes, from the Banfield branch of the family."

"Yes, the Banfields from Wiltshire," she mused. "I haven't seen hide nor hair of your side of his family in years. Though to be quite honest, I have not heard from any side of his family until his return last week." Her smile was cold.

Aunt Mildred managed a nod. "We were all so scandalized by his behavior when he left London, we hardly knew where to look."

"Perhaps you could have looked to his young bride, left at the wedding bed," the duchess suggested.

"Yes. I suppose we could have." Aunt Mildred paused. "I apologize, Your Grace. My behavior was inexcusable and I have long regretted my actions. I had meant no slight to you. You have ever been above reproach."

"Have I ever been?" she said thoughtfully. "How dull that sounds."

"A duchess is never dull," Aunt Mildred said with great authority.

She smiled. "I suppose not. I do appreciate your visit to me now." She fixed an eye on Nora. "I do not think we have had the pleasure of an introduction."

Aunt Mildred hurried the introduction, and Nora fought to hold back a blush as the duchess scrutinized her.

"You seem to be a very quiet person," she said after some time had passed. "I imagine you're here in London looking for marriage?"

"Yes, Your Grace," she murmured.

"Lady Honora and I have been diligent about finding her a suitor this season," Aunt Mildred said. "I think a quiet man who likes country life would be best for my niece."

"There is no shortage of gentlemen who fit that description," the duchess said. "I am sure you will have the success that you are seeking."

Aunt Mildred leaned forward. "In truth, Your Grace, she has been less than successful," she confided. "I had hoped for more for her."

Both women looked at Nora in silence. She sat as still as she could, embarrassment cloaking her so tightly that it was difficult to breathe.

"What is the issue?" the duchess asked with interest. "There has been no scandal attached to the Banfield name since my husband left

London. I cannot imagine there was much opportunity for scandal in Wiltshire."

"Scandal! Of course not. But my niece has a docile temperament, Your Grace, which may be mistaken by some as shyness."

"What of it? Some gentlemen prefer a quiet miss," she said.

"Yes, but many more seem to prefer a certain sort of spirit or encouragement these days."

"She is no antidote. I am sure by season's end she will find some husband or another."

The silence was deafening. Nora could almost hear her aunt's internal struggle as she clearly wanted to say that she needed more help, but couldn't quite bring herself to say the words. Nora felt grateful.

The duchess rose. "I do thank you again for the visit. I will pass your greetings to my husband when next I see him."

"Oh, I think they are capable of passing on their greetings to me themselves?" A rich voice punctured the air with silken danger for a moment before the duke appeared in the drawing room.

If the duchess was the definition of icy serenity, then the duke was the very picture of arrogant warmth and ease. He entered the room with the authority of a king. Tall, lean, and dark haired, he had firm chiseled lips and a thin blade of a nose.

His smile spread across his face like warm honey, and Aunt Mildred simpered at him like a bee. "Cousin Mildred! Well, it has been an age, hasn't it, my dear?" With almost alarming grace, he pulled her to her feet and bent low to kiss her hand.

A smile as Nora had never seen before crossed her aunt's face, lighting her face with pure delight. "Duke! Welcome back to England, my boy. Why, it does seem like forever since I last saw you. I suppose the occasion of our last meeting was on the happy event of your marriage," she said with a nod toward the duchess, who stared at her.

"Cousin Mildred, I shall always recall with great fondness the sheer variety of sweets that your cook kept in the pantry. And the vast array of frogs at the lake of your estate, perfect for a young boy's lazy summer afternoons."

"You were a scamp," she said with obvious affection.

"Do forgive us," he said to the room at large, "it is always so important to reconnect with family, but I apologize for carrying on and ignoring the rest of you. And who is this charming young lady?" He sketched a bow at Nora, who curtsied in return as Aunt Mildred introduced her.

"Lady Honora," he murmured, and his eyes sharpened as he looked at her. Nora looked at him curiously. It felt as if he recognized her. But perhaps he had this intense magnetism with everybody he met. "Another cousin," he mused. "Well, well, it is good to see the family growing, no matter how distant the connection."

"And of course they wish to grow the family further," the duchess interceded. "Lady Honora is in need of a husband."

"Yes, you do look the right age to be casting a wide net," the duke drawled. "Cousin Mildred, I am astonished that you have not packed her off into marriage already. I recall you being an absolute stickler for tradition."

"You are a dreadful tease, Your Grace," she told him. "And I don't mind telling you that, even though you are a duke now! My poor niece has had a family tragedy which has delayed her coming out."

"If you are here for marital assistance, I don't know how helpful we would be in this regard," he said. "The Hawthorne dukedom may be one of the highest in the land, but there are many who think me quite disreputable."

"More than many," the duchess snapped. "A veritable trove find you reprehensible."

He bowed in acknowledgment. "Yes, a trove of naysayers dog at my feet wherever I go."

"Those naysayers could never come close to being half the man that you have become, Duke," Aunt Mildred said staunchly.

Nora thought that this was rather a wonder. Aunt Mildred could have no idea of the man whom he had become, having just been reunited with him for all of ten minutes. Still, she couldn't deny that the duke had a certain brash authority that instilled confidence.

"I would imagine a duke's endorsement of me would carry some weight," Nora said, and watched as three pairs of eyes locked on her.

He turned to the duchess. "From my information, my dear, I do believe we should endorse Lady Honora."

The duchess looked at him for a long moment of unspoken communication. Finally, she shook her head and sighed. "I am planning a ball in three weeks' time, and will be sure to invite you," she said. "I have plenty of relatives who need marrying and might as well add Lady Honora to the list."

"A ball?" the duke asked with interest. "I did not hear of these plans."

"Well, now you have," she replied.

"No matter, I would not dream of ruining your plans by being present," he said. "You may have your ball, and pray make it as lavish as you wish."

"Thank you very much for an invitation, Your Grace," Aunt Mildred announced, breaking the tension. "Might I ask you for the favor of inviting the granddaughter of a dear old friend of mine? She is much the same age as my niece, and it would be so nice for the girls to spend a grand evening together."

"Another wallflower? Yes, of course." she said absently. "Do leave their names with my secretary and he will arrange it."

Nora shot a sharp look at her aunt. She had not told her of Miss Lockhart's behavior at the last ball and her desire to distance herself from her. But if she looked past the pained memory of that night, she knew deep in her heart that she was thrilled at the opportunity to see those green eyes up close again.

CHAPTER ELEVEN

The public market along the Strand was always busy. Jacqueline loved the thrill of being in the middle of the crowds, thick in the hustle and bustle of the city. People of every rank and station were here, shuffling along the gravel street to haggle over everything from hatpins to belt buckles to handkerchiefs to meat pies. She could smell the savory scents, and her stomach rumbled, but she didn't want to stop at the food stalls and risk losing focus on her purpose at the market today.

The dangers involved in milling around with the masses and poking around the goods offered in baskets and on tables instead of visiting the grand shops on Bond Street with their endless shelves of neatly bundled merchandise made it all the more exciting. She grinned as she examined the displays before her.

"You're like a magpie, flitting over the most useless fripperies," Phin told her. "I swear, you spend more time choosing ha'penny bows than I do deciding on entire suits."

"You knew what you were getting into when you agreed to escort me on a shopping expedition," she retorted. "If I wanted to shop on Bond Street, I would have taken Bea. But I wanted something more exciting, so I chose you and the Strand. Besides, the right bow can make all the difference in a lady's appearance."

Phin shook his head and cradled her elbow in his broad hand, casting a hard look at anyone who got too close to her. He had also insisted on bringing two hulking footmen with them, who trailed half a stall behind them. Jacquie sighed happily. It was nice to feel cared for, for once.

The fog lay thick on the city, and she had almost decided to postpone her errand to another day. The mist was cool against her face and left tiny dewdrops on her eyelashes. If she had stayed at home, the guilt would lie heavy on her heart as thick as the fog swirling on the ground, and she wouldn't be able to sleep again tonight.

It was the memory of Lady Honora's face that haunted her. She had looked so cold and unflappable when they were arguing at the Countess of Marchfield's ball, but Jacquie sensed that she had been hurt when Bea was needling her.

Jacquie didn't want to hurt Lady Honora. She would prefer if their arrangement could be as amiable as possible. To appease her mother and to be sure that she didn't meddle in her life, she was planning to spend a considerable amount of time with Lady Honora, and she would rather that it wasn't contentious. Most importantly, she admitted to herself, she *liked* Lady Honora. She wanted to spend time with her.

She felt the stirrings of remorse. She hadn't been kind, and neither had Beatrice. She could reflect upon many times in her life when she hadn't been a nice person, but it had not often troubled her before now. It had always felt like herself and Bea against the other women in society—though she couldn't quite remember now why it had always felt like a war.

Maybe because even from the beginning, they had suspected that their lover's relationship was not how most women felt, and they felt threatened. She remembered entering her debut season feeling so secure in her beauty and realizing with shock that she was not the Incomparable Toast of the Season that her parents had always told her she would be. She became popular, but never in the circles that she had expected to be in. In retrospect, she could admit that reacting with poor behavior against other women hadn't been the best way to handle those feelings.

The issue had never been the other women. It had been her own conceited expectations, and her struggle to understand her place in society if she couldn't be at its top. Jacqueline had found a comfortable place for herself and for Beatrice in the social hierarchy during that first season, when they had still clung to each other like lifelines, but they had never had a comfortable relationship with a lot of the other women who had still felt like competition to them. Perhaps the threat had simply been in their minds. And perhaps it was time to allow herself to be more open to other people, to let more opportunity for growth and friendship blossom inside her.

Lady Honora had done her a kindness by inviting her to the countess's ball. It has been a very shabby return of the favor by allowing Beatrice to taunt her, and then ignoring her for most of the event. It was not well done of her. That was no longer the kind of person that she wanted to be.

Jacqueline hesitated over a basket of fans, etched with pastoral scenes. Lady Honora was from the country and spoke often enough of returning there. Would a fan be an appropriate gift to thank her for the invitation, and to appease her ire about Beatrice?

Phin snorted. "Don't you have enough fans, Jacquie dearest? I vow you have a different one for every gown."

"One can never have too many," she sniffed. "But as it happens, it isn't for me."

"Are you looking for one for Bea?" He waggled his eyebrows at her. "Hoping to beg your way into her bed again now that you are finding yourself bereft of lovers?"

She scowled. "No, not for Beatrice either. She has even more fans than I do. Including the most ridiculous one bedecked with ostrich feathers, of all things. What even *is* an ostrich? Have you ever heard of such a creature? Honestly, it's completely ludicrous." She shook her head. "No, it's for—well, I want to purchase something for Lady Honora."

"The country mouse? The plot thickens. Have you bedded her yet?"

"She's not a country mouse," she snapped. "And no, of course I haven't. We're just…well, I suppose I don't know what we are. Not friends, exactly. We're more—sort of working together."

"Working?" Peals of laughter erupted from him. "Miss Lockhart and Lady Honora, in all their London finery—*working*? At what, pray tell? Coal mining? Farming?"

"Phin, you are the worst tease. Do not be ridiculous, please." She picked up another fan and unfolded it, admiring the painting on its delicate leaves. "I suppose you could say that we're conspiring together, in a certain way."

"Conspiring? Is the prime minister safe? Is it Guy Fawkes who you've been secretly adulating all these years?"

"Is nothing sacred with you?" she asked, tossing the fan back into the basket in exasperation.

"Sacred, as in church and state? I suppose not, but let it be known that it isn't I with a bevy of gorgeous conspirators for whom I'm purchasing gifts."

Jocular shouts and rowdy laughter erupted from a dozen meters away. Someone was in the stocks, feet shackled to the wooden structure as onlookers jeered. Jacqueline was glad that she had decided against a meat pasty as her stomach churned.

She could hear the other market goers asking with mild curiosity what the crime was, and heard someone reply with a spit that it was just another filthy molly caught with another man by an innkeeper nearby.

"Pants down and all!" the man chortled. "What a sight that would be for the missus, eh? Two men in the altogether like that?"

Phineas's lips thinned. "I cannot understand why the stocks is still thought of as a solution or a punishment for such things," he muttered.

She averted her eyes and focused on the goods offered before her. Fingers trembling, she stroked a selection of thin ribbons edged prettily with picot stitching. There was every color imaginable in the baskets in front of her, a beautiful rainbow of color on a dismal day.

"Do ye like what ye see, lass?" the old woman behind the table asked her, smiling.

Jacqueline glanced back at the crowd around the stocks. *No, I do not,* she wanted to say. But instead, she took a deep breath and started haggling. She got a good price for them—she always did—and she scooped the ribbons and bows into her reticule.

When she turned to tell Phin that she had enough of shopping, she realized that she was alone in the crowd with only his footmen nearby. Fear hit her like a bullet, ricocheting against her heart. *Phineas.* Craning her neck and raising onto her toes, she searched the area but did not see him.

Knowing that there was only one place he would be drawn to, Jacquie swallowed her fear and pushed her way through the throng to the stocks.

Phin was standing beside the wooden structure, talking to a pair of constables with a fierce frown as they were releasing the man from the wooden structure. The crowd was booing, and Jacquie felt a restless energy from them. She saw a woman spit at the ground in disgust.

Nervously, she approached them. Phin glared at her. "Get back to the carriage," he snapped. He looked at the footmen. "What are you thinking to allow her to come near? Escort her away, now!"

"Come on, miss," one of them said to her. "You don't want to get mixed up in this."

"Perhaps I do," she said coldly. She looked at the man who was being released from the chains. He was filthy, hair matted with blood where someone had struck him or thrown something at him, and he was covered with mud and excrement.

He looked at them, wary and tense enough to flee.

"We are not all against you," she told him, her voice quiet enough that only he could hear her in the crowd.

His face eased, and he looked surprised. "Thank you, miss," he said to her uncertainly.

She reached out and touched his dirt smeared hand, then allowed herself to be whisked away by the footmen through the angry throng of people.

"Miss, you shouldn't have done that," one of them murmured to her. "Begging your pardon, but you don't know the type of crowd that lingers here. You could be in danger if you are seen to associate with him."

"And yet here I am, quite fine," Jacqueline snapped. "He is as human as any of us and deserves compassion."

She saw them exchange uneasy glances, but she knew she couldn't explain further. How could she say to them that she had the same desires that this man was accused of? How could she explain that if they despised him, then it meant that they despised her too?

She waited in the carriage for Phin and was overwhelmed with relief when he launched himself into the seat across from her.

"I'm so glad you're unhurt," she exclaimed. "I was worried for you."

He shook his head and rapped on the roof of the carriage to start moving. "I am well," he said shortly. "But more importantly, he will be all right. He wasn't hurt much by the mob. I was able to speak with him after the police left. His name is Mr. Robinson and he's a cook at the market who decided to take a break from the market with a candlemaker in a nearby inn. There was a raid on the inn and the candlemaker got away, but Mr. Robinson wasn't so lucky."

Jacquie moved from her seat across from him to sit beside him and leaned her head against his shoulder. She squeezed his hand. "What kind of raid?" she asked.

"The police break into establishments where they suspect men are congregating with other men. Somehow, they seem to have a fairly accurate list of places who are sympathetic to mollies, or which are run by us." His face twisted. "Although I don't know Mr. Robinson, I do know many who have taken their leisure in such places. God knows I've been in them myself enough times."

She frowned. "But you don't need to worry about frequenting such places and courting such danger to yourself."

"Jacquie, it doesn't matter if I have the luxury of avoiding the public inns and tap houses," he said in frustration. He raked his hand through his hair and slumped against the plush seat. "Many people that I know don't have the means to express their desires in more private places, and it isn't right that I can avoid this danger but do nothing to help those who are in peril every day."

Jacqueline was quiet for a moment. "I have never had to worry so much about it," she confessed. "No one seems very concerned by women's relationships."

He sighed and rested his cheek on top of her head. "And I'm glad for it. It would break my heart to think of you in danger."

"What will happen to Mr. Robinson?"

"I gave him my address in case he wishes to be employed somewhere where he doesn't need to fear for his safety. Whether or not he takes my offer remains to be seen. I could use another cook."

"You can't employ the whole world, Phin."

"But I can try, can't I?"

CHAPTER TWELVE

Nora sat in the elegant morning room, occupying herself with nothing. Despite her calm exterior, she felt at sixes and sevens. She was ready for the next social engagement, whatever it may be, but the focus on entertainment and the pressure to find the quickest path to nuptials was wearing on her.

She was grateful for her life of relative leisure, though it had left her with little in the way of worldly knowledge. She had learned more in one afternoon from the ladies at Gina's salon than she had in a decade in Wiltshire.

There must be something she could do to contribute to the causes that Gina's friends were so passionate about. She could be passionate about *something*, couldn't she? She allowed herself a moment of respite and sank against the pillowed back of the sofa.

Aunt Mildred sailed into the room. "A lady does not lean!" she snapped, and Nora felt her back straighten and her shoulders fall back at the sound of her voice.

"Will you be ready at four for the musicale at Lady Watson's?" she said. "I hope you haven't forgotten. She has two unmarried sons. I think the elder and heir would be an excellent match. But the younger is quite respectable as well. No title, but wealthy in his own right, and well decorated from the war."

She didn't wait for Nora to reply before she swept out of the room again. Aunt Mildred never waited for a reply and always assumed her will would be followed. Nora picked at the braided edge of the sofa cushion. She would rather like to be heard. If not by Aunt Mildred, then by *someone*. But what did she have to say?

A footman arrived with a small package. "This arrived for you, my lady," he said and presented it to her. He bowed and left the room.

Even the servants didn't wait for her to speak, Nora realized.

Curious, she plucked apart the paper wrapping to reveal a note and something tucked into a soft cloth. She unfolded the cloth slowly and found a beautiful array of ribbons.

Carefully, she lifted the bundle from the cloth. There were thin ribbons, thick ribbons, some plain, some edged in lace. Scarlet ribbons, sky blue, daffodil yellow, inky navy. They were beautiful to look at on such a dismal afternoon.

Keeping the rainbow of ribbons on her lap, she unfolded the note while her heart beat faster with anticipation. There was only one person she could think of who might be sending her a gift. Someone to whom she had sent a certain pair of slippers, not long ago.

My dear Lady Honora,

I saw these ribbons and thought to buy a smile from you with a gift. I apologize if you thought my behavior insincere and my friend impertinent. In truth, perhaps your thoughts were accurate. But I am a woman of my word and I stand by my promise to help you woo the Earl of Sinclair.

To prove to you that my intentions are honest, I offer you my help in the area that I am most useful—please give me another chance and meet with me at my modiste tomorrow morning, so we can craft for you a wardrobe more enticing to an earl than to a vicar!

Your obedient servant,

Miss Jacqueline Lockhart

The name and address of the dressmaker was scrawled in the corner of the note, with the time of the appointment. Tomorrow morning, eleven o'clock.

Nora stroked the glossy ribbons. She had been so angry when she left the Countess of Marchfield's ball, so hurt with the feeling of being neglected when she had thought that she and Miss Lockhart were developing a friendship.

The joyful display of ribbons in her hand argued against the ache in her heart. Maybe the friendship *was* earnest. Maybe she *could* put her trust in Miss Lockhart. Maybe she could allow herself to feel a glimmer of hope that they could begin anew.

Nora did want new dresses. And who better to purchase them with than a new friend? Aunt Mildred had already authorized a new wardrobe of high necked pastels, believing that demure and modest dresses would win the heart of a true nobleman. Nora thought wistfully of the types of dresses that Miss Lockhart and Miss Everson favored—bright, fashionable frocks, daring necklines and tissue thin fabrics. She thought of elegant Lady Gina and her pretty ethereal gowns, romantic and frilled and feminine.

Perhaps she could find something better suited to her than sturdy dresses in pale pastels. And cloaked in a new frock, maybe she could find the courage to find herself. A self with passion. With a voice unafraid to speak to anyone. Someone who would be listened to.

If Miss Lockhart could help her do all this, then it was a friendship most invaluable.

Nora lost herself in a dreamy fantasy of dancing in a delicate muslin dress weighing no more than a feather, feeling light and free and happy instead of stressed and worried and fatigued. She would whirl about the room and not feel the lack of anything. Not friends, or flirtations.

Her eyes snapped open. The only problem was that she was all too willing to collapse the boundaries of friend and flirtation with one Miss Jacqueline Lockhart.

She knew she wanted something much, much more from her, and it wasn't loneliness that prompted her desire. No, it was Miss Lockhart's laughter that sent shivers up her spine, and her warm smile that made her knees weak with longing. She wanted to press her lips to hers in a sweet kiss, she wanted to run her fingers through that gorgeous mane of midnight black hair.

Nora was positive that Miss Lockhart felt the same way. Apart from their precarious alliance, she felt the pull between them. Could it ever come to fruition? Maybe, just maybe, they could find the time to enjoy each other fully, intimately, before Nora left London.

Nora looked down at the ribbons and bows in her lap and felt a rush of pleasure. She was attracted. And though she had never gambled in her life, she was willing to bet that these ribbons meant that Miss

Lockhart was, too. Her breathing quickened and she clutched the ribbons to her chest.

This was something that she could feel passionate about.

Nora was going to take a leap of faith and believe in both the power of their friendship and the strength of their attraction.

They would have enough venues in which to pursue an attachment, wouldn't they? Aunt Mildred had already arranged an invitation for the Duchess of Hawthorne's ball, which would be one of the season's biggest events. And there were so many more invitations that overflowed Aunt Mildred's desk in the library.

Maybe Miss Lockhart would tire of their agreement before they could act on their desires. Nora could not be quite sure of her steadiness of character or her reliability, despite the attraction that surged between them.

She might have more to lose than to gain. But it was a risk she was finally willing to take.

CHAPTER THIRTEEN

The private consultation room at Madame Beaulieu's sewing atelier was dominated by a large work table scattered with bundles of fabrics and trims, and by a wood-framed full-length mirror leaning against one corner. Large arched windows let in plenty of natural light and made a comfortable chamber where women could discuss such intimate details as their measurements and their bills.

Jacqueline sipped a cup of tea and wondered if her invited guest would show, or if it was only herself who would order a new gown today. She wasn't often nervous, but today she was and she discovered with surprise that it made the anticipation all the sweeter. Here, then, was something worth waiting for. Something intriguing. Enticing.

This was something that could truly *be* something. Until now, Jacquie had been seeking entertainment, and respite from her mother's lectures. But amusement had been replaced by desire. And desire could in turn be replaced by deeper emotions.

Lady Honora arrived within a quarter hour. Jacqueline heard her voice first, low and musical as she entered the establishment, and felt the quiet thrill course through her. Soon, she was rewarded with the sight of the woman herself, pausing at the doorway, the picture of grace and beauty.

Jacqueline rose and curtsied for the pleasure of Lady Honora's slow smile. Relief flooded her at the sight of that smile, but the guilt that had haunted her since the Countess of Marchfield's ball twisted her stomach. The pride that she had to swallow wasn't sitting easily.

"Thank you for meeting me here," Jacquie said, feeling vulnerable as she met Lady Honora's steady gaze. "I wish to apologize to you for the way I behaved when last we saw each other. You were gracious enough to arrange that invitation, and I not only behaved poorly, but I did not uphold my end of the bargain."

Lady Honora nodded. "Thank you for your apology, Miss Lockhart. That evening was not my most cherished experience in London thus far, I must admit. But it is over now, and I appreciate the lovely ribbons that you sent over with your invitation to join you here."

"May we start anew, then?" Jacquie asked.

"Yes, let us start fresh. In the spirit of friendship, this time," she said with a smile.

Forgiveness had Jacqueline feeling light as a feather. "I am so glad to have you with me on this most important task," she said in a giddy rush.

Lady Honora gave her a look. "What you deem to be an important task, most of us merely call dressmaking," she said, but her pleasure at Jacquie's greeting was evident.

"You underestimate the importance!" Jacqueline exclaimed. She twirled, delighting in the feel of her skirts flying against her legs. "Today I wish to commission a gown to complement the most meaningful gift that I have received in recent months."

Lady Honora rose a brow.

Jacqueline raised her skirts well above her ankles and presented her foot, revealing a pink satin slipper with beautiful ribbon rosettes along the toe.

Lady Honora smiled in recognition. "So you *did* like the dance slippers, Miss Lockhart," she said, pleased. "They adorn your foot beautifully. I don't think there is another foot in London so suited to pink satin as yours." She paused. "Perhaps not even in Paris."

"Paris? Now I know it's flattery," she cried. "London, I could accept. These are indeed the prettiest slippers in all of London, I am convinced. But Paris! Why, I should be astonished if you could prove the verity of your claim."

"But the proof is here before my eyes, Miss Lockhart," she said. "I could not imagine a lovelier foot. And I feel sure that it is connected to the loveliest leg in all of London, as well. And the very loveliest hip, and the prettiest waist. But all *that* remains to be seen, of course. I can only be sure of the foot."

Jacqueline's body was aflame with desire to hear Lady Honora talk about the intimate parts of her body. Especially the idea that someday—hopefully *soon*—she would indeed see her waist, and all the treasure that lay beneath her skirts. It delighted her to hear the sly banter between them. Her attraction was not one-sided, it seemed.

The modiste bustled into the room. Madame Beaulieu was a middle-aged woman with black hair, a wide smile, and a sharp eye that caught every detail of fit and figure. This was Jacqueline's favorite fashion establishment in London and she had been a dedicated patron for years.

Her goal had often been to be the belle of every ball. Although she could not admit to success on that score, Madame Beaulieu had always wildly succeeded in crafting gorgeous and intriguing dresses for every occasion.

"Have you decided on the cut of the gown that you would like, Miss Lockhart?" Madame Beaulieu asked. "Has your friend come to help you out with the decision?"

"Indeed she has," Jacqueline replied. "This is my sixth season, after all, and I was thinking something daring. I am no blushing debutante, after all."

The modiste nodded. "You need to compete with those young things, and a daring look will attract the men away from the young ones, whose mamas like to have them trussed up to their ears in voile and lace if they can manage it."

Jacqueline leaned over the fashion plates that she had selected upon her arrival. "I was thinking something like this one—off the shoulder, dipping low across the chest."

"Your mother won't object?" Lady Honora asked. "That bodice looks to be hardly an inch wide."

Madame Beaulieu snapped open her measuring tape and placed it against Jacqueline's bust. "There is much more than an inch required to cover up this bosom," she declared. "Don't you worry, we won't have your friend's gown falling down and exposing her!" She scribbled measurements into a small book.

"Well, I suppose we could err on the side of caution in order to prevent my mother from having a fit when she sees the dress," Jacquie said.

"Or we simply shouldn't tell your mother," Lady Honora replied, and Jacquie caught the hint of a smile on her face.

The modiste agreed. "Your friend is quite right, Miss Lockhart. Mothers can be the very worst sort of saboteurs when a young miss is facing another year on the shelf. We will have you prettily presented, and all the gentlemen will be at your mercy yet again! Now, which color were you thinking for your dress? May I suggest lilac, or a pale spring green?"

Jacqueline met Lady Honora's eyes. "Pink," they replied in unison, and Jacqueline laughed in delight.

"Look at my darling shoes," she said to the modiste, lifting her skirts and showing off her shoes. "Are they not the most delicious shade of pink that you have ever seen? My fondest wish is to have a dress to complement them."

The modiste pursed her lips, then nodded. "I have the very thing," she announced, and she hurried out of the room.

"You may well set a new fashion," Lady Honora said. "I can just see the gossip columns with news of lady's bosoms falling out all over London."

Jacqueline laughed and leaned closer. "Perhaps that would not be so very bad for society," she said. "I can think of several benefits to the situation."

"I can only see the benefit from viewing a very particular bosom," she replied, her eyes burning into Jacqueline's.

Jacqueline's breath caught, and she leaned ever closer over the table. She was so close, close enough to feel Lady Honora's breath on her cheek, close enough to feel the warmth from her body, close enough that she thought she could count the very hairs on her head.

Close enough for a kiss, to finally feel those perfect lips against her own.

Madame Beaulieu returned, chattering about the silk voile that she had in stock. Jacqueline jerked back as if scalded. Certain her cheeks were bright with the fire that raged within her, she forced herself to look at the sheer fabric. It was a beautiful pale pink, banded with opaque darker pink stripes.

Jacquie leaned over the table and shook a length from the fabric roll, grasping the yardage in both hands to feel its cool silky texture, sensual against her skin. The delicate fabric weighed almost nothing, with less heft than a butterfly's touch. She raised the skirt of her day dress to the thigh and draped the pale pink cloth over her thin white petticoat, peeking again at her rosette covered shoes.

"It's perfect," Jacqueline breathed.

The modiste tossed her hair and allowed a superior smile to show on her face. "We do know what we're about here," she boasted. "We are the most elegant dressmakers in the district. We always know what will best suit a woman."

Madame Beaulieu honed her sights on Lady Honora. "Now that we have your friend all settled, are you also looking to have a dress made up?"

"Why, we were just talking about such a thing," Lady Honora said. "Of course I would wish to patronize your shop, after seeing such beautiful results on my…friend. I need a whole new wardrobe, I think, but I shall start with one dress. I received some very beautiful ribbons as a gift yesterday and would love to see some of them affixed to a gown."

Jacquie darted a glance at her, but Lady Honora was the picture of innocence, standing by the table with her fingers trailing over a pile of lush velvet.

"I would very much like to see your patterns," she said, and Madame Beaulieu started to show her the various styles that they were making for various patrons.

"Oh, but Lady Honora is a new customer," Jacqueline piped up. "Should you begin by taking her measurements, before looking at any patterns?"

Lady Honora looked at her sharply, but the modiste nodded. "Of course, we need your measurements in order to make your gown to specification." She exited the room for a brief moment and returned with two assistants.

"My lady, may we remove your gown in order to measure you?"

It was phrased as a question, but the assistants were already moving toward Nora. Asking was a nicety. Naturally, Nora would need to be measured in her undergarments, the same as she would at any other modiste she had visited either here in London or in the country.

The only difference was that Nora had only ever been measured by herself, or with her aunt nearby, or a cousin now and again as they arranged gowns for the neighborhood assemblies.

Never had she disrobed in a shop with an audience in the corner who perched in her seat looking like a cat with the cream who was now contemplating a plump canary. Never with someone whose very presence made the hair on her arms rise with anticipation. Never with someone as gorgeously and outrageously sensual as Miss Jacqueline Lockhart.

She wanted those eyes on her, caressing every inch. But she hesitated. She felt she should give Miss Lockhart the opportunity to remove herself if she was in any way uncomfortable. Although to judge from her grin, she didn't look at all ill at ease.

"Of course, Madame Beaulieu," she said slowly. "But I wouldn't want to take up any more of my friend's time than she had planned. Miss Lockhart, please feel free to leave if you need to return home. I would hate to keep you any longer than you had planned to be on your errand."

"Don't mind me," chirped the most tempting mouth Nora had ever seen. "I always have plenty of time for dressmaking. We're all ladies here, and I daresay you would be wanting my opinion anyhow. If you need to disrobe, please go ahead."

Nora smiled in return. This was the reply she had hoped for. She craved Miss Lockhart's opinion, and not only on clothing. She had hoped to gain it in different circumstances, perhaps in front of a gentle fire cracking in the hearth and a steaming bath drawn for two. But this new twist, though unexpected, was not unwelcome by any means.

The assistants busied themselves around Nora as the modiste described various necklines and fabrics and hem lengths. They nipped their hands down her buttons and up her skirts and soon she stood there, exposed in her half stays and sheer chemise and cotton drawers.

The modiste looked at her. "You will look lovely in the modern style, my lady. Miles of skirt will make your legs seem endless, and the square bodice will show your chest to every advantage."

Nora looked in the full-length mirror while the assistants began to move measuring tapes up and down her limbs and across her body. She felt proud and daring and wonderful, with a delightful awareness of the power of her own body, standing in deshabille with a beautiful woman gazing at her.

She could see Miss Lockhart in the mirror, her face poignant with desire. She caught her eye and held it, loving the look of admiration and wonder in her face.

It felt scandalous to be standing there in her stays, excitement crackling in the air. Exciting and a little wild. Words that she would not have chosen to describe her life thus far, but words that she wanted to embrace to her scantily clad bosom.

She knew without a shadow of a doubt that although no specific words had passed between them yet, they would soon be lovers. She smiled in the mirror and knew by Miss Lockhart's returned smile that she knew it too.

After she had been measured, the dressmaker presented her with fabrics that had Nora sighing with pleasure. At last, here were elegant soft fabrics in colors that she fell in love with. No more pastels. No more sturdy tailoring primly encasing her body. Instead there would be long soft swaths of fabric that would drape and cling to her body, beckoning and enticing.

"With your peach coloring, my lady, I would suggest a dramatic blue," Madame Beaulieu said. "Darkest navy muslin, light as gossamer, with silver embroidery. We could pleat the fabric over the bodice to show off its texture. Your blond locks will shine like pure gold against this color, and your gray eyes will be complemented by the fabric."

The assistants bustled with yards of sheer fabric to drape over her, with swatches of lace and ribbon and trim. "Yes, I think a Vandyke lace will be beautiful at the hem and the edge of the puffed sleeve." She pursed her lips. "And we will add the ribbons you brought under the bust line to accentuate the lines of your figure, and along the hem."

Miss Lockhart smiled from her perch in the corner. "You will be exquisite."

Nora smiled. "I hope you will like what you see," she murmured, and was rewarded with a sly smile that awakened a thunderous desire within her.

Nora swiftly attired herself in her white day dress with the help of the dressmaker's assistants, and they left the shop in high spirits.

"Shall we go to Gunter's for an ice?" Miss Lockhart asked. "If you are new to London, then I would think you have not yet gone. I cannot allow you to return to the country without tasting our city's finest treat."

How could she pass up the opportunity to prolong their day together? Nora agreed with the suggestion in an instant, and they walked down the crowded street together toward Berkeley Square and its popular tea shop, their maids trailing behind at a respectable distance.

Gunter's was a busy establishment and Nora thought that half of London must be inside its small shop. They were soon seated at a table near the back of the room. Nora felt her eyes widen as she saw the confections being served to patrons.

This was turning into an excellent day indeed. "This dress will look perfect at the Duchess of Hawthorne's ball," Nora said happily.

"The Duchess of Hawthorne is in town? And she is hosting a party?" Miss Lockhart said in surprise.

Nora blinked. "I apologize, I had forgotten that I have not yet mentioned it." She paused, then decided that she wished to be honest. It was difficult to say the words confronting her new friend, but she took a deep breath and said, "In fact, Miss Lockhart, when I received your gift of the ribbons and your note to accompany you to the dressmaker's, I was not sure if I would even tell you about the duchess's ball."

"Not tell me?" said Miss Lockhart, frowning. "But I thought we had an arrangement! However else will I arrange the earl to court you?"

A waiter brought a small tray of delicacies to them, including two ices nestled into glass cups, and an array of candied fruits.

It was difficult, but Nora continued. "You and your friend Miss Everson were—well, you were cruel to me at the Countess of Marchfield's ball. I was not sure if I wished to see you at another engagement. I thank you for your apology earlier, but your behavior truly hurt me."

Nora was unaccustomed to addressing another person's rudeness and was embarrassed at needing to speak of it at all. She dipped her spoon into a dish of violet flavored ice and tried to savor its cool syrupy sweetness, but there was an uncomfortable pit in her stomach.

Miss Lockhart had the grace to blush. "I was a beast," she admitted, leaning close to her. "I cannot explain it away, I cannot justify it. I was upset that night, and angry at the situation. But you—you deserve much better treatment than my actions that night. I am sorry. I am so sorry for hurting you."

"I only ask for your respect and for a dignified exchange between us," Nora said quietly. "And that we help each other with some degree of kindness."

"You can ask for so much more," Miss Lockhart murmured with a little smile.

"Well, how do you act with your other friends?" she asked, deciding to ignore the look of desire that was heating up her blood despite the cooling effects of the ice.

Miss Lockhart considered. "Most of the people I socialize with are not quite friends," she said, and Nora realized by the play of emotions on her face that it was a recent realization. "I behave with them in the same way that I have with Miss Everson, or how I have behaved with you—we laugh, and tease, and compete, and it might not always be in the spirit of kindness. I have taken what I wanted without much thought of how it has affected them, whether it was stealing a dance or more. In the end I suspect none of us feel close to one another, and it leaves us all feeling a little fragile."

Miss Lockhart nibbled at a candied orange. "I could use a friend," she said, sounding surprised, and her bright green eyes met Nora's.

"So could I," Nora replied, and smiled as she picked up her spoon again.

Chapter Fourteen

The afternoon sky was a brilliant blue, the sun was shining, the birds were chirping, and Jacqueline's thoughts whirled around a woman whom she had not yet kissed. Snugly ensconced in a deep window seat in her bedchamber, she propped her chin on her hand and gazed out the window at the lush green trees of the garden outside. A gentle breeze stirred their leaves.

It was a perfect day, filled with the promise of opportunity.

After their encounter at the modiste and their afternoon at Gunter's, Jacqueline knew that she couldn't wait much longer. They had not discussed it in words, but it was clear from the sizzling looks between them that there was a deep attraction that needed to be addressed.

The wounds that Lydia had left on her heart were still fresh, but fading fast despite the depth of emotion that Jacquie had thought she felt for her. Ever since she had bumped into Lady Honora at that ball weeks ago, her blood had been at fever pitch every time she thought of her.

It demanded satisfaction.

Lady Honora was unlike anyone else in Jacquie's social whirl. She was kind, she was dignified, and she was honest. Jacquie was starting to like and admire her more than anyone she knew.

Her head knew it couldn't be love. It wouldn't even be a long-term affair. Jacquie had committed to helping her find a gentleman to marry. It was not a path destined to end with them being together forever.

Her foolish heart, however, was dreaming about lazy mornings waking up beside her, taking long rides in Hyde Park together, and visiting the haberdashery for a new hat with ribbons to match the exact colour of Lady Honora's gray eyes.

Jacqueline sighed. She was unwilling to dream too far into the future, knowing that such a reality could never be theirs. She had no idea how much experience Lady Honora had, or even if she had any at all. Had she ever been in a romantic situation with another woman before?

If she could plan things just right, perhaps tonight she would know for certain.

She drummed her fingers against her chin. Tonight was the Duchess of Hawthorne's ball. There was no better time like the present to put a plan into motion to learn what she wanted to know about Lady Honora.

Jacqueline was as swift and precise as a general to put all the pieces of her plan in place.

At breakfast, she carved her kippers and chattered with her parents about the opportunities that she could have if only she cultivated the right friendships with the right social classes. It was such a shame that the sticklers of the *ton* didn't like her, based on youthful indiscretions.

She heaved a few well-timed sighs and paired them with longing stares into the middle distance, and then mentioned that her mother had been right about Lady Honora Banfield. Her connections were exceptional—hadn't she been able to give her the invitation to tonight's ball, hosted by no less than the mysteriously reclusive (and exclusive) Duchess of Hawthorne? What a thoughtful young woman.

At luncheon, Jacquie enjoyed a cold chicken cutlet and observed that Lady Honora's aunt was a woman of remarkable fortitude and strength to be chaperoning a young woman about town so tirelessly at her age. It would be such a kindness to allow her to rest, but of course Lady Honora would need to attend the duchess's ball tonight. It was so important to be in the good graces of Her Grace, and of course she was a dear cousin by marriage to Lady Honora.

At a light midafternoon repast of hot tea and sweet biscuits, Jacqueline was well rewarded.

"You will never guess where I have been this past half hour," her mother declared, choosing a thin biscuit covered in lemon drizzle. "I paid a call at Lady Mildred's home. She is looking well, but she admitted that the fast pace of the season was catching up with her."

She took a bite of her biscuit and hummed in pleasure. "These are delightful—Cook will need to make these again!"

Jacqueline impatiently crumbled a corner of her own biscuit.

"Well, as we were talking, I told Lady Mildred that we would be happy anytime to chaperone her niece. It would be no trouble at all, given that we attend so many functions ourselves! And even more so these days, with the help of her and her niece's invitations. I assured her that we are ever so careful with you and that she need not have any cause to worry about a thing."

Satisfied, Jacqueline finished her biscuit. "I am sure she was pleased, Mama," she said.

"Why, I even told her that it would be the easiest thing in the world to have Lady Honora stay with us after a long night at a ball, to save her the worry of thinking of her niece coming home so late to a dark and shuttered house. Our townhouse is snug, but we have quite enough rooms that it would be no trouble at all to have an overnight houseguest now and again!"

Jacqueline blinked. She was glad she had finished her biscuit, or else she would have choked on it in surprise. This was more than she had dared to hope—but it was perfect. "Such a generous offer," she managed to say.

"Yes, well—it is such a kindness to Lady Mildred! I am astonished not to have thought of this before. It can only help your standing in society if people comment on how close you and Lady Honora have become. They will see that a decorous and well-bred young gentlewoman would only have friends who fit into high society." She sipped her tea. "I thought it best to insist upon putting my plan into action right away. Tonight our carriage will pick up Lady Honora on the way to the duchess's estate, and then she shall spend the night here."

Perfect. Perfect, perfect, *perfect.*

Jacqueline felt the thrill of anticipation course through her, and she wondered what Lady Honora would think of her plan.

❖

Nora was standing in her dressing room gazing into her wardrobe. The dress that she had ordered at Madame Beaulieu's establishment last week was finished and hanging with her other gowns, as rich and splendid as a peacock amid sparrows.

The memory of being measured for the dress sent a shiver of pure delight through her. If Miss Lockhart had been so affected by the sight of her at the modiste's, she would be enthralled to see her in the gown that they had planned together. Ruefully, she admitted that she was more excited to see Miss Lockhart than she was about the potential of dancing with the Earl of Sinclair.

Aunt Mildred came into the room and sat on a chair near the door. "My dear, I just received a most interesting offer."

"An offer, Aunt Mildred? Whatever about?" Nora asked, riffling through the dresses in the wardrobe.

"Mrs. Lockhart came by the house and offered to take you off my hands whenever I might be too tired to escort you about town."

Surprised, Nora dropped a handful of skirt. "You? Too tired?"

"It has been known to happen," she admitted. "I am not a young woman any longer, my dear, and it is a tough pace to keep up at my age. I have launched many a lady into society and thought nothing of helping you with your debut, out of respect and love and the memory of your mother, my dear sister." A shadow crossed her face. "But the last time I sponsored anyone was many years ago now. I find it all too easy to forget my age. Maybe I have been pushing myself too hard."

Contrite, Nora crossed the room and grasped her aunt's hand. "We can scale back our engagements," she said earnestly. "I don't mind. We attend plenty of gatherings and we can well afford to be more selective in the ones that we accept."

Aunt Mildred patted her hand. "No, my dear. Now is the time to redouble your efforts to make a name for yourself in society. It is important to attend these things and not to slight any of the hostesses. There are those who find the smallest slips worthy of gossip, and there is nothing more important than your good name."

Nora nodded, but wasn't sure if she agreed.

"That Miss Lockhart may be pert, but one cannot deny that she attracts attention everywhere she goes. The gentlemen swarm to her, and as her friend, you could attract those in her sphere."

It wasn't a ringing endorsement of either of their characters, Nora thought. But Aunt Mildred didn't think of such things. She thought of goals, and how best to achieve them.

"At any rate, I have asked the Lockharts to escort you to the duchess's ball tonight. They were even so kind as to insist that you spend the night with them, and you will come back in their carriage tomorrow. You also have been having many late nights, and it is time to start thinking more healthfully of your rest."

"Tonight?" Nora repeated in surprise. The Lockharts had invited her *tonight*? This was strange and sudden. Or was it? Did Miss Lockhart have a hand in her mother's invitation?

"Yes, Honora, tonight," Aunt Mildred said, and rose to her feet. The gentleness and vulnerability in her tone was stripped away and her imperious nature returned in full force. "You need to attend the Duchess of Hawthorne's ball so that you do not give any hint of a snub to her. She has the Prince Regent's ear, you know. So you shall attend with the Lockharts and you can tell me all of the news tomorrow. Who you danced with, and what title they had. All of the important details."

Aunt Mildred paused in the doorway. "And, Nora, I saw that new dress of yours. It is quite modern, and I do not know if I approve of it. But it could be just the thing to attract the Earl of Sinclair." With that last word of advice, she swept out of the room and down the hall toward her own chambers.

Nora looked at the sea of pale debutante colors spilling out of her wardrobe, with the navy ball gown standing out in their midst. Her mind raced with questions and her heart yearned for answers. Miss Lockhart must be behind this somehow. She had not mistaken the naked desire on her face when they were together at the modiste's establishment. It would have been impossible to mask the appreciation that she had seen in her glittering eyes.

She pulled out the new dress, with its rows of ribbons and lace adorning the hem. The deep blue color was striking with her coloring and hair, just as the dressmaker had predicted.

Tonight, she and Miss Lockhart would have the opportunity to seize time with each other. Even if it was only for one night, she would be able to carry the memory with her forever as she settled into a new life soon as a nobleman's wife.

It was unfortunate for her aunt that the head that she planned to turn was another woman's, and not the earl's.

But it was most fortunate for her.

CHAPTER FIFTEEN

The Duchess of Hawthorne's ball was an absolute crush and therefore heralded as a smashing success before Jacqueline and Lady Honora even reached the end of the receiving line. Half of the conversations that they could overhear were admiring comments about the size of the crowd and the preening boasts that they were part of it.

The other half were about the duke—or more to the point, the duke's continued public absence from his duchess's side.

"I swear, I hear all sorts of gossip about the dullest of people, and as soon as it turns interesting, it's as if I know no one of any importance who knows anything at all," Jacqueline muttered. "I do hope we get more of the story tonight."

They inched their way forward. Slowly, they indeed gained more information through half-heard exchanges and whispers.

The duchess was not young, but still young enough to bear a passel of children if the duke would only stay in England now and do his duty.

The duchess was well regarded, but no one could claim to know her with any intimacy.

The duchess was beautiful and could have any paramour that she chose, but instead remained faithful to her absent husband.

The duchess had not entertained in London for several years, and this was the first ball she had held in all that time.

The duke had returned to London, but was rumored to be not in attendance tonight, at a ball hosted by his own wife and in the ducal estate that he resided in.

Finally, they reached the front of the line.

The Duchess of Hawthorne cut an intimidating figure. The first thing Jacqueline noticed was her posture, which was impeccably correct, and then her sapphire eyes, which bore into her with an intensity that startled her. The duchess was the most beautiful woman that she had ever seen in her life, but with a coldness and remoteness as if she had been carved from marble.

Jacqueline curtsied unsteadily and felt as though all her secrets were laid naked before her.

"Welcome to Hawthorne House," the duchess greeted them. With a regal nod of her head, she dismissed them.

They entered the house in silence, awed by its grandeur and intimidated by its mistress.

But within the ballroom, the atmosphere was livelier. With the sight of a packed room and people she recognized, Jacqueline felt her tension ease. She was close enough to Lady Honora to give her arm a familiar squeeze without anyone else noticing. "I'm so glad your aunt agreed to allow you to come with me," she murmured.

They had traveled in the company of Jacqueline's mother in the carriage, and had waited in the receiving line with her for the past hour. Immediately upon entering, her mother had found her friends, and this was their first chance to talk alone.

Lady Honora's smile lit up her whole face. "I am sure that you are not as glad as I am. My aunt is a wonderful woman, but being her constant companion has been difficult at times."

"I am happy to be your companion for the evening," Jacqueline told her. She hesitated, then said in a rush, "I hope I do not presume too much. If I am in any way mistaken...that is, if you do not feel a certain—*warmth* toward me, I want to assure you that you are under no obligation to do anything despite my creating this happenstance between us. We can always enjoy the ball as friends, and you can return to your aunt's house tomorrow."

Lady Honora watched her, unsmiling, as she stumbled over her speech. A long moment passed in the crowded room, and the chattering din around them seemed to become a dull roar.

"Your presumption is entirely warranted," she said finally. "You intrigue me, Miss Lockhart. And I would like to find out more about you tonight. I assume our chambers are close to one another?"

Jacqueline assured her that they were.

"And dare I presume that they are in quite a separate area from your parents' suite?"

Jacqueline nodded reassuringly.

"Then there is only one other thing I wonder. Would you perhaps have a habit of rising late and no one would think it the least unusual if we two linger over gossip and a light repast all morning before I must take my leave of you and return to my aunt?"

Jacqueline grinned. "These things can be arranged."

"Then I think we have a wonderful dozen hours before us at the very least, and I look forward to each and every one of them," Lady Honora declared.

Jacqueline's heart sang. "I am in wholehearted agreement." She smiled. "But if we are to be intimate, you must call me Jacquie."

"Then please call me Nora," she replied and her smile in return was shy and sweet. "But do not think that this means that our arrangement is off. I still need a husband, after all, not just a lover." But she was smiling as she said it, and Jacquie was thrilled to be teased.

Jacquie laughed with delight. "By all means, we shall find gentlemen to flirt with even if we shall go home with each other tonight." Her mood sobered. "But let us be clear—I would not seduce you if your heart is engaged with another. As soon as you are serious about any of these men as a suitor, all of this must be over between us." She thought of Lydia. "I have been with unfaithful lovers, and I can bear no more of it."

Nora frowned. "But we could at least remain friends afterward?"

Jacqueline hesitated. "If we become lovers, then I don't think I could be your friend after your wedding," she said.

Nora was quiet. Finally, she replied, "It would be worth it all to be in your arms tonight."

Her sweet sincerity warmed Jacquie's heart. "Then we shall make it a night to remember."

They watched in silence as pairs arranged themselves for dancing.

"Do you know anyone here worth dancing with?" Nora asked. She bit her lip. "That sounds terribly snobbish, doesn't it? My aunt has been ever so focused on making a good match."

"So is my mother," Jacquie said with a sigh, and gave her mother a cheery little wave from across the room. "She is watching us, so I suppose we should make our move towards the dancing."

Scanning the crowd, she brightened. "I do know that marquis! We should be able to attract him over here for the next set."

"How?" Nora asked, looking uncertain. "I'm wearing the most daring frock I've ever purchased, but I have no idea how to act in order to live up to this gown's promise."

Jacquie's gaze lingered over Nora's gown. She remembered in vivid detail how she had looked in her undergarments while being measured for her new dress. A tiny shiver of anticipation went up her spine. The navy dress had an empire waist that was gathered under a lovely expanse of bosom, putting all the focus on her breasts and her long legs. Her shoulders were bare, with an airy puffed sleeve perched on her upper arms. The ribbons she had purchased for Nora marched in neat rows beneath her waistline, and accented her hem, and Jacquie smiled.

"It's very easy. You must act as if you are the most beautiful woman in the room," she said. "Because that is what you are."

"I think that honor belongs to you alone," Nora said. "And I am delighted to see you wearing my gift. The shoes look splendid on you."

Jacquie gave a little twirl, her new pink striped gown rippling around her. It was a fragile shell of a dress and she loved the effortless way the fabric flowed. With a saucy wink, she said, "If I may be so bold, my lady Nora—I think *you* shall look perfect on me."

Nora laughed, happiness brightening her face as the marquis drew closer and dropped a bow before them.

"May I have a dance with this angel before me?" he asked. "Miss Lockhart, it has been an age. I didn't expect to see you here tonight at the duchess's ball."

"Perhaps I am but a vision, and you should seek a more corporeal companion," she said, grinning at him. She gestured to Nora with her fan. "Lord Andrews, have you met Lady Honora, of Wiltshire? She is a cousin to the duke. And currently one of my favorite people in London."

He smiled at Jacquie. "Any friend of Miss Lockhart's must be an accomplished dancer and great fun to swing around a ballroom."

"You are in good hands, Lady Honora," she said. "Lord Andrews is a perfect gentleman, even if he can be too exuberant during a cotillion."

"Duly warned," Nora said with a smile, and Lord Andrews whisked her away.

Jacquie watched as they joined the other dancers. She hadn't anticipated how good it would feel to help a friend and to encourage her to dance, instead of flirting with the man to ask her to dance instead. This could be penance for all the dances she had stolen from other women over the years.

"Jacqueline Lockhart, as I live and breathe," a seductive voice cooed at her ear.

The Countess of Straund stood there, a tall gleaming column of perfection. Slim arms reached out to her, pale blue eyes shone at her, and the very fabric of her pleated Grecian gown seemed to breeze toward her to wrap about her legs and ensnare her.

"Lydia," she acknowledged her, and she stepped away from her arms to avoid the familiar embrace.

"I didn't expect to see you here, Jacquie dearest." She smiled at her, all too knowing, overly sweet. "I presumed the duchess had higher standards than to allow the very bottom of society to attend her events." She paused, tapping a long manicured finger against her chin. "But then of course, our darling hostess wouldn't know what you are, would she? A lover of other women? Someone should warn her."

"You are looking well, as always," Jacqueline said coldly. "Your venomous heart has not yet eaten away at your beautiful face. But your wit is as mutton-mannered as ever. You can spread no ill will toward me without damaging your own name."

Lydia's smile was calculating. "I think you are quite, quite wrong about that, Jacquie. I have the power to do a great many things. I have wealth, a title, and very many friends who would repeat anything I told them."

Jacqueline rolled her eyes. "Your 'very many friends' are the reason that your word would be discredited in an instant. Whose arms are you in these days? Baron Beaufort? And who was before me? Wasn't it Mr. Walters, from the publishing house? My lovers are not the only interesting gossip that could be spread."

Lydia scowled at her, but then her face relaxed again into a smile. "Why must we be so acrimonious, dear? We had something once, something special. I thought we could even do it again sometime."

The thought of those lying lips on her body, those faithless arms around her, enraged Jacqueline. "You told me that our lovemaking was a sin, that I should be cast out from society for my unnatural lusts. You told me that no one else in England could have made you do such loathsome things in the bedchamber. And how is it that now you say it was special and you could want it again?"

Lydia bit her lip and looked away. For the first time, her act fell away to reveal vulnerability.

Jacqueline's eyes narrowed. "Your other lovers can't give you what I could, can they?"

Lydia turned soulful eyes toward her. "Your touch was... magnetic," she whispered. "But how could I desire such a thing? I didn't think that I could want that kind of love, but since we parted ways...it's all I can think of."

"And you can't find another woman to satisfy you?" she snapped. "There are women everywhere. Be patient and *look*."

"But what we had was so good. I am so sorry, Jacquie dear. Help me through this. *Love* me through this," she said urgently, and placed a cajoling hand on her arm.

Jacqueline shook it off. "I cannot help you to accept yourself for who you are, Lydia," she said, and backed away from her. Her anger gave way to exhaustion. "Accept yourself, and then you can reach out to others. But don't expect others to do the work for you."

Jacquie wove her way around acquaintances and friends and former suitors. The laughter and talk of the crowd overwhelmed her and all she wanted was to be in Nora's calm presence, to find quiet peace and understanding with her.

A familiar hand grabbed hers and Bea's shining face came into view. "What a crush!" she cried. "Is this not the most splendid ball this season? Is not our hostess the most elegant creature you have ever seen?"

Jacqueline impatiently shook her hand free of Beatrice's grasp, then stopped short as she remembered what Lydia had said about her reputation. "Bea, have you heard any unsavory rumors about me this season?"

"Unsavory? Never!" But her laugh was unconvincing and her gaze wavered.

Jacqueline's lips parted in an exhalation of dismay.

"You've never cared a jot what the gossips say. Why the long face now if some old biddy thinks you've been a bit too familiar, that maybe you drink and flirt too much? It's not as if you're trying to impress anyone."

Jacqueline shook her head. "I don't care," she agreed, but her words sounded hollow.

Bea bustled away to another dance partner, leaving Jacquie behind without a second glance. She turned away and set her course again toward Nora at the other side of the room.

It had been the truth for so long. She hadn't cared about her own reputation, as long as she was invited to enough parties to fill her evenings and had an entertaining time. And somehow, despite her pert ways, she had always been invited. Right now she was in the ballroom of a *duchess*, for heaven's sake. No one with a truly tawdry reputation would be allowed anywhere near a duchess, no matter what strings Nora had pulled to get her here.

Gossip had never bothered her before. But now that it might affect Nora, she felt wretched. She didn't want to taint Nora's name, to ruin her chances of marriage. She must be above reproach if she ever wanted to succeed on the cutthroat Marriage Mart.

Coming here tonight with Nora might have been a dreadful mistake.

For her own good, Jacqueline should tell Nora that they could never see each other again.

Her selfish heart ached.

Overwhelmed with fatigue and sadness, she pushed her way to an alcove at the edge of the ballroom. There were several such shallow rooms in this part of the room, far away from the heated crush and the dancing. One was occupied by middle-aged men debating politics, and another was overstuffed with a gaggle of fresh faced debutantes who burst into giggles when Jacqueline stalked by.

The last alcove was blessedly deserted and also the most secluded, behind several large plants as well as a heavy half-drawn curtain. She pushed thick velvet fringe off her face as she entered, then sank onto the cushioned bench. Defeated, she leaned back against the pillows and closed her eyes.

Her mind was spinning so she didn't bother to focus on any thought in particular, but the words "unnatural" and "sinful" kept repeating. Jacquie knew in her heart it wasn't true. She had met too many other women who wanted the same thing, had read the poetry of Sappho and the literature of the Greeks. There had always been women who loved women, and men who loved men.

But sometimes it was a heavy truth to carry among the ballrooms of London, when others hurled such words at her.

"May I join you?" Nora's soft voice was a soothing balm to her nerves. She felt the cushion dip as she sat beside her. "I saw you dart in here after you talked to that woman." There was a long pause. "I would do anything to give you comfort, but I can offer you privacy if you need that instead."

"Stay," Jacqueline said, and opened her eyes.

Nora's face was close to hers, her gray eyes full of concern. Her blond hair was swept away from her face in an elegant coiffure, but a few curls had escaped and framed her face. Jacqueline reached up and brushed one of the golden tendrils behind her ear, wishing she could feel the silky smoothness of her cheek beneath her fingers instead of through the glove's barrier.

"Stay," she repeated again, her voice softer.

Nora smiled. "Of course I'm staying," she said. "I'm here. As long as you need me."

"Oh, I need you," she said. She hesitated, but Nora was so lovely and calm, and she was already leaning toward her, her lips parted, her eyes inviting.

She shifted on the bench and leaned in, Nora's rose petal perfume flooding her senses, her lips now mere inches from her own. Jacqueline's lips pressed against Nora's soft pair, tenderly at first, then fervently.

Her kiss electrified her senses and she felt giddy, invincible. Her lips slanted against hers and Nora's tongue slipped against her own. This was even better than she had imagined—and she had imagined a lot since she had met Nora. She was soft and warm and welcoming, and the kiss set off sparks from the tip of her head all the way down to her toes, which were curling delightfully inside her satin rose dance slippers.

The kiss seemed like an eternity. It surely had been only a moment.

They broke apart, and Jacqueline touched her forehead against Nora's. They smiled at each other, the secret shy smile of lovers.

"Well, well, well," drawled a male voice from the alcove's entrance. "Such an interesting evening this is promising to be."

CHAPTER SIXTEEN

Jacqueline sprang away from Nora, her heart pounding.
A tall man with broad shoulders pushed aside the heavy curtain and walked into the alcove. He seated himself between them and leaned back against the cushions, draping one arm behind Nora. He had a face made equally for laughter and for sorrow, deep grooves etched into his cheeks and around his eyes. Dark eyes peered at them beneath heavy eyelids. A smirk hovered on his lips, and those eyes were amused.

"I thought you were not in attendance tonight, Your Grace," Nora said.

Jacquie gasped. This was the Duke of Hawthorne? The one man her mother had warned her against? The man whose name was on everyone's lips tonight? "Your Grace. We shall leave you to your thoughts," she said, her own thoughts racing toward escape.

His teeth glinted at her as a smile spread across his face. "Alas, but you should not. Not when my thoughts are so very pertinent to your situation."

Taut with fury, she wished she could flee but knew she could not.

His insouciance turned to sincerity before her eyes, and he straightened in his seat. The duke reached out his hand, palm facing her, and his expression grew serious. "Truce. Please stay," he said, as if he could read her mind. As if they had the option to leave, which she knew they did not.

He said nothing further, merely gazed at her from hooded eyes that gave nothing away. Yet his sudden change in manner convinced her.

"And of course I am enchanted to see you again, Lady Honora, my dearest long lost cousin," he said as he brought her satin gloved hand to his lips. "Though it is my irreproachable wife who is the host of this gathering, not myself. You are correct that I have not yet made an official appearance at this ball. I do expect it is meeting with your satisfaction?"

"I am pleased to see you again, Your Grace." Her voice was polite, but hesitant and thin. Nora had gone pale, and Jacquie wished she could hold her hand and comfort her. The duke smiled.

"Now that we are all reacquainted, do tell me more about this delightful encounter that I was interrupting." His voice was commanding, but without even the hint of lechery in his voice.

Jacqueline felt strangely inclined to confide in him.

"Who are you, exactly?" Nora asked instead. Her face was expressionless, a mask of her usual self.

Hawthorne eyed her and seemed to consider her question. "I could be your greatest friend. Or a dread enemy. The choice is yours to make."

"I suppose only a fool would choose you to be an enemy, Your Grace," Jacqueline replied.

"*Au contraire, ma cherie.* I count some of the very best people that I know as enemies. After all, so much in life is a matter of perspective, wouldn't you agree?"

Nora clasped her hands in her lap, so tight that her knuckles were white. "I'm not sure that I understand or appreciate your riddles, Your Grace. Regardless, what do you seek to gain from this encounter? Money? Favors?" Her voice was unsteady.

"Oh, I have enough of both to last me several lifetimes. The only thing I want to know from you is details, my dear, so I can help you beyond your wildest dreams."

"And why should we give you any details at all? What is your benefit, Your Grace?" Jacqueline countered.

Hawthorne relaxed again on the bench, as if they were all old friends. One Hessian booted leg stretched out in front of him. "The benefit to me is the joy of helping those around me, of course."

Jacqueline laughed without humor. "Surely you don't see yourself as some Good Samaritan, lounging around your own ballroom in order to help those unfortunates around you?" she taunted.

"Ah, but what if I am one of the same unfortunates that you speak of? Of course, I don't see it that way at all. As I mentioned earlier, my dear ladies, it all depends on perspective."

Jacqueline narrowed her eyes. Did he mean...?

"Yes. I am a lover of men."

Silence fell over the alcove. Jacqueline could hear the men still discussing politics a few feet away, and the debutantes with their shrill giggles, but all she was really aware of was the *thump, thump, thump* of her own heart. Her eyes darted from Nora, her hands twisting in her lap, to the smirking duke, who looked as if nothing on this earth could startle him.

So this was the scandal. This was why the duke had fled England and lived abroad for so many years. Jacquie was dumbfounded.

"In fact, I believe my latest lover is a dear friend of yours. Sir Phineas Snow?"

Jacquie reeled back. "But he has said nothing of this to me," she said, trying to absorb the news. "And he tells me of all of his lovers." Didn't he? She struggled against the feeling of betrayal. Phin could have warned her of this.

Hawthorne shrugged. "Some of us are perhaps more discreet than others," he said, raising a brow at her. "Nevertheless, we all should look out for each other, shouldn't we? That is why you are here, after all. My dear wife extended this invitation to Lady Honora only after I suggested it. Phin had dropped a word in my ear about the two of you, and I thought it a kindness for the dukedom to lend its support to you."

Nora's face was white.

"Oh, don't fret. Your secrets are safe with me, as long as you practice a modicum of restraint. The alcove is only half-curtained, you know. I spied you here in this corner and thought it behooved me to interrupt before you went any further." He smiled beatifically. "I am nothing if not an angel of mercy."

"I think you misunderstood the situation," said Nora.

"Did I?" he asked, his eyes assessing her and then Jacqueline. A smile curved his lips. "I think perhaps I did not."

"Why, husband dear," a voice as cold as charity spoke from beyond the curtain. "How delightful to see that you have joined my party."

He rose from the padded bench with admirable elegance and bowed deeply enough to fit a queen. "You have always thrown the very best of entertainments, dear heart."

The Duchess of Hawthorne stood before them, dreadful despite her beauty. Jacqueline fought the urge to shiver.

"When I saw you, I thought to have some private discourse. But instead I find a very cozy and inappropriate tête-à-tête." The duchess glanced dismissively at Jacquie and Nora. "In my *own* house, Duke?"

He smiled at her. "When you invite the world to your kingdom, my dear, all cannot always go as you plan."

"And yet everything is possible," she replied. Her eyes held a wealth of meaning, clearly intended solely for her husband.

Hawthorne dipped his head in response.

The duchess turned away from him, fury clear in every line of her body. "Miss Lockhart, Lady Honora. I expect you ladies would wish to partake in the cold supper being laid in the adjoining hall? I should be remiss in my duties if either of you felt less than welcomed and satisfied as guests in my home." Her tone was scrupulously polite.

Nora seized the moment with alacrity and curtsied so low that Jacqueline was surprised that she didn't topple over. "It is most generous of you, Your Grace. Thank you so much for your kindness."

Jacqueline scrambled to her feet and followed her lead, rendered silent by the quiet danger that sang in the air between the duchess and the duke. They removed themselves as fast as they could, fleeing the alcove and their hostess while trying not to draw unwelcome attention to their haste.

As soon as they spied a door leaving the ballroom, they ducked through it and into the hall, though it was nowhere near the cold repast that the duchess had mentioned. It was enough that it was empty of guests and servants. Staring at each other, they found themselves in a paroxysm of laughter.

Nora laid a shaking hand on the wall of the hallway, her other hand on her belly. "I don't know how I can be laughing when I feel like at any moment I could pass out with fear!" she exclaimed breathlessly.

Jacqueline wheezed in reply, doubled over in a fit of laughter. "I have never been so nervous!" she gasped. "And I could *murder* Phin for saying anything at all about me to Hawthorne. He knows of my interest in you, but I swear I never thought he would tell a soul."

Nora looked thoughtful. "The duke seems trustworthy. He did come over to tell us that we might be visible to others."

"It was decent of him," Jacquie agreed. "Did you see how frightening the duchess looked when she interrupted us? I wonder what their relationship truly is."

"I suspect we will never know. I would be shocked if we would ever be invited to another gathering here at Hawthorne House," Nora said with a smile. "Distant family relations can only take one so far in life."

"I don't know about that," Jacqueline said. She reached out her hand and touched Nora's cheek. "But it wouldn't be a bad idea to attend, if we were ever invited back here. The duke seemed to be very understanding of our situation. The way he spoke…The fact that he is with Phin…He must be trustworthy. I think he would know other people who are inclined the same way. Maybe we could meet them too."

Nora stared at her. "Would you want to be so public in your affections?"

Jacqueline shrugged. "If we could have the opportunity, then of course I would want to be public. I am not ashamed of who I am. Why should I be?"

Nora didn't say anything. Jacqueline bit her lip and looked away, embarrassed by her emotions. In so many ways, she was falling headlong into this new friendship and it was easy to forget that she didn't know so much about Nora as she might like.

"Forget it," she said lightly, and tugged on her hand. "Let's go in search of the repast before too many people wonder where we have been this past half hour."

The rest of the night was a blur to Nora. She felt hot and cold and dizzy, in turns and sometimes all at once. It was a credit to her dancing tutor that she faultlessly executed each dance that she was asked to dance, relying on muscle memory and instinct. It was a credit to her indomitable Aunt Mildred that she was still able to make small talk while barely aware of the topic at hand.

And of course it was a credit to Jacqueline that she was so unable to focus on any of the evening at all. A credit to her beautiful form and figure, swaying across the ballroom on so many gentlemen's arms, a credit to her wonderful warmth when she had told her that she wanted to dance with her and her alone if only it was acceptable. That warmth was so foreign to Nora, who had felt so little of it since her parents had passed away. She had felt so cold and so alone for so long.

Nora feared that she had pushed Jacqueline away by being unresponsive to her emotion. And yet she did feel very uncertain about the strength of her feelings for Jacqueline, and how willing she was to throw proprietary to the wind in her presence. Kissing in the duchess's alcove!

This was not what she had envisioned when she had thought to pursue a dalliance with Jacqueline. She had something much more circumspect in mind. Stolen kisses in a private carriage, or discreet hand holding beneath the table at Gunter's.

But Jacqueline seemed so much more experienced than she was. Could she have meant what she said, that she would be public with their relationship, if such a thing was possible? Nora had never considered such liaisons in terms of permanency. In her experience, they were brief private encounters. Secrecy was of paramount importance. But was it possible to have more? Emotion flooded her heart.

At the end of the evening, they settled into the carriage on their way to Jacqueline's home. Her mother was uncharacteristically quiet, likely reliving the evening in the presence of nobility. Jacqueline reached for Nora's hand under their reticules, a clandestine touch that made Nora aware of just how cold she was. How cold she had been for a long time. She squeezed her fingers, then gently stroked her soon to be lover's palm.

How quiet the streets of London seemed, and how loud her beating heart.

It wasn't long before they found themselves at the Lockharts' fashionable townhouse. Jacqueline's mother bade them good night and a maid escorted them upstairs.

"Here you are, my lady," the maid announced with a curtsy. "I hope you find every comfort here during your stay with the family."

Nora's cheeks felt as pink as the pretty wallpapered room as she slipped inside the bedchamber. Her own hairbrush was already on the dresser, and the maid was shaking out her nightclothes. Her aunt had arranged an overnight case to be sent over to the Lockharts' earlier in the afternoon.

The maid drew off her navy evening gown reverently, with a low exclamation. "Your dress is ever so nice, my lady," she exclaimed. "Such a beautiful color! I imagine you and our Miss Lockhart made a pretty picture together in your finery."

Nora looked at her sharply, but the maid was busy carrying the dress to the wardrobe. "So many suitors you must have had between you!" she said wistfully. "My Thomas is the footman who was with you tonight and he says the crush was unimaginable with all the carriages. There must have been so many men to dance with!"

She slipped the fine white cotton shift over Nora and tied the silk wrapper around her waist. "Of course, no one can hold a candle to our Miss Lockhart for dancing, so I'm sure she must be exhausted. I imagine you're more than ready for bed yourself! But you ladies must have so much to review together, and I know she had tea and a few biscuits brought up to her rooms so you can have a good gossip before bed. It was ever so when Miss Everson stayed the night as well," the maid prattled on. "Come, here is the way to her rooms."

Nora allowed herself to be escorted into Jacqueline's sitting room, where a small fire crackled in the hearth, and a pot of tea gently steamed on a small table.

"Welcome, Nora!" she cried out as if they hadn't seen each other in days, instead of a mere half hour. "Thank you for bringing her, Sally. You're a true treasure."

The maid grinned and pocketed the coin that Jacqueline slipped to her. "Enjoy your evening, miss!" She bobbed a curtsy. "Milady." She left the room.

Nora took in the scene. Jacqueline beamed at her with the radiance of the sun, lounging on a small settee in her nightclothes and showing an enticing amount of creamy décolletage. The sitting room had been strewn with artfully placed cushions and soft blankets. Candlelight flickered, bathing the room in soft amber light. Behind the teapot, she spied a plate of strawberries and an ice bucket holding a bottle of champagne.

It looked perfect.

It looked practiced.

"Miss Everson?" Nora said quietly.

Jacqueline's face fell for a moment before the smile reappeared, but it didn't quite meet her eyes. "Sally mentioned it, did she? Bless her, she does mean well. She *knows*, of course. Sometimes I reckon all the downstairs *knows*. But you would think she would have the sense to keep some things private."

She reached out to Nora, who had not taken a step farther from where the maid had brought her. "Come, sit with me," she said. "I know I had not mentioned Beatrice, but surely you knew that I had past lovers? She is not the only one that I have been with intimately. Haven't you kissed any pretty women at home? Kissed…and maybe more?"

"Yes, I have had lovers," Nora replied, her voice low and urgent. "But I seduced no one with the efforts that I had practiced with another."

She strode forward and in a fluid motion, grasped Jacqueline by the hand and yanked her toward her so abruptly that Jacqueline stumbled and pressed against her. They were near enough the same height and stood eye to eye.

Nora saw her own passion answered on Jacqueline's flushed face. "I want your desire to be for me alone and not for the memory of another woman. I want to love you without thinking of anyone else in the world."

"You make me feel like we are the only two in existence," Jacqueline breathed.

Nora pressed her lips against hers and felt the world dissolve around them. All she could focus on were the lips beneath hers.

Jacqueline drew back and tucked a lock of Nora's hair behind her ear. She smiled. "Come to my bed, darling. Come lie with me."

Nora followed her without hesitation. In contrast to the prepared sitting room, the bedroom had not been arranged as part of the seduction. Plain bed covers were neatly drawn up. There was no fire laid in the fireplace. A book of poetry lay half open on the night table, and the pair of rose satin slippers had been kicked off underneath the open window.

"Welcome," Jacqueline said quietly.

Nora smiled at her. "Thank you," she said, and leaned in again for another kiss, her eyes closing in bliss.

She felt hands caressing her shoulders and then a pair of arms wrap firmly around her waist as the kiss deepened and grew more urgent. A delicious pressure built inside of Nora. She moved her lips over Jacquie's neck and untied her frilled bed jacket, sliding her hands between the gauzy covering and the cotton shift and pulling her close, delighting in the press of another woman's body against her own.

It has been so long. Years had passed since she had a moment like this. Worry tugged at her mind. Had it been *too* long? Could she remember how to pleasure another? But her body seemed to know what to do. Suddenly, she knew that her instincts wouldn't fail her. Jacquie trusted her enough to be in her arms. She could trust herself to relax and enjoy the moment.

She swept her hands restlessly over Jacquie's hips and heard an answering sigh.

Nora drew her head back, her arms still tight around Jacquie. "I wish your maid had left you clothed," she said.

A half smile played on Jacquie's lips. "Not words one wishes to hear in a moment like this, my dear. I don't know how they do things in Wiltshire, but in London we look for rather *fewer* clothes in the bedroom. I feel quite shockingly overdressed as it is."

Nora laughed. "I loved how you looked in your dress tonight," she said. "There was the sweetest little posy of flowers tucked between your breasts."

She looked down at Jacqueline's chest. Freed from the confines of the stays that had pushed them up all night beneath her evening dress, her breasts were small and sweetly shaped. Her shift was loose, the neckline dipping low to reveal the lovely valley between her breasts. The weave was so fine that Nora could see the dusky shape of her nipples through the fabric and the faint shadow of her navel.

Thoughtfully, Nora leaned forward and placed a kiss between her breasts. "From memory, I would place that posy here," she said.

Jacquie's eyes were luminous. "Maybe it was lower," she said, her breath catching.

Nora raised a brow. "Lower? Well, sadly, your maid took the dress away, so I cannot be sure of such details. But you might be correct." She placed a kiss on her right nipple and heard a quick intake of breath. She tilted her head. "I'm not sure if it was quite so far over." She kissed the left nipple as well.

"Oh, let us be done with games," Jacqueline gasped. "I cannot bear such teasing."

Nora slid the bed jacket down Jacquie's arms, letting it pool around their feet, and grasped a fistful of her shift and pulled it up over her head. And there she was. The most beautiful woman in England. No—in all of Europe. Standing in the nude before her.

London had been a very good idea, Nora thought dazedly, if only for this moment.

"I feel quite alone now," Jacquie complained, "and there is no fire as I thought we would be in the sitting room. Do come closer, dearest."

Nora grinned fiercely and kissed her, bringing her body as close as she could, and suddenly her own clothing had disappeared under the magic of Jacquie's light touch, and then they were in the bed with their limbs tangling in such a way that she didn't know anymore what was happening except that this was the happiest she had been in a long, long time.

She traced her lips again over Jacquie's breasts, and slipped her hands joyfully down her body, across her waist, around the curve of her bottom, and finally down her thighs. Jacquie's hips moved beneath her touch, and her arms were tight around her. Nora slipped her hand between her thighs and found a delightful warmth welcoming her, waiting for her, and she took as much pleasure from pressing her fingers against her sweet pearl as Jacquie did, judging from the cries that left her lips as she increased the pressure and then slid inside her. She loved her gently, then thrust more firmly, and it didn't take much longer before she swept her fingers once again across Jacquie's most sensitive spot and she shivered under Nora and cried out once more and then went limp.

Nora smiled and pressed a kiss to her forehead. "And *that* is how we do it in Wiltshire," she told her, before snuggling beside her and laying her head on her shoulder.

Jacquie giggled. "I could become used to country manners," she said.

She sat up, the wool blanket falling away from her chest and Nora wondered if she would ever become accustomed to the sight of her in deshabille. Jacquie in a day dress was inviting, in a ball gown was enticing, and in nothing at all was nothing short of incredible.

"We are polite folk in London, so do let me show you *our* customs in return," she said, her eyes brimming with laughter.

"I am only too eager to be educated," Nora told her, and she lay on her back while Jacquie moved over her and surrounded her with breathy sighs and lush kisses and sensitive, delicate touches. The scent of sweet oranges filled her nose from the perfume that she favored, and in delight Nora realized that she knew now exactly where she had dabbed it on her body. Secrets that she hugged close to herself as she inhaled deeply, burying her nose in the crook of an elbow and against her neck and in that glossy cloud of curls.

It was difficult to separate the physical sensations from the emotions that overwhelmed her, and Nora reveled in the loss of control, giving herself entirely into Jacquie's knowing hands, holding nothing back from her.

Then she felt the heat of Jacquie's lips and tongue licking its way like wildfire low on her belly and across her hip bone and lighting onto the top of her thigh, and her hands were parting her legs so that the fire could spread from those glorious lips directly onto her center. Nora gasped as Jacquie's tongue swirled around her, dipping into her and bringing her ever closer to ecstasy. She gently eased a finger inside and that sweet pressure combined with those honeyed lips brought Nora toppling over the edge, stars in her eyes and a fever racing through her blood and sounds of joy from her lips.

Her eyes closed as she listened to her panting breath start to even out, and Jacquie moved beside her and drew the covers up again. Only then did Nora realize that she had thrust them away as the fire had overwhelmed her senses. She felt Jacquie curl up close beside her, a hand resting on her chest, a leg drawn up over her thigh, and she sighed in deep contentment.

"London ways have their charms, too," Nora said drowsily, and heard Jacquie's low laugh in her ear as she drifted off to sleep in her arms.

CHAPTER SEVENTEEN

Nora opened her eyes to the pale dawn light shining through the window and onto the bed where Jacqueline lay sleeping beside her. Jacquie was on her side, and her hand was pillowed under her face. Black curls lay in beautiful disarray across the pillows.

Nora sat up and gathered the blankets around her, gazing down at the beautiful sight in front of her. She twirled a lock of Jacqueline's hair around her finger lazily. Her heart was full, and she reveled in the luxury of relaxing beside her.

Last night had been revelatory. She had never felt so open with anyone before. With Jacquie, she felt wild and free and powerful. How swiftly her feelings had moved from friendship to so much more.

For a moment, she railed against the injustice that would prevent them from being truly together, before she collected her thoughts. Their situation was much the same as any unmarried pair who had hastened to the bedchamber, she tried to convince herself. Any man and woman who lay together outside of matrimony would need to act with the same secrecy and discretion. No unwed couple could stay together without scandal.

Part of her wanted to cry over the unfairness that as two women, they had no option for matrimony together, unlike the fictional and theoretical unwed couple that she had thought up. But the more practical side of her tamped down the rampant emotion. This was never meant as a serious relationship—she had embarked upon it as a dalliance and nothing more.

Even if her lover were a man—if Miss Jacqueline had actually been Mr. Jack—it still would be no use. The Lockharts didn't have the money or station to match the Banfields. Their two families would never unite in matrimony, regardless of gender.

Live in the moment, she told herself. Right now, sitting in this bed, beside this sleeping woman, after a night of the most glorious lovemaking she could have imagined, life was good and all was well. She didn't need to borrow trouble from tomorrow.

Jacqueline stirred. She opened her eyes slowly and smiled. "Good morning, Nora," she said and bounced up in the bed. "What a perfect morning after a beautiful night!" She laughed and then hugged her, toppling them both off balance. They fell back among the pillows.

Nora laid her head on Jacqueline's shoulder. "I believe I was promised tea and gossip this morning," she said.

Jacqueline laughed again. "You could have had both last night, but you spurned them, so why should you get any now?"

"I was after a much more interesting prize last night. Now that I've had it, I rather fancy some refreshing tea and civilized conversation," she said, trying to keep a smile off her face.

"Liar," Jacqueline murmured. "I think you are like me, and you want more of the same. Who am I to deny a woman her morning's pleasure?"

Her mouth descended upon Nora's, and it was quite some time before they were satisfied.

Midmorning, they rang for the tea to arrive. "Sally will handle everything," Jacqueline declared, stretching. "She will rearrange the sitting room and will bring us a light repast."

Some of the joy fizzled out of Nora as she remembered Sally dressing her last night and mentioning Jacqueline's other lover, and she looked away.

"You aren't jealous of Beatrice, are you?" Jacqueline asked her. "We haven't been lovers since before you and I even met."

She sighed. "I suppose I shouldn't be jealous. You were right that I have had other lovers. It's just that they are far from here, and you haven't met them, so it doesn't seem the same to me. I'm not saying that it's right," she added hastily.

"Just how many lovers did you have?" she asked.

"Only two," she replied. "One was a friend of my cousin's, visiting from Scotland. We spent a few weeks together, years ago.

After my parents passed away." She bit her lip and looked away for a moment. It was still so painful to remember that time. Jacqueline squeezed her hand in sympathy.

"The other was only for one night, when I traveled to Bath for a cousin's wedding. I met a woman there who was also attending the wedding and we passed the evening together at the inn where we both stayed."

Jacqueline grinned. "I've had more than two, as you may have guessed. I have been in London for a long time, and there are more willing women than you might originally suspect here. I have had the misfortune of falling in and out of love so many times...I feel as though my love life has been a lifetime of beautiful mistakes and heartache."

"How many?" Nora demanded. "And do I know any of the others?"

"Well, Beatrice, as you know. And also Lady Perry, though it was the summer before she married."

Nora raised her brows. "Really? Lady Perry? I wouldn't have guessed!"

"You don't even know who Lady Perry is, do you?"

Nora giggled. "No, of course not. But it seemed like the worldly sort of thing to say."

"Yes, very worldly," Jacquie said, and Nora just had to kiss that pert little nose in front of her which was wrinkling in laughter. "Anyway. It was the merest dalliance," Jacqueline said, with a dismissive flick of her hand. "She seems happy with Lord Perry, and I do wish them well."

"Anyone else?"

Jacquie paused and frowned. "More recently...Lydia, the Countess of Straund. She was the woman I spoke with last night, before our discovery by the duke."

Nora opened her mouth to reply, but then shut it when Sally came into the room.

"Good morning, miss! My lady! I hope you had a restful night. Don't you worry, Lady Honora, I've already been to your room and rumpled the bedclothes so the other maids don't guess what's going on."

She settled a covered tray on a table beside the window and drew the curtains. "But if you could just nip over to the sitting room for a quick minute, I do have a few footmen on their way with hot water for a nice bath. It wouldn't do if you were here in the bedroom with Miss Lockhart while they came in."

Nora did as she was bade, grabbing her silk wrapper to cover herself as she waited for the bath to be arranged. She sat on the settee that Jacqueline had sprawled on last night. In the light of day, it was an airy bright chamber, quite unexceptional, very unlike the den of seduction that Jacqueline had arranged last night.

She smiled. In truth, she wouldn't mind an evening before the fire, feeding each other delicacies. She simply hadn't been prepared for it last night, and not with the thought of Miss Everson so present in her mind. But last night had been so wonderful, and now she could dismiss the thought of the other women that Jacquie had loved from her mind.

Bathing with the glorious Jacqueline was sure to be a highlight of her London season when she only had the memories to cherish during the long cold winter. She supposed she would be married by then. If all went according to plan, someone this season would make her an offer to make him the happiest of men.

Jacqueline had mentioned that she had spent a summer with Lady Perry. Their liaison hadn't lasted after the lady had married. It meant that one brief season of passion was all they had before them. Not long enough, but it seemed impossible to dare wish for more.

Through the closed door, she heard her name being called as Jacqueline waited for her to return to the bedroom.

Nora frowned. Being with Jacqueline temporarily didn't sit right with her. And yet, what other option did she have?

Jacqueline peeked through the adjoining door. "Come on, Nora! The water will be cooling. Join me!"

Pushing her fretful thoughts from her mind, she rose from the settee and headed toward her temporary lover.

Chapter Eighteen

The air in Aunt Mildred's townhouse felt too still and silent after the dizzying night that had started in the Hawthorne ballroom and ended in Jacqueline's bedroom. Nora restlessly played on the pianoforte to fill the house with sound and vibrancy, but it failed to lift her spirits. She dropped the lid on the keys after half an hour of distracted practice.

She had heard that over a million people lived in London. Their townhouse was ensconced cheek to jowl among a string of others, all of them inhabited for the season. It was so strange to think of loneliness when there were so many neighbors, but she didn't know any of them the way that she knew all of the prominent families around Rosedale Manor.

Nora felt far lonelier here in London, pressed against people wherever she went, than she ever had in the country, with the next house over two kilometers away from her own.

However, today she knew that she was lonely because Jacquie wasn't by her side. Last night had not been long enough to learn every nook and cranny of her, to fill herself with memories to last through the cold nights that would come with her eventual marriage.

Sighing, Nora wandered into the library where the daily papers were brought after Aunt Mildred reviewed them in the mornings. She was in sore need of distraction from her thoughts. Since her last visit to Gina's salon, she had found herself entranced by newspapers. Miss Alice Andrews, one of the other women who attended the salon, was a journalist who wrote extensively about the wars against Napoleon.

Speaking with her and hearing her passion for the topic had sparked Nora's interest.

Only now was she realizing how much she had relied on her papa when he had been alive to tell her what she needed to know of the goings-on overseas. She had never bothered to read the news for herself or to form her own opinions on what was being reported. She had listened to what other people told her, and absorbed what they thought about it all.

Nora gazed out the window. She had considered herself well educated enough for a country girl who had never attended a formal school, but through her ongoing association with the salon every Tuesday, she was repeatedly confronted by her lack of knowledge. Nora was tempted to think that it was the very air of London that inspired her newfound interest in the world beyond her childhood home, but knew she owed much to the influence of Gina's salon, and the energetic curiosity that Jacquie seemed to have for everything.

Despite the loneliness that she felt in the throng, she had never felt more connected to individuals than the ones she had met here in the city.

Nora frowned down at the paper and smoothed its crinkled pages over her knee as she continued to read Alice's article. The papers were expensive, as Aunt Mildred had complained just the other morning as she consumed the society pages. Nora wondered what it would be like to go to a gentleman's club to read all the different newspapers and talk about the goings-on of the day. Would it be similar to the afternoons at Gina's salon? Wistfully, she wished she could peer inside a club, just once, to see what it was that women were missing.

Nora kept a wary eye on the door to the drawing room. Aunt Mildred could come barging in at any moment to whisk away the paper. She was convinced that too much focus on politics would make Nora a less desirable conversation partner in society. With a wry smile, she wondered what Aunt Mildred would think if she ever learned that she was discussing much more than politics when she went to visit Gina. Her visits would just need to stay secret while she remained in London with her aunt.

A shadow fell across the doorway and she thrust the newspaper behind her on the windowsill, making sure the curtain was drawn.

"Miss Lockhart is here to see you," the butler announced, and Nora's heart fair leapt out of her chest with happiness.

Jacquie bustled in, all smiles and laughter, her gait so quick that her hips swung from side to side in a most entrancing pattern. Her fine muslin gown swirled around her legs, and an embroidered shawl was draped around her arms. Every corner of the room expanded with energy and light and life.

"What an elegant little house!" Jacqueline cried, flinging her arm up in a wild gesture at the room. "The colors are absolutely last decade, but the furniture is darling. And so tasteful. I do think you have one of the loveliest abodes in Mayfair, Nora."

She leaned in, and Nora inhaled her orange blossom scent as she grasped her hand. "I missed you," Nora breathed, uncaring that they had only been apart for a matter of hours.

"And I you," Jacquie said with a smile. "How sweet to think of you all nestled up in this little house, missing *me* of all creatures! I do hope you weren't pushing aside a crust of bread and a cup of water, wasting away with grand emotion. And of course, gnashing your teeth. No lover's sulk is complete without teeth gnashing."

Nora shook her head. "You are an irrepressible tease."

"Then repress me not, fair Nora! Let me prattle on and on and none shall come to harm." Her grin was brilliant.

Aunt Mildred entered the room. "Miss Lockhart, how kind of you to pay us a visit."

Jacquie sprang to her feet and entered an elegant curtsy. "Lady Mildred, you have raised a perfectly darling niece, and my parents have tasked me with bringing their raptures and praises to you. Lady Honora was a delight to all who encountered her at the Duchess of Hawthorne's ball last night."

Nora felt her cheeks burn as Jacquie sank back onto the sofa.

"Lady Honora was in our tender care all evening," Jacquie continued. "We had such an enjoyable night."

Nora smiled. "Yes, there was a lot of dancing."

"Most invigorating, I would say."

Nora blushed again. "It was my most memorable evening in London thus far," she said, and was rewarded when Jacqueline beamed at her.

Aunt Mildred sniffed, but it was clear that she was trying to hide a smile. "Well, I must confess that I had no hand in raising Honora. That was my dear sister and her husband, and a fine job they did. Honora is the very image of her mother."

Nora swallowed hard. Thoughts of Mama were still difficult, but never more so than when Aunt Mildred looked at her with that mixture of pained loss.

"They were wonderful models," Nora said quietly. "I wish they could be here now to escort me about and to see how London has changed since their heyday."

Too late she realized how unappreciative she sounded, and she watched helplessly as Aunt Mildred drew herself up as straight as a poker. Quickly she added, "Of course I am grateful to be here under my aunt's sponsorship." She touched Aunt Mildred's hand and was rewarded with a quick smile from her.

"Your elegant manners do your parents an endless credit," Jacquie said. "And I am sure Lady Mildred is an excellent example of behavior as well. Now if only some other ladies had half of your comportment and a fraction of such a sterling example in their own lives!"

Aunt Mildred rang for tea and settled into a chair. "You do not need to remind me of the ill behaviors of these young girls," she huffed. "Half of the young things on the market are without sense, and the other half without caution."

Jacquie leaned forward, eyes sparkling. "Did you hear the news about Miss Bradshaw? Her bosom was practically falling out of her gown last night. It did give her an advantage when choosing a partner for the dancing—a more appreciative crowd of old roués as I had never seen before all flocked about her."

Aunt Mildred let out a sharp laugh. "I cannot imagine such a thing! Well, I am glad that my Honora is a sensible creature. I am grateful not to be escorting someone just out of the schoolroom with all the modern notions of ill manners and poor discretion. And it is good to be together with other young ladies of a similar age," she added. "If you could but garner a collective group of levelheaded ladies, I daresay society would be a good deal more sensible."

"Certainly more enjoyable," Jacquie said with a look at Nora.

"Miss Lockhart has been instrumental in helping me on the dance floor," Nora said. She broke into the conversation, wishing she didn't feel so awkward when she had something to say. Knowing it was disrupting the flow of conversation, yet yearning so much to join in and be part of the group. Wanting to belong.

Jacquie nodded. "Your grace on the dance floor is a credit to your own talents," she said. Nora felt herself ease, allowing Jacquie's warmth to settle over her and comfort her.

"Honora will be a beautiful bride and will look lovely dancing at her wedding," Aunt Mildred said with affection. "And you must be looking for yourself, of course, Miss Lockhart. Did any gentleman secure your hand for the supper dance last night?"

They exchanged secret looks. They had been careful to avoid the supper dance so that they could share their meal together, tucked away in a corner while they sampled sweets and savories and let their anticipation build toward the night that lay ahead of them.

"No particular man has caught my fancy," Jacqueline said brightly.

"It will be just a matter of time. If only my Honora had your lively disposition! You lighten my spirits, Miss Lockhart. It is a pleasure to know that you two have struck up a friendship. You should spend more time together," Aunt Mildred said. "Why, I remember being quite inseparable from my girlfriends during my London seasons. It is nice to see you making more bosom friends, dear."

"Yes, I am constantly seeking ladies as bosom friends," Nora said, and Jacquie glanced at her with a knowing smile.

"You seem the sort of fashionable young miss who always has an exciting social engagement to attend, Miss Lockhart." Aunt Mildred took a sip of her tea, her eyes bright and inquisitive. "What sort of entertainments do you have coming up this week?"

Nora frowned. She had expected her aunt to be dismissive of Jacquie's pert manners, but instead she surprised her by appearing fond of Jacquie.

Jacquie considered the question. "I am going to Vauxhall later in the week."

Aunt Mildred blinked and frowned, and Nora felt more settled. This was the judgmental aunt that she had been living with for almost two months now.

"Vauxhall?" Aunt Mildred echoed, and exhaled slowly. "Do they still have the hot air balloons? And the fireworks?" Her face was rapturous, as if she was transported to a different time.

Nora set her teacup in its saucer, reeling with disbelief. Her aunt had fond memories of *Vauxhall*? "I thought you had considered it gauche," she said.

"I would never describe it in such a way," Aunt Mildred countered. "I spent many nights wandering about the pleasure gardens in my youth."

Jacquie smiled. "Vauxhall is all you remember it being, and more," she declared. "It is my very favorite entertainment in all of London. Lady Honora, have you been to the gardens yet?"

"I have not." Her mind was still whirling over the fact that Aunt Mildred considered Vauxhall respectable enough to visit, with all the potential dangers to one's reputation if one strayed too far from the lit paths.

"We shall go together tomorrow night. I am sure we could ask a few gentlemen to accompany us to dinner in one of the boxes," Jacqueline said. "A nice private conversation with our beaux will be the very thing to spice the air with romance and win over the heart of an eager swain."

"I would like for Honora to enjoy herself with a young set for the evening," Aunt Mildred announced. "Thank you for your kindness in arranging such an outing. She would be delighted to accompany you."

"Yes, delighted," Nora assured Jacquie, but inside she was frustrated that her aunt had once again made the decision for her.

"Lady Honora, I have brought some fashion plates if you would like to peruse them with me." Jacqueline reached into her reticule and retrieved them, then waved them about.

"You girls should go on and look at the plates together in your sitting room, Honora." Aunt Mildred rose to her feet. "That dress that you wore last night was not at all what I would have chosen for you. But I cannot deny that it might have helped gain you attention from the gentlemen. Perhaps you should choose more gowns together, if this is the final result."

Nora stared. Aunt Mildred had made it clear many times that she thought perusing fashion plates was a frivolous waste of time, and a pastime most enjoyed by emptyheaded young misses.

They retreated Nora's sitting room as soon as they bade Aunt Mildred farewell.

Jacqueline flung herself onto the settee. "Finally, my dear Nora! I thought we would never be left to our own devices."

Nora sank to the floor and rested her cheek on the settee next to her. Jacquie stroked her hair, and Nora thought how lucky she was to be here with the most beautiful woman she had ever met.

"My aunt is quite taken with you," she said, still in disbelief.

"Oh, aunts often are," she said. "Mothers never quite like me, but aunts are very fond. It's funny how it always seems to be true."

"She wishes I were more like you. Then she would be rid of me sooner."

"Rid of you?" she cried and sat up. She scowled down at Nora. "Lady Mildred loves you and is doing all she can to make you happy. My parents are trying to steer me into a path that I do not want in the least, but your aunt is working with you at every step to ensure the exact future that you are seeking. However could you say that she wishes to be rid of you?"

Nora shook her head. "I meant nothing by it."

"No, do not say such a thing." Jacqueline eased herself onto the floor beside Nora and pulled her hand onto her lap. Her soothing touch on Nora's fingers relaxed her. "I know you now, Nora. I have seen you shrink away from conflict and from speaking your mind. You do not need to do such a thing with me—I will listen to you, no matter what you have to say."

Nora saw only kind encouragement reflected back at her in Jacqueline's shining eyes. "Thank you," she said. "I feel sometimes trapped by Aunt Mildred's expectations. And my own. And I suppose I am jealous of your easy way with my aunt. Everything we say to each other is so weighted by the hopes that we have for me to marry well, and sometimes it seems that I don't know her as well as I thought I did." Nora shivered. Talking about her deepest fears, however vaguely, sent a prickle of dread over her skin. Leaning against Jacqueline, she rested her head on her shoulder.

"Your aunt loves you," Jacquie repeated softly. "She is easy with me because we do not know each other, and we have nothing important to share. Your relationship with her is so essential, so of course you are both careful with what you say. But never think that you are alone when you have her here with you."

Nora frowned. "I wish we could find a way to connect again."

"Maybe you just need to relieve your mind of such worries and trust that they will work out. That's what I do," Jacquie declared. "Vauxhall will be the very thing for you. It is a garden of pleasure, and your head will be so full of novelty that you will scarcely have time to worry about anything." She squeezed her hand. "I promise you, I will make sure that you will enjoy yourself."

Nora raised her head and placed a sizzling kiss on Jacqueline's soft lips. "I am so glad that we met," she said fervently.

"Me too."

"I wish it didn't have to end when I marry. I will miss you," Nora whispered.

She had never known anyone like Jacquie, so free and open and spirited. She thought of the men that she had been introduced to during the past few weeks, and none of them could compare at all with the woman in front of her.

"Perhaps...maybe after I marry, we could continue to see each other?"

Jacquie pulled away, her face serious. "I could never bear to be with you while you spend your nights in another's embrace. I want all of you, or I will have none of you."

Nora kissed her deeply. "I will take what I can have of you now, then."

But she was starting to wonder if memories could ever be enough.

CHAPTER NINETEEN

The pleasures of Vauxhall Gardens never failed to brighten Jacquie's mood. When she was in poor spirits, it was a balm to her soul and provided her a calm respite from the troubles in her world.

After presenting her burnished silver season's pass to the ruddy faced man at the gates, a thrill slipped down her spine as she walked past the threshold and into the gardens. At Vauxhall, she was free to be Jacquie, true to herself, with the wild abandon of her desires. Away from her mother, away from the stuffiness of the ballroom. The fresh air and endless gardens were invigorating.

So was the woman walking beside her. Jacquie watched her walk, posture correct and proper, hips barely moving more than necessary. Nora was prim in her evening dress, bundled in a royal blue shawl, but Jacquie grinned with delight at the memory of those hips moving beneath hers with unrivalled passion.

The party was chaperoned by Beatrice's cousin Mr. Wilfrid Byrd and his sister Eliza, who had married a well-to-do lawyer and became Mrs. Carter several years ago. Neither Beatrice nor Jacqueline spent much time with Bea's relatives, as they were thoroughly unpleasant. However, they were also lax chaperones, and Jacquie had been able to get a favor from Beatrice to make up a party on such short notice for Vauxhall. Since Eliza's marriage, Jacqueline and Beatrice had often attended the garden's entertainments with parties made up of their mutual friends, understanding that a chaperone close to their own age would allow them far more freedom than if they were with their parents.

Jacquie thought of the many times where she had been lost on the winding paths, caught up in a lover's embrace. Lydia in particular had loved the anonymity of the gardens.

As if aware of the tense mood that crashed on Jacquie, Nora reached out and squeezed her hand.

The evening summer air was cool and sweet upon Jacquie's face, and she closed her eyes. Just for a moment, she wanted to forget about everything and everyone in her life. She could feel the light fabric of her chemise and her dress floating over the light pinch of her stays, the uneven cobblestones under the thin soles of her shoes, the firm and exciting press of Nora's hand on hers.

She opened her eyes. What she liked best about Vauxhall was its endless possibilities. Tonight, there were acrobats and singers. Tomorrow afternoon, a hot air balloon exhibition. Three nights from now, a comic troupe was scheduled. There was always something happening, some amazing wonder to impress and amaze.

"There is nothing quite like a pleasure garden," Bea said languidly. "The air is ever so inviting." She rolled her eyes at Jacquie.

Jacqueline had needed to do some serious cajoling to set up the evening with Bea and her relatives, but she had informed her that it was the very least that she could do to try to make up for her horrid treatment of Nora at recent social engagements.

They strolled for a quarter of an hour before entering the dinner box. A lovely feast was spread before them and they partook of the delicacies. Jacquie's heart was full, her head enchanted. Nora sat beside her and Jacquie was anxious for her to try all of her favorite tidbits from Gunter's picnic basket, which she had ordered specially with her in mind for tonight. She thought of the ices they had shared together on the afternoon after their visit to the modiste.

"Miss Lockhart, your head is in the clouds today," Eliza sneered at her.

Jacqueline's attention snapped back to the table. "I apologize, I was woolgathering," she admitted.

"Wondering which gentleman's arm to claim for a turn about the garden after our repast, no doubt," she continued with an indulgent smile.

Wilfrid sniggered. "That decision is indeed what our Miss Lockhart is ever occupied with."

Resolute, Jacquie gripped her soup spoon and glared at him until he quieted. She then smiled as sweetly as she could. "I do believe that is the purpose of most of these society engagements, is it not? To be in the company of dear friends, and to make an advantageous match?"

Eliza huffed as the waiter came around and platters of fruit and cheese were served.

"You've had six long years to make an advantageous match, and you've squandered each of them. Why, I've been married for half that time and I'm not even in my twenty-second year. So there is no doubt in my mind that you've naught planned but empty promises and insincere affections, if indeed that is *all* that you have planned!"

"Miss Lockhart has done nothing to disgrace herself," Nora said quietly, but with such calm authority that the table silenced to listen to her. "She is a credit to any party that she belongs to. Including this one, even if the manners displayed by *some* are somewhat less than what one would expect of good society."

She had never sounded more like Lady Mildred. Jacqueline felt her breath catch and struggled to suppress tears from welling in her eyes. She gazed at Nora with gratitude. She knew how difficult it was for Nora to speak up among strangers, and she was touched that Nora had sprung to her defense at once. For so long, her only defenders had been Bea and Phin, and it was an unexpected joy to have Nora join their ranks.

Jacqueline breathed deep and reminded herself that Eliza had always been insufferable. She should remember that well, she thought with an inward wince, as during her debut several years ago she had beaux who had dropped her to swarm around Jacqueline every chance they got. It was hardly her fault, she thought, but then remembered that she had begged as many waltzes as she could from each of the gentlemen. And not just once, she recalled. At every occasion. But they had looked so handsome, and she did love to dance—and yet she could have been more considerate of Beatrice's cousin. It was possible that Eliza could have married a gentleman instead of a lawyer if not for Jacquie's flirtations.

But then, perhaps not. All she had done was dance, and Eliza's snappish personality was enough to turn the most dedicated suitor off. Jacqueline had apologized for her behavior at the end of that summer, but by that time Eliza had chosen wealthy Mr. Carter and had gleefully rubbed Jacquie's nose in her unmarried status ever since.

Wilfrid snorted. "Well, our cousin Beatrice is no better. Our parents despair of her ever being married."

"I shall be long married before any woman consents to be wedded to a boar such as yourself," Beatrice snapped.

Jacqueline saw a sympathetic look or two thrown her way from the group, but she saw more disapproving glances than not. Hoping her cheeks were not red with embarrassment, she nibbled on a pear and tried not to sulk. She had nothing to be ashamed of.

Jacqueline glanced over at Nora, who gave her an encouraging smile, and she felt herself relax and remember why she had begged Bea to arrange the party. Time spent with Nora was worth it. Nora was so kind and so caring, and supportive.

Dreamily, she looked at the glass lamps hanging in the trees, sparkling like fairy lights and illuminating her desires. She could see Nora taking in the atmosphere and was delighted to be sharing the experience with her. When they had finished their supper and someone suggested a fortifying stroll, she grasped the opportunity.

"Come, let us walk behind the others," Jacquie urged Nora. "Let us be alone."

In a large group, it was easy to fall behind and even easier to slip away onto an unlit path. The sounds of the crowd seemed to hush, though there were hundreds of people close by. Away from the glittering lanterns, it was so dark that it was difficult to see each other.

"It was clever of you to find an opportunity to be together like this," Nora breathed.

"Thank you for speaking up to Eliza for me," she said. "I appreciate it. So much. More than you can imagine."

"It was no more than the truth," Nora said. "You are one of the finest people I know."

Jacqueline did not possess a shy bone in her body, but something about the magic of the evening made her feel vulnerable, exposed. She wished that she did not have to steal moments away with Nora in the shadows, instead of walking beside her on the bright paths, flirting like other lovers. "It—it's like another world here at Vauxhall," she said, struggling to find the words. "I know some might think that it's tawdry or common, but it never fails to stir something inside me. It makes me think that anything can be possible."

"I don't think it's tawdry," Nora murmured, and in the darkness Jacquie could see the glint of her teeth in a smile.

She shook her head ruefully. "Every season I insist on purchasing a season's pass with my pin money, and every season I drag Beatrice here time and time again. I have had more intimate encounters than I can even remember out here among the garden paths, and have stumbled upon just as many other lovers by accident."

"Is it just a place for trysts, then?" Nora frowned, and Jacquie was glad to see that the evening meant more to her than that as well.

"No, not at all," Jacquie said, eager to explain her love for the gardens. "I have heard music here that would stir the soul, and I have heard troubadours and poets. I have been in hot air balloons soaring high above the gardens, and I have lain in the grass and tried to count the stars. It is a marvel here. And…and I am so happy to share it with you."

"I understand," Nora said. "I have spent much of my time in the country, and for many years my entertainment was in the books I read. I have imagined many wonders, but how amazing it must have been for you to have seen those wonders with your own eyes, and to have experienced them in person!"

"It has made me feel…involved. Alive. Part of something bigger than myself." She was glad that the darkness hid her blush, and she sought to change the subject away from feelings. "However, that being said, I did have my share of trysts here."

"Would you care to have another one?" Nora asked, and leaned forward to press her glorious mouth against her own.

They kissed for an eternity, tasting, loving. Nora's hand brushed her waist, and Jacquie pressed herself against those curves that she longed to see again. Impatiently, she grasped at the skirt that was in her way and gloried in the soft warm feel of Nora's bare thighs beneath her thin dress. She inched her way higher and finally felt the sweet heat of her center against her fingers. Kissing her deeper, she stroked her firmly.

A loud boom startled her, and she broke away from Nora to see a shattering explosion of light above them in dazzling spray of colored sparks.

"Oh, fireworks!" Nora exclaimed, delighted. Her face was illuminated by the shimmering colors in the sky, and Jacqueline thought it was the most beautiful sight she had ever seen. Shadows and light played across her face, her eyes shining.

"You can be as loud as you like here, darling. No one shall here you above the firecrackers."

Jacquie pressed a kiss to her neck and continued her exploration beneath Nora's dress, bringing her to sweet ecstasy as the fireworks boomed and cracked and exploded above them, the sound indeed masking Nora's cries of pleasure.

Nora lay against her for a moment, then pushed away. "That was amazing," she said, wonder in her voice. "I had never dreamed of such an experience."

"Only in London," Jacquie said lightly, but the moment had dazzled her too. She felt something deep and wondrous inside her. Afraid of the depth of her feelings, she sought to hide them away.

Nora leaned forward and kissed her again. "It seems hardly fair of me to have my pleasure alone among the gardens, when I can think of another secret garden that I could be exploring."

And she sank to her knees before Jacqueline. She was so quick that before Jacquie could comprehend what she was doing, she had disappeared underneath her skirt and her mouth had found her center. Knees buckling, Jacqueline gasped as Nora brought her to stunning heights of bliss, so swiftly that her waves of ecstasy crashed upon her almost immediately upon contact with her lips.

Nora rose and drew Jacqueline close to her. "You are delightful, my sweet Jacquie."

Jacquie felt overcome and could only press her face to her neck in reply.

They stood together for a long moment before hearing the crackle of footsteps upon twigs and foliage.

Beatrice appeared with the Earl of Sinclair in tow and looked none too pleased to see them. "My dear Miss Lockhart and Lady Honora," she greeted them with false enthusiasm. Clearly, she had wanted a secret rendezvous of her own. "Why, we were just looking to rejoin my party and here is half of it already."

Sinclair bowed to them. "What a fortunate happenstance. Shall we go to see the tightrope walker?"

Jacqueline managed a smile. Had they been seen? It was impossible. Surely if the earl had noticed anything amiss, he would be reacting with shock instead of bowing before them with as much elegance as if they were in the ballroom.

They followed him to one of the main pavilions, where a large crowd was gathered. Their own party was chatting noisily, with Wilfrid leering at whomever he could. The earl's group was there as well—a small gathering of former and current military men, the earl told them as he made the introductions.

"You are always the lucky one, Captain, always with the most beautiful women around you," said a bluff faced young man. "Or I should say 'my lord' now, of course!" He laughed. "To be truthful, these fireworks remind me so much of gunfire that it's difficult to remember that we are back in England."

Sinclair grasped him by the shoulder and gave him a friendly shake. "No need to worry about enemy fire here, is there, Roberts? Not like the old days at all with danger all around us. There were times I didn't think any of us would get out alive."

"You are all very brave men," Beatrice broke in. "We are the lucky ones to have such men defending us abroad!" She batted her eyes at all of them, but especially at Sinclair. Jacqueline noticed with trepidation that he wasn't paying attention to her at all, and worried about what that would mean for her courtship of the earl. She darted a glance at Nora, who was looking at the group of men in quiet contemplation.

"We had our share of sticky wickets to get through, but by God, we persevered," another man said.

Sinclair nodded. "We were spared when so many weren't. And here we are, after all is said and done." He shook his head. "I never expected to be back here so soon."

"I, for one, am thrilled that you are back on British shores," Beatrice said in a low voice that Jacquie recognized as her most seductive pitch. She was trying so hard, and Jacquie felt a rush of sympathy. Jacqueline had been the recipient of that intense focus in the past, and although it made for a passionate exchange in improper circumstances, it was decidedly too much in company.

Nora stood quietly beside her. And Jacquie had promised she would help her with the earl.

"Gentlemen, the entertainment is starting. Let us be quiet and allow the ladies to enjoy themselves," Sinclair admonished them.

A reprieve. For at least as long as the performance. Jacqueline's knees felt weak with relief.

Astonished, they watched as a woman high above them walked along a rope as slender as one could imagine, as nimble and quick as a cat. The entertainer did all manner of daring movements upon the rope.

Nora gasped aloud and edged closer to Jacqueline. "I have never seen anything so mesmerizing!" she proclaimed, her eyes wide and shining. "Have you ever seen such a graceful woman? Have you ever even imagined that one *could* walk upon a rope?"

Jacquie dared to lean against her for a moment. "I confess to wondering about a great many improbable things about women with a happily flexible nature."

Nora giggled. "I may not be so flexible, I am sorry to admit."

"You make up for it with inimitable grace and presence," she said, and was rewarded by a shy smile that made her heart skip a beat.

But inside, Jacqueline was tense, the specter of the earl's courtship looming over her head and her heart. The last thing she wanted was to help either Beatrice or Nora with the earl, at the expense of the other. Especially not Nora, not after she had brought her to such pleasure mere minutes ago.

But there was only so long that the tightrope walker could remain up there performing her tricks. Jacquie felt with sick certainty that it would be her own turn very soon to create a magic trick of some sort if she wanted to keep Nora as her lover and Beatrice as her dearest friend.

There would be no better opportunity to promote love than when the earl was here beside them, and no better place than Vauxhall to encourage romance.

But if Jacqueline helped Beatrice to flirt with the earl, then Nora would lose faith in her. On the other hand, then she would have Nora for longer as a lover, as they would cease to be lovers as soon as Nora was engaged to anyone.

If she helped Nora, then Beatrice would be furious with her. She needed to marry well and fast so that her father was spared debtor's jail, and the earl was her clear preference.

Jacquie had spent half a lifetime helping Bea and fighting dragons together with her. It had been them pitted against the world for as long as she could remember. She had known Nora for less than a summer, but was sure deep in her heart that she would volunteer to ward off dragons for her anytime that it was required.

"You're frowning," Nora said in her ear, startling Jacquie.

"I'm worried about how the woman is going to descend from that rope," Jacquie said, but in reality all her worries were for herself. She watched as the woman far above them completed her flips and twists to thunderous applause.

"What a performance!" Sinclair and his friends joined in the applause.

Now it was time to make her choice. With a deep sigh, Jacqueline smiled at the earl as warmly as she could and tried the oldest trick that she knew in order to gain a man's sympathy and attention. "My lord, poor Lady Honora is feeling faint from the excitement," she said, giving Nora's elbow a squeeze.

Nora looked startled, then after a swift glace at Jacquie she placed the back of her hand against her forehead and her knees buckled. "Oh yes, I am in need of some air," she said, "away from the press of these crowds. I have never seen such astonishing things in the country and am overset with emotion."

It wasn't the most convincing scene that Jacquie had ever seen, but the earl gallantly placed an arm at Nora's waist and the other cupped her elbow, supporting her. "My lady, I will escort you back to that bench over there where you may sit and recover." His stern countenance cleared people from their path, and Jacquie was impressed at how fast the fashionable earl became the military man who could serve and protect.

"I too am more accustomed to the country life and find the noise of London too much at times," Jacquie heard him say to Nora as he drew her away from them.

Beatrice found her way to Jacquie's side and pouted. "Sinclair was most attentive to me until he saw your wallflower." She sulked. "I should have been the one to feel faint." Her voice was accusative. "I would have been much more believable."

"Bea, she is not *my* wallflower." But her protest was tired. Jacquie felt defeated. She saw Nora and Sinclair sitting together on the bench, two blond heads together. They looked like the perfect couple. Jacquie reminded herself that this had been the goal all along. She had promised to help Nora. Even if it now turned out that it hurt herself.

"Yes, and you so often take women who are not in your interest to the primrose paths? I am sure that nothing untoward would ever happen to you in the gardens of Vauxhall." Her tone was sarcastic. "Admit it, you are putting her interests first."

Although it was all true, the commentary rankled her. "Bea, be happy for me, please," she said.

Beatrice scowled. "I am trying my hardest to find a man to throw his fortune at my family, and the *only acceptable man* that I could bear to marry is paying court to your lover? Instead of me, your best friend? How is it that Lady Honora has both you and the earl? How much luck can the woman possess?"

Jacquie sighed. "She only has me until she has the earl," she confessed. "As soon as she is spoken for, our affair will end." Saying the words aloud shot a little dart into her heart and she winced.

Beatrice slid her arm around her waist and pressed a kiss to her cheek. "I know you are too sensible to be in love with such a bore," she declared. "You have better taste, Jacquie darling. Really, it's too soon after the countess to go through such emotion again."

Anger shot through her. "Nora isn't a bore," Jacquie snapped. "Maybe I am in love again, Bea. But it's tearing me apart because she is so dead set on marriage. Why am I never enough for the women that I love?" Her voice warbled, and she bit her lip hard.

Beatrice paused. "Then encourage her elsewhere, away from Sinclair. For God's sake, don't promote her relationship with him. She makes you happy, Jacquie. Don't you wish it to continue?"

"I promised to help her, Beatrice. I won't go back on my word," she said fiercely.

"Even if she could be the love you are looking for?"

"I want to help with whatever she is looking for. Even if that appears to be marriage," she said.

They looked over at the Earl of Sinclair, who was bowing low over Nora's hand as she laughed up at him on the bench. It was almost nauseatingly sweet.

Jacquie took a fortifying breath. "I wish to make her happy," she said, though her head thudded in discontent.

Beatrice smiled in sympathy.

Chapter Twenty

Aunt Mildred hid her smile behind her teacup, but Nora knew that a less well-bred woman in her position would be crowing with glee at this very moment. The London sun was shining, there was a growing pile of calling cards on the silver salver in the hallway, and the Earl of Sinclair was in their sitting room remarking on the state of government and society.

Nora wasn't paying attention. Instead of his cultured voice discussing politics, she heard Jacqueline's low throaty laugh, and instead of the scene before her, she saw the soft curves of her body.

The Earl of Sinclair had paid her a call to check on her health after last night's "fainting" spell, which had to be explained to Aunt Mildred as Nora hadn't told her about Jacquie's scheme to get her and the earl together away from the rest of their party.

She should be delighted right now to be the focus of the earl. This goal that she had been chasing since her arrival in London seemed well within her grasp. It had been a brilliant tactical maneuver on Jacquie's part, for as soon as she and the earl had sat together, he had been attentive and caring. To her surprise, they had found a great deal to talk about. Sinclair was a good match for her, but she felt no joy in the discovery.

The courtship that she had wished for now filled her with sadness because it would end her relationship with Jacqueline. Of course, she wasn't sure anymore what Jacquie had felt. Nora had been swept up in the romance when they had made love on the dark walks of Vauxhall, but then Jacqueline had pushed her so easily toward the earl. If she cared for Nora, wouldn't she have hesitated to throw her in the arms of another?

And as soon as Nora had gone with Sinclair, she had noticed Miss Everson press close and kiss Jacquie's cheek. She knew they had once been lovers. Was it possible that Jacquie was still in love with her friend, and would return to her as soon as Nora was engaged? Had that been her plan all along?

Instead of triumph over the earl, she felt an itchiness in her soul. She yearned to be away from this elegant house and its impersonal magnificence. London was no home to her, and she was sick at heart for the rolling hills of Rosedale.

"Lady Honora seems to be far away," Sinclair commented.

Nora started. "I was lost in thought," she apologized under the disapproving eye of Aunt Mildred.

"I wonder if the antidote might be a ride in my new curricle? Lady Mildred, would you be so kind as to spare your niece for an hour? I promise she will be safe and secure in my care. I wouldn't dare allow so much as a bee to buzz too closely to her."

"Of course my dear Honora is free to accompany you, my lord! Why, she would be delighted by nothing better. Anyone can see that she needs more color in those cheeks of hers."

Nora knew her own assent was unnecessary, so she nodded and gave a shallow curtsy before heading to her chambers to change into a costume more suitable for an afternoon's ride in Hyde Park.

Sinclair settled her in his curricle with attentive care. "Your aunt often thinks she knows what is best for you, Lady Honora."

"Yes, Aunt Mildred has decided opinions," she said.

He laughed. Even his laugh was perfect, charming, not too loud or too long. He really was a perfect suitor. "I want to let you know that whenever we are together, I encourage you to have a voice in your life. You can choose what you want to do or where you want to go. I know she did not ask you your preference this afternoon, and I wanted to ride with you so I did not stop her from accepting on your behalf. But you always can have a voice with me, Lady Honora."

Sinclair seemed to stop short of declaring himself beyond those words. Nora was flustered. She wasn't ready to make a commitment just yet. She was starting to be uncertain of what she wanted to commit to.

Perched high in his curricle, watching his steady hands expertly work the reins, all Nora could think about was Jacqueline's delicate fingers and soft touch on her body.

"You are even quieter without your aunt. I thought this might be a welcome respite for you, but I apologize if I misread the situation."

"It is I who should apologize, my lord. I have been inattentive, but I confess I was enjoying the ride so much." It wasn't quite a fib, she told herself. The weather was lovely, and it was nice to be riding through London.

She willed herself to relax, to focus on the moment. The Earl of Sinclair was a nice man and he didn't deserve to be treated with poor manners, no matter how much she wanted to be elsewhere.

"My estate in Yorkshire is a peaceful place. Enough neighbors that it is a lively enough society if one wishes, but filled with nature walks and gardens if one prefers to repose. It is a beautiful corner of England." He glanced at her. "Perhaps someday you will see its pleasures for yourself."

Nora replied cordially that his grounds sounded lovely, and then thought she should change the subject away from any discussion that might indicate interest in a shared future at his estate.

"Your friends that we met at Vauxhall were very nice," Nora said, settling on a neutral topic. "Have you plans to keep in touch with your fellow servicemen now that you are in England?"

"The military is like a brotherhood," he said. "I would trust those men with my life, regardless of whether or not we are currently serving our country abroad. It is hard for me to imagine that I will not return to war and fight at their side again." His lips tightened, and he touched the whip to the horses and turned a corner. "It's a community that I never thought I would find, and it's an odd thing to go from their company to my fellow lords of wealth and leisure here in London."

Sinclair cleared his throat. "You can see why I would be eager to return to Yorkshire. You have spoken so highly of your own country estate and the peace that you experienced there, so I know you understand."

"I do find the country restful," Nora admitted. "And yet, I have found much to admire in London. More so than I expected. I couldn't imagine what wonders could be found here, so I never wanted to visit the capital before. But now I can't imagine never seeing these things again."

She thought of Jacquie, enthusiastically embracing every diversion and amusement she could wrest from London life. And she thought of Gina, who had created a salon where every opinion could be considered and debated. Nora had never dreamed that such a wide-open world existed here, and that she could surround herself with people she could connect with.

"London is not without its pleasures," Sinclair said. "And business will keep me here often enough that I will have plenty of time to enjoy them. But the country is where I see myself settling down, with my family. I have two younger sisters, chomping at the bit to finish with school and set London on fire, no doubt." His tone was warm and indulgent. "Cecilia, the elder, is sixteen and will be coming out into society next season. I believe she has deemed it an absolute eternity from now."

Nora smiled with genuine warmth. "She sounds spirited. I'm sure she will captivate the *ton* when she arrives."

"I hope so. Life will be easier when she is wed and thus another man's problem," he said cheerfully. "But I jest. Ceci is a handful, but a charming girl nonetheless. It is one of the reasons that I am seeking a wife this season. It is time for me to settle down now that I have inherited the earldom, and my sisters have almost grown into ladies. I need to find a partner to help chaperone them around society. Our parents have been gone for many years, and my brother died before he could marry. I have no close female relatives upon whom to call for such a task."

"I understand," Nora said. "There is no replacement for family."

He gave her a sidelong glance. "I'm glad you agree. We are of the same mind there. Of course, I'm not wholly altruistic, thinking of my siblings' benefit. The old house will seem so quiet without my sisters. If they are successful in their seasons, then soon enough I'll be left to rattle through the large house alone. I would rather fill it with joy, with a wife to dine with and with children running through its storied halls."

Nora murmured her agreement. Several months ago, this had sounded like the ideal future for herself. In fact, it was more than she could have dreamed of. But could she see herself as his sister's chaperone? As his wife, the Countess of Sinclair?

A desire for family was what had prompted her to come to London to seek marriage in the first place. It was the only reason she had accepted Aunt Mildred's offer to bring her out in society when her aunt had visited her in Wiltshire. A ready-made family of a husband and two sisters sounded like the perfect situation for her. Why wasn't she happier at the thought?

"My cousin, the Duchess of Hawthorne, speaks very highly of you," he added. "I would trust her with my life. She says you have integrity."

Nora blushed, thinking of the subterfuge that Jacquie had used in order to lead her to the earl's notice last night at Vauxhall.

They drove along through Hyde Park, stopping frequently. The Earl of Sinclair knew a great many people, and more than one young miss fluttered her lashes at him and persuaded him to at the very least touch his hat in greeting.

"These young women have been beside themselves all season to grasp at my attention," Sinclair murmured to Nora. "I do not mean to sound conceited, as I have enjoyed dancing with many of them. I was raised to do my duty, whether it's on the battlefield or the ballroom, after all. But I am looking for a more like-minded woman. Someone I could trust with my family. Someone sensible, who I could grow a life with."

Dread gripped at her heart with every word.

It turned to elation when she saw Jacqueline across a sea of people, walking with Miss Everson, and every nerve she possessed tingled with longing for her touch. Crossly, she reminded herself that she was with Sinclair and not at liberty to leap from his curricle and into Jacqueline's arms.

Still, they could at least greet each other. It was perhaps a paltry thing to bring her such joy, but she relished the sound of her name from her lips. She perched at the edge of her seat and tried to figure out the best time to call out Jacqueline's name. Not quite yet, she calculated. She was still too far away and Jacqueline hadn't seen her yet, but soon—

"I must greet my uncle," Sinclair said, startling her, and he steered the curricle expertly in a ninety-degree turn.

Nora's lips parted in surprise. She wrenched her head back as the horses galloped down the path, and saw Jacqueline standing there, stricken with shock. Disappointment coursed through her as she turned to face forward in her seat again. Jacquie will understand, she told herself, but she was worried. After Jacquie had arranged her to spend time with the earl last night, they had not had the opportunity to speak to each other in private. *I could not have stopped the curricle. I could not have gone to her though I wanted to.*

"Is your uncle here?" she asked, struggling to maintain a neutral tone. "I do not believe I have met him."

The Earl of Sinclair stared straight ahead. "I thought I had seen him, but alas I must be mistaken."

"In that case—"

He interrupted her. "I must bring you back to your aunt. We have been gone almost an hour and I recall her strictness on matters of time." He smiled at her and whipped his horses onward.

They spent the ride home in silence. Nora thought to herself how disappointing it was that Sinclair had professed to want her to speak her mind with him, and yet had refused to allow her to speak when it truly mattered to her.

Chapter Twenty-one

In the middle of the fashionable crowd, Jacqueline felt alone. She felt the sting of Nora's rejection as if it were a slap across the face. The cut direct! She had been snubbed before, but never so publicly and never by anyone she cared for. So vividly did she feel the hurt that she raised her hand to press against her unharmed cheek.

A reassuring hand brushed her shoulder. "Don't worry about her," Beatrice said. "She has made her choice to throw herself at the Earl of Sinclair. You will get over her."

"I don't know for sure that she wants to be with the earl." She turned and strode down the paved walkway, leaving Beatrice to hurry behind her.

"You know I am wearing my new walking shoes and can't go so fast," Bea said once she had caught up. "And you know that I am not in the wrong here, so you needn't go stomping off away from me. And just because Lady Honora is pursuing the earl does not mean that Sinclair has made a decision yet about matrimony."

Jacquie sighed. "I know, and I am sorry. I am just feeling overwrought."

"Well, even if you have not helped me nearly as you ought to with the earl, you know that if there is anything I can do to help you, you must let me know." She nudged Jacqueline with her shoulder, solid and reassuring. "You are more family to me than dreadful Wilfrid and awful Eliza," she added with a little smile.

Jacquie forced a smile onto her face. "I am fine," she lied. "I will be fine. I survived Lydia, and I shall survive Nora."

Bea looked doubtful but did not continue to press her. Jacqueline tried to allow the sights and sounds of the park entertain her. She was almost always ready to be amused, but today no longer held any joy for her. The memory of Nora's face as she turned in the carriage to watch Jacqueline after the cut direct was unbearable.

As soon as Nora had her opportunity last night to gain Sinclair's attention, she must have done it thoroughly enough to beg a ride in his curricle today. She hadn't given a second thought before snatching what she wanted.

She was just like Lydia, Jacquie realized bitterly. She had only used Jacquie until she could move on to a man's embrace. Then she bit her lip. No, the reality was worse. Nora was just like *Jacquie*, in her previous opportunistic seasons, stealing what she could from other women in order to serve her own selfish desires. The thought cut deeply. Was this how the other women had felt, when Jacquie had stolen dances promised to them, and flirted with their beaux?

"Look, there's Phin!" Beatrice said, pointing to where he was strolling with the Duke of Hawthorne. "The perfect man to cheer you from your doldrums. Phin, do come here!" Bea caroled out.

Jacquie scowled. She was in no mood for men, not even if he was one of her dearest friends.

Bea poked Jacquie's shoulder. "You adore Phin. And we have not yet seen him together with his lover. You must be dying with curiosity to see them together."

Jacquie sighed as Phin loped over and grasped each of their hands in his, bringing them in quick succession to his lips. "My darlings, I am in alt to see you." He bowed. "I believe you have already had the pleasure of meeting the Duke of Hawthorne?"

"Not the pleasure that you may have had, sadly," Beatrice said, eyeing the duke's muscled build. She curtsied as Phin introduced them.

Hawthorne looked down at her. "Miss Everson, I am enchanted."

"Phin has told us so much about you," Beatrice said, batting her eyelashes.

Phin crossed his arms. "Neither of you have any sense of secrecy," he complained. He nodded to the duke. "I assure you, everything was complimentary."

"*Everything* was complimentary," Bea repeated, and she winked at Hawthorne and glanced pointedly below his waistcoat.

The duke smiled. "My compliments are seldom presented, but they are always well received," he retorted, and Beatrice giggled in delight at the riddle.

Phin frowned in concern. "Jacqueline dearest, you look long in the face today."

"Jacquie? She is crossed in love." Beatrice paused. "Again."

"A lover's quarrel?" Hawthorne raised an elegant brow. "Shall we trounce the fellow? I could arrange a trouncing in a trice."

"Please do not," Jacquie said flatly.

"Oh yes, where has my memory gone?" the duke said. "It is not a fellow at all, is it?"

Beatrice glared at Phin. "And you say *we* are without secrecy? Where is your honor?" she hissed at him.

Phin backed away a step, his hands up. "I said nothing," he protested.

Jacqueline sighed. "Leave off, Bea. The duke saw Nora and myself in a compromising situation at the ball that the duchess held, weeks ago." Hearing Bea's shocked gasp, she hastened to add, "Oh, it was nothing! Merely a kiss."

Bea hummed in disapproval. "In public? And you were caught? Jacquie, it's not like you. You may be a flirt, but you are at least discreet!"

"Nothing ever escapes my attention in my own home," Hawthorne said with gravity. "And you ladies should be aware that *nothing* escapes the notice of society for long."

"I can't explain it," Jacqueline said. "When I am around her, I feel so alive. And I can't turn away from truly living, can I?"

The four of them stood together in quiet contemplation. Even though they were in the middle of the fashionable set in one of the most crowded places in London, Jacquie felt safe in their midst. Safe to expose her secrets, to seek their advice. Bea was right, she thought. This was family. It didn't matter if they weren't related to her by bloodline. They were related to each other by heartline.

"Shall we see you at the party tomorrow?" Hawthorne asked.

"They don't know about the parties," Phin muttered with a warning glance at him.

Jacqueline blinked. "I thought we knew everything about you, Phin," she said in surprise. "What are you talking about?" When Phin was quiet, she turned her eyes to the duke. "Your Grace?" she asked.

Phin shook his head and lowered his lips near to Jacquie's ear to murmur, "Since that day we saw Mr. Robinson in the stocks, when you were purchasing ribbons for Lady Honora, there have been a few of us meeting up together at my townhouse. People of...similar persuasions."

Her brows shot up. "And why have Beatrice and I never been invited?" she whispered in outrage.

"Because both of you are gossips," he said. "You love nothing more than talk and chatter and you might say the wrong thing to the wrong person."

Bea whispered heatedly, "We know better than that. I have never gossiped with anyone about such intimate matters unless I was *quite* sure that we understood each other."

"You might not even realize that you are speaking to someone who is unsympathetic. There are informants everywhere," Hawthorne said gently. "They pretend to be allies, but they are paid by different organizations to betray us."

Jacquie was bewildered. "I still don't understand—"

"Because I have told you time and again that it's different for men," Phin snapped. "Maybe you *can't* understand. Our lives are in danger. Three of our sort were hanged this month, Jacqueline. For sodomy. For love."

Hawthorne placed a hand on Phin's shoulder. "It's all the more important that we all stand together and trust each other," he said. "When I held such gatherings in Paris, I turned no one away from my door, and as a result I met priceless friends through the years. We all of us have need of somewhere to feel safe."

Phin glared. "I have been telling you, I am not sure if it's wise to hold such parties in England. People here have not the same tolerance as France. And how can you be sure that we will be safe?"

"Because I am a duke," Hawthorne drawled, and Jacquie realized with a start that every regal inch of him glittered with gold or was draped with velvet or was embellished with rubies. Hawthorne wore his ducal trappings arrogantly. Defiantly. "I will protect my own," he swore, his deep voice threatening. "None dare touch a man of my station."

Sighing, Phin relented. "Beatrice and Jacqueline, you are welcome to visit me at my home tomorrow afternoon at three o'clock," he said. "Tell no one. Bring no one but your most trustworthy maids." Clearly less than pleased, he sketched a bow and departed with the duke.

Beatrice let out a long sigh. "I wasn't expecting any of that," she admitted, as they started walking again down the path.

"Neither was I," Jacquie said.

"We cannot go to such a gathering, of course," she said. "I imagine there are plenty of indecencies."

Jacqueline grasped her hands. "Please come with me, Bea. Please?"

"Why ever do you wish to?" she asked in surprise. "You heard Phin. He obviously does not wish for us to go, and we have no need to. He's right, you know. I have never heard of a woman being persecuted or hanged for an intimate relationship."

Jacquie sighed. "Because I want to know more people who are like I am. Bea, I am not like you. You know that I never wish to marry. I cannot bear to think of being with a man in that way. I can speak honestly about my romantic relationships with you, or with Phin. But—I would like to speak more openly, sometimes. Maybe Phin's friends would have advice for me on how to maintain a longer relationship than the ones that I have had, because all of my lovers keep leaving me for the security of wedded bliss."

Beatrice hesitated before replying. "If there is even a hint of— of *nudity*, or debauchery, we are turning around and going straight home!" She heaved a dramatic sigh but gave Jacqueline a look that spoke volumes about how delighted she was, underneath her outrage. "We're in this together, Jacquie. Just like always."

And she grabbed hold of her arm and didn't let go until they were back to the carriage.

❖

The late morning sun streamed in Jacqueline's bedchamber window. She was pacing in front of the wardrobe with an intensity that she was convinced would wear a groove in the thick carpet, but she walked on, back and forth and back and forth.

What did one wear to an afternoon gathering such as this? She really should cancel her plans with Beatrice. Phin would understand. He didn't even expect to see her there. She whirled around to grasp her pen and a sheet of paper to send a note, but tossed them back onto her escritoire.

No, she couldn't cancel. If she had any chance of repairing her relationship with Nora, these would be the people to offer advice.

Jacquie's curiosity was also burning with an intensity that shamed her. She shouldn't be so wound up about who would be attending, when she knew she would hate for others to be wondering the same thing about her.

Jacqueline had known many ladies over the years who had flirted away the hours with her. She had not lied to Nora about her number of sexual partners, but she hadn't revealed just how many she had kissed. If she saw some of those ladies at Phin's party, she wasn't sure how she would feel. She had tried to never end her flirtations with bad feelings on either side, but it had not always worked out that way.

She shook her head and wrenched her wardrobe open. She and Beatrice would both go, it was certain. And it didn't matter what she wore, she knew she looked charming in all of her dresses—the moment Jacquie tired of any gown or had any doubt about how they showcased her, she cast them off to Sally.

Getting dressed would take her mind off of the situation. Jacqueline called for her maid and stood tensely as Sally dressed her and arranged her hair.

"My lady, you must relax," Sally urged her. "Or else you will get dreadful furrows in your face." She smoothed her hand across Jacquie's forehead. "You are too young for such stress."

"I am not stressed," she snapped. "And what of it, even if I am?"

Sally said nothing, merely finished with her hair and curtsied. "Will that be all, my lady?" Her mild tone spoke volumes about her hurt feelings, but Jacqueline was too out of sorts to pay her attention.

"Yes, you may leave," she said, despising her own imperious attitude.

Alone with her thoughts again, she regretted sending Sally away, but couldn't bear to bring her back. There was still a quarter hour before she was to meet with Beatrice, which seemed like a terribly long time. She seized a book from her bedside table and tried to read poetry, but instead the verse reminded her of Nora.

Thinking of Nora was fresh agony for her mind to fret over, and tears threatened to spill onto her cheeks if she didn't rein in her emotions. Nora! What did it mean that she had ignored her in the park? She knew Nora had seen her. The curricle had been coming straight toward her and Bea, and hadn't she turned to watch as she destroyed Jacqueline's happiness?

Her foolish heart wanted to believe otherwise. It had been two days since Vauxhall. But an entire week had passed since they had been in Jacquie's bed, gloriously and completely together in an intimacy that had never felt more right. Seven days since she had the luxury of skimming her hands over smooth creamy skin without worry of discovery, of inhaling Nora's scent of rose petals and femininity. A sennight since Nora had run her hands through her curls, pulling her close for another kiss.

Over one hundred hours since she had wanted to tell her that this could be love.

Jacqueline took a deep steadying breath. Love! Who knew if it was really what she felt? All she felt now was a painful confusion.

She checked the clock on the mantel again. It was time to meet Beatrice.

Shoulders back, chin up, she strode out of her bedchamber toward the great unknown.

Half an hour of light traffic later, the carriage pulled up in front of Phin's home. They made no immediate move to signal to the footmen to open the door. Instead, Beatrice and Jacqueline exchanged measured looks.

Bea spoke first. "It looks no different from when we have been here at dinners over the years."

"Is that a hint of disappointment that I hear?" Jacqueline teased her. Being in Bea's presence steadied her, and she felt her earlier emotional maelstrom ease.

Bea sniffed. "It is not! But I am surprised that a den of iniquity can appear so unassuming."

Jacqueline laughed. "We shall not be entering into anything nearly so scandalous as a den of iniquity! Now—are you quite confident that you can trust the footman and the driver not to gossip about our whereabouts?"

Bea gave her a look. "The footman is Sam, whom you may recall we caught sneaking kisses with our friend Miss Frances last year. He is devoted to both of us since we never revealed his impertinence to the butler." She considered. "And Miss Frances never ceases to profess her gratitude to us either."

"Oh yes, I am fond of Sam." Jacqueline nodded. "Let us go in!"

Bea rapped on the carriage roof and Sam opened the door with alacrity. He helped them down the carriage step.

If Jacqueline could have found a discreet place to cast up her accounts, she would have taken the opportunity. But instead, she gripped Bea's hand, walked up the brick path, and rapped on the ornate wooden door.

Wilson, Phin's butler, opened the door. Average height, middle-aged, quite elegant, and entirely supercilious.

"Wilson, hello. We are here to see your master," Jacqueline announced, and was proud to hear that her voice sounded confident and didn't tremble once.

"I will inquire if the master is at home, miss," the butler replied. With a slight bow, he left them in the hallway.

They exchanged looks.

"I didn't expect Wilson to act as if he didn't even recognize us," Jacqueline confessed.

"Nor did I. Ought we have asked Phin if there was some sort of password?" Bea asked.

They waited another long minute, and Jacquie's nerves soared.

Wilson returned with such little noise that Jacqueline was positive that he had floated back to them. "If you would like to follow me, ladies, I shall escort you to see Sir Phineas."

This was it. This is what they had come here for. A thrill of excitement rippled through Jacqueline. They followed Wilson down another hallway toward the back of the house, where they could hear the faint strains of a piano growing louder as they approached.

They entered a large room with a pair of French doors opened onto a balcony, light cotton curtains billowing in the breeze. Four men conversed near the piano, which was played by an unexceptional looking young lady. Two women were near the fireplace, chatting over a cup of tea. And Phin was smoking a cheroot near the French doors with the Duke of Hawthorne.

The scene was completely and utterly ordinary.

Beatrice looked disappointed.

Hawthorne grinned and sauntered over to them. "Miss Lockhart and Miss Everson. How delighted I am that you cleared your calendar to attend our little gathering."

Phin joined them. "Greeting my guests as if this is one of your own many estates?" he said to the duke, then smiled at Bea and Jacquie. "Welcome, ladies." A serious expression came over his face. "I apologize for yesterday. Of course you are both welcome wherever I go. I should never have questioned it. May I have the pleasure of introducing you to my other guests?"

Phin took them around the room, introducing them as they went, going through the motions of polite society. And in truth, to Jacquie's wonder, the gathering really *was* polite society.

The young lady at the piano played a vivacious piece and two men started an energetic dance together across the drawing room. The other men smiled indulgently. Phin was smoking his cheroot, lounging against the mantelpiece. Jacqueline felt his eyes on her and sipped her tea, wishing that there was a splash or more of a stronger libation in her cup.

And yet, this was far more sedate than she had imagined. No one was behaving boorishly, and she could see no one taking a liberty that would not be enjoyed in any ballroom of London.

A willowy auburn-haired man named Mr. Smith came over to her, wine glass in hand. "I come bearing a gift, Miss Lockhart," he said, presenting her with the wine. "I have it on good authority that you may be in need of it."

He ran his hand through his messy pompadour, and she was charmed.

Jacquie accepted the wine and saw Phin nod at her from across the room. She lifted the glass in acknowledgment. "Thank you, Mr. Smith," she said. "This is a welcome gift indeed."

He had a beautiful face full of freckles, a pointed chin, and a graceful manner, and as he bent over Jacqueline's hand, she froze. He looked familiar, though she was sure they had never met.

"Please, call me George. I insist."

Nodding in surprise at his immediate informality, she sipped the wine.

"You look like you have much on your mind," he said in a cultured treble voice. "If you care to tell me, I will happily listen to your troubles." He smiled at her and gave her a little wink.

Jacquie hesitated. But this was why she had wanted to come to the party, wasn't it? Hadn't she wished for an opportunity to discuss her relationship with Nora among people who could understand her situation?

Taking a deep breath, she summoned her courage. "I think I'm in love with a woman. And I don't think she feels the same way."

George nodded, and Jacquie was relieved that he seemed both sympathetic and unsurprised. "A tricky situation. Have you spoken to her about your feelings, or are you unable to be direct with her? Does she know that you are of the lavender persuasion?"

Jacquie blinked. "Lavender—what?"

"It's a term used for women who seek these arrangements with other women," George told her. "I apologize for using cant that you may not know, but I have been long in this community and am used to our ways."

"She knows my feelings. We have been intimate." She told him everything and felt the weight ease from her chest. "So I do not know if she will marry another, or if she would consider waiting and seeing how our relationship could grow."

"You would be asking her to give up a lot," George said. "You may have never planned to marry, but this could be her one opportunity to wed."

"I know, I am being selfish," she said impatiently. It was no worse than she was used to being called.

"Not selfish at all." He smiled. "There is no greater risk than asking for one's deepest desire, but also no greater reward. You should consider asking her what she wants. You may be surprised by her reply."

"Or I may be devastated," Jacqueline pointed out.

"If you are devastated and ever need anything at all, Miss Lockhart, I hope you will allow me to help you. I am always ready to help a lady." He held out his hand. "Have we a bargain?"

Jacquie pondered his question as she shook his gloved hand. Then she blinked and looked closer at him. She did know that face. She did know those eyes. Mr. George Smith! This was *Lady Georgina Smith*! She had met Lady Georgina many times over the years and had never been interested in furthering their acquaintanceship into friendship. She had always seemed too intellectual for her and Bea. Jacquie tried to absorb the shock and Mr. Smith turned to kiss Beatrice's hand in greeting.

Jacqueline blinked again, then flounced off to grab Hawthorne's arm and steer him to a corner of the room while Beatrice started to flirt with Mr. Smith. "What is the meaning of this?" she asked. "*Mr. Smith?*"

"Smith is a particularly good friend of mine," Hawthorne warned her. Jacquie felt the full power of a ducal glare and she shivered. He looked down at her in disapproval. "What do you think we invite people here for? Petit gateaux and gossip? No. This is a place where everyone is free to express who they are. Who they *truly* are. The same courtesy that is extended to you is extended to all of these people."

Abashed, she struggled to find words. "But…I do not understand this," she whispered.

He raised a brow. "Do you not? Be careful, Miss Lockhart," he said with a hint of steel in his voice. "There are so many who would say that they do not understand *you*. Can you not accept that there are people in this world unlike yourself? Your lack of understanding does not, in fact, have anything to do with them. It only has to do with you."

She blushed and averted her eyes. "I suppose this is true."

"I suggest you drink your wine and converse with our guests," Hawthorne said icily.

Jacquie joined Phin by the doors. She finished her wine, and out of long habit, he handed her his own glass. "I suppose you are still Hawthorne's lover?" she asked. She was still indignant from the duke's rebuke about Mr. Smith—or was it truly Lady Georgina? She was unsure now of everything she thought she knew, and she struggled to understand.

"Yes. We have been rather inseparable since he returned to England. He's a good man." His eyes lingered over the duke.

"Good for you," she congratulated him. "You could not have reached much higher—a duke is always a catch, whether it's matrimonial, monetary, or amatory. It's a good thing to have him by your side. His Grace, your bedroom steward." She wiggled her brows at him.

"Now, minx, be serious," he chided her, then grinned. "He's also my steward of the carriage, and the music room, and once in the gardens."

"Entirely too much information," she said with an airy wave, and took another puff of his cheroot.

Phin leaned forward and gave her a brotherly kiss on the forehead. "Be happy for me, please." Then he paused. "Come, I wish to talk to you in some measure of privacy." He tugged her through the French doors and into the garden where they could be quite alone.

"You look serious," she said.

"I don't know if you will care much," he said. "But I feel you need to know. Jacquie, the betting books at White's have wagers in them that concern you."

Relief caused her to laugh out loud. "Phin, there are always wagers about me and some man who claims that he shall wed me! You've told me for years of the ridiculous lengths men will go to place a wager."

He puffed on his cheroot and her laughter slowed. "The bets aren't about marriage." He gazed at her, his blue eyes sober. "The wags in the clubs think you aren't looking for a ring at all. They think you've been loose in your affections."

"I've never once sneaked off with a man," Jacquie said fiercely.

"My dear, the rumors aren't about being loose with men," he said.

Shock rendered her speechless. Incapable of thought, only sounds were registering in her mind—the chirp of a bird, the tuneless whistle of a street sweeper, the distant murmur of laughs and conversation of people inside the house.

She swallowed. "Well, I suppose this was always a risk," she said with a bravado she wished that she felt. "The wagers specifically mention women?"

Jacquie plucked Phin's cheroot from his hand again and frowned down at it, turning it over and over before snuffing it out.

Phin covered her hands with his own, his eyes sympathetic. "Yes. The wagers are betting on how long it will take you to run off with a married woman," he said. "I'm still with you. Myself, Bea. The duke. You have allies."

"How popular is this piece of gossip about me?" she whispered. She smiled bitterly. "I suppose I can't classify it as gossip, can I? How many people are learning the *truth* about me?"

"So far, it's one comment in the betting book at White's. But it's a salacious tidbit. I wouldn't be surprised if more people become interested." Phin sighed and looked deep into her eyes. "I'm not sure what this will mean for you."

"Gossip sometimes slows down," Jacqueline said. "If I do nothing to feed into it…I am not a noble, I am a nobody to so many of the gentlemen in those clubs. My name can be quickly forgotten." She managed a smile. "It is good that I never did plan to marry."

"You won't be invited to many events."

"Except for Lady Honora's charity, I am hardly ever invited anywhere these days."

They sat in silence.

"Are there any rumors about Lady Honora?" she asked, afraid of the answer.

"Only that the odds are good that Sinclair will ask for her hand in marriage before the month is up."

She nodded, absorbing the news. It was nothing that she hadn't expected. She would have to make sure that no rumors touched Nora or ruined her chances with the earl.

"I wonder if it was Lydia spreading these rumors," Jacquie said. "She has been trying to court me again."

"Strange way of courting."

"I cannot think of who else would wish to smear my name. I do not know to what lengths her jealousy would reach. When I last saw her, Lydia seemed to want nothing more than to win me over again."

She was quiet.

"I have an invitation to a ball tonight," Jacquie said. She didn't know how to feel about it. She was too numb to feel anything at all. "Maybe it shall be my last one. Or maybe the wags will not have any effect on my reputation." She breathed deeply. Steadily. "But even if they do talk, I am going. And I will be at every event I choose, until the day the invitations stop coming."

On the carriage ride home, Bea chirped happily about Mr. George Smith, oblivious to his secret. The Jacqueline of yesterday would have revealed Lady Georgina's identity and settled in for a cozy gossip. But Jacqueline today understood so much more, and so she nestled in her corner of the comfortable carriage seat and listened to Bea's praises.

Chapter Twenty-two

A ballroom held no pleasure without Jacqueline in it. Nora danced with whoever asked her, with little interest and less enthusiasm. The Earl of Sinclair wasn't even in attendance, and Nora wished she had pleaded a headache earlier and stayed home.

Aunt Mildred was delighted because noblemen were finally paying attention to Nora, enough to fill over half of her dance card for the first time since her arrival in London. Clearly, she would soon have an eligible gentleman for her hand in marriage, no matter who it was that asked for it.

Annoyed with herself for feeling so vexed, she sipped a glass of tepid lemonade and fanned her heated cheeks.

She wasn't paying much attention to her surroundings, or she would have seen the Duchess of Hawthorne approach long before she said her name in her cold, cultured accents.

"Your Grace, good evening," Nora said, surprised.

The duchess was attired in heavy satin and adorned with jewels fit for a queen. Diamonds winked from her ears and rubies shone around her slender neck. Her magnificence was dizzying. And terrifying.

"You are looking well, Lady Honora," the duchess said. She perused her. "But I think a trifle warm. Shall we stroll on the terrace together for some air?"

She waved a finger at Aunt Mildred to indicate that she would stay with Nora. Her aunt sent a triumphant look toward Nora. It was one thing to have paid a social call on the duchess, but quite another to be singled out for her favor at a public event.

Nora deposited her lemonade cup on a nearby table and neatly hooked the braided loop of her fan handle around her wrist.

"By all means, Your Grace, let us stroll."

The terrace was a wide stone walk that wrapped around the entire first floor of the estate. Flickering torches crackled in their wall sconces to light the way. There were very few people outside, although the night was beautiful and the evening young.

Nora waited for the duchess to address her, her heart beating frantically.

After a few moments of pretending to admire the trees and appreciate the night air, the duchess seared Nora with a look. "Your friend is not in attendance tonight," she noted.

It didn't seem a casual remark. "I have several friends present," she replied.

"Need we keep up with pretenses? I thought you cleverer than that, Lady Honora." Her voice was amused. "You know which friend I am referring to. The black-haired beauty with whom you have a less than chaste relationship."

Nora's heart skipped a beat. "Consoling a friend in a ballroom is no grounds for such censure." She fought to keep her composure.

"Did I sound censorious? Oh dear. No, I don't judge or condemn you, or anyone else."

"Of course not, Your Grace," Nora murmured.

"I seek to give advice where I can, to ladies who seem inclined to listen." The Duchess of Hawthorne paused, then added, "I do *not* include your friend in that category."

Nora lifted a brow. "Because she has not the title of lady, or not the temperament, Your Grace?"

The duchess laughed, a low throaty sound that sparked something deep inside Nora. "There, I knew you were clever," she said with rich approval. "Your friend draws too much attention to herself, and rumors follow her. She is the wrong sort of woman to pursue. You need to be more careful."

She felt a flash of anger but tamped down her emotions. It didn't seem safe to let the duchess know how her true feelings.

"I believe you are being pursued by a cousin of mine, the Earl of Sinclair," the duchess said. The change in subject was abrupt.

"The earl has been most solicitous," Nora admitted, "but he dances attendance on many ladies. I would not presume any particular pursuance on his part toward me."

The duchess smiled, and her radiance magnified. Yet the smile didn't lend any warmth to her countenance. "I believe you to be quite safe to presume away," she said. "I have encouraged his suit of you. Sinclair is an excellent man and would do well as a husband."

Nora had heard much the same from anyone who had spoken to her of the earl, regardless of how well they knew the man, so she simply nodded at the praise that she heard so often.

The duchess's eyes sharpened. "He would be an ideal partner, Lady Honora. Sinclair spends as much time in London as one could wish, but when in the country he will keep occupied with the hunting season."

This was a little more unusual.

"The earl would not trouble you if you kept your own agenda," the duchess said. "You could have everything. Wealth. Independence. Security."

"Marriage is indeed a union to be much desired," Nora agreed.

"Are you being deliberately obtuse, Lady Honora?" she said in exasperation. "With Sinclair, you would be free to do as you wish, live your life how you wish. You would have the power and the means to make a difference in the lives of other women. You could provide a safe haven for those women to love as they wish without raising an eyebrow from society."

Nora stared in shock.

Was it possible that she heard correctly? Was the duchess trying to encourage her to marry the earl, but to keep relationships with other women at the same time? She opened her mouth to speak, but had no words.

The duchess sighed. "You do not need to be coy with me. Trust me."

They stopped and stood at the elegant stone balustrade. The duchess looked out over the dark gardens, her hands braced on the wide railing. "I understand the life you are struggling with," she said. "I have seen it happen time and again in society." She turned to Nora.

"I am simply urging you toward marriage to make your life easier, more pleasant. You will have options. You can even have your friend, and no one will be the wiser."

Nora couldn't hold it in any longer, despite her shyness. "Her name is Miss Lockhart," she said with as much dignity as she could muster.

The duchess waved an impatient hand. "Do the intelligent thing and hide your liaisons. You risk not only your own reputation and Miss Lockhart's, but you risk casting aspersions on any number of ladies who may have the same desires as you have."

She leaned closer. "Do you understand the jeopardy you are in? We must protect our own, Lady Honora. Unwed, and cavorting around ballrooms as you did at mine, you will create more scrutiny toward any lady who laughs too loudly or stands too closely to a friend. And this is what you should be working to prevent. You have the means, you have the opportunity, you have the intelligence to create a better life for so many. Marry soon and marry well. If not the Earl of Sinclair, then there are plenty of noblemen who would have you. I could scare up a proposal for you in a heartbeat from any number of my acquaintances."

Nora's mind whirled. This was not a discussion that she could have predicted having with anyone, let alone the duchess. A woman's proper place in society had always seemed to require a great many lectures regarding obedience, from authorities ranging from family to the church to friends. But this was the first time that anyone had approached her and told her that she could have anything that she desired, as long as she had the appearance of obedience to society's strictures.

"I do not know what to say, Your Grace," Nora said. Nor did she know how to feel.

Maybe the duchess was right and Nora's place was to marry a gentleman this season. Maybe she *could* convince Jacqueline to continue as her lover while she was married.

"Think of what I have said, Lady Honora," the Duchess of Hawthorne said to her. "Think of me as a friend, and take my words seriously. I can help you—but you need to understand what it is that

I am able to offer. And you should have a care with how you behave. Wise actions can protect you. The wrong choices, particularly ill-advised relationships with the wrong sort of women, can destroy you. Be circumspect in your behavior."

The duchess seemed content to have delivered her diatribe even without a reply from Nora and seemed to feel no awkwardness or embarrassment at the situation.

The duchess walked with her back to her Aunt Mildred, who curtsied deeply. "Thank you for walking with Honora, Your Grace," she said. "We are most cognizant of the deep honor you do our family."

The duchess smiled. "You have a lovely niece, Lady Mildred. It is a pleasure to walk with a sensible young lady." She leaned in and dropped her voice to a murmur. "I do have one small piece of advice, however. If I were you, I would keep poor influences away from such a sterling character as your niece."

"Poor influences?" Aunt Mildred gasped.

"Yes, indeed. My cousin, the Earl of Sinclair, would be a wonderful catch for her. He takes my counsel quite seriously. Family connections are so important, are they not? But heed my words. There are certain young ladies who do not have the breeding or character to match her elegance. Lady Honora needs to choose her friends more wisely."

The duchess turned and walked away, leaving Aunt Mildred looking bemused. "Honora, what is the meaning of this? Which friends of yours does the duchess disapprove of?"

Then it clicked. "That pert Miss Lockhart." Her face twisted, and Nora remembered how she had bonded with Jacquie over memories of Vauxhall. Then Aunt Mildred straightened and a fierce look came over her face. "Miss Lockhart must be a bad influence on you. I should never have allowed such a low connection, even if I was friends with her family at one time. You can no longer socialize with her. Your future with the Earl of Sinclair is at stake!"

"Aunt Mildred, you exaggerate. I do not think a man of the earl's stature would care if I have a friend or two that his cousin might disapprove of."

"The duchess was clear in her censure. Where a duchess censures, everyone shall follow. I don't think Miss Lockhart will be invited around much after word gets out."

"There is nothing to get out," Nora protested. "Her Grace said nothing. It was the merest quibble."

"No, it isn't." Aunt Mildred's face was grim. "I confess to have heard one or two things about Miss Lockhart and her forward manner. I gave her the benefit of the doubt and was willing to give her a fair chance, especially given how you have blossomed with her friendship. But you don't need her anymore. Look at your dance card tonight! And with the duchess's endorsement, I would be very surprised if the earl doesn't come up to scratch within the sennight."

"What did you hear?" Nora asked, a sense of dread settling over her.

"Nothing fit for a young woman's ears," Aunt Mildred huffed. But under Nora's unrelenting gaze, she sighed. "It has been said that she likes to flirt a little too much and be too bold in her favors. You are not to see her again."

Nora took a deep breath. "I will see her if I choose to," she said, startled at her own nerve. "I am capable of managing my own friendships. I will not abandon Miss Lockhart based on the caprices of a duchess."

Aunt Mildred bristled. "I am doing this for your own good," she said. "It is nothing personal against Miss Lockhart, but you need to think about yourself first. Your future."

"If the Earl of Sinclair chooses to marry me, then he will need to do so knowing of the company that I keep," she said steadily. "I do not believe that Miss Lockhart has done anything to be ashamed of."

"You see her influence? You would never have spoken to me like this before you met her." Aunt Mildred's tone was sharp.

They stared at each other. Nora had never spoken against her aunt's wishes, and her heart was hammering in her chest. Would she lose the affection of the last close relative that she had? She tried to swallow her fears.

"I respect your opinions, Aunt Mildred," Nora said with dignity. "But I expect you to show mine the same respect, even if we disagree."

Aunt Mildred's face was flushed with outrage. Nora reached out to touch her hand, but her aunt moved away. The movement felt like a dagger into Nora's heart.

They hardly spoke for the rest of the evening, and Nora went to bed that night sick with fear that she would soon lose everything—her aunt's love, Jacquie's affection, and the potential for marriage.

Chapter Twenty-three

Jacqueline closed her eyes as Sally brushed rice powder over her face and applied a thin line of black kohl around her eyes. Lightly, she dabbed a tinted salve to her lips. Breathing deeply, she opened her eyes and looked at herself in the mirror.

Battle armor, was her first thought. Better to be prepared for action, she thought, instead of sitting by as a damsel in distress.

Her eyes were large and luminous, her lips rosy and dewy. Her curls fell in a tumble around her face and neck, spilling onto her shoulders. The daring pink gown that she had ordered with Nora covered her curves, showing a large expanse of bosom. The posy that Nora had so admired was pinned to her bodice.

She looked no different than before. But inside, she felt worlds apart from who she had been just yesterday.

Yesterday's woman was carefree. Today's woman was scandalous. She hoped tomorrow's woman would not be completely ruined.

Sally brought out a pair of dancing shoes and Jacquie shook her head. "The rose slippers," she said.

She nodded and fetched them from the shelf. Jacqueline looked at them, admiring the workmanship and the beautiful rosettes. She felt comforted as she slid her feet into the shoes that Nora had sent her as a gift. It seemed so long ago now.

Smiling at Sally, she picked up a lace fan and snapped it open. "I am ready," she announced, and dropped a low curtsy to Sally, who giggled.

"You look ever so lovely tonight, miss," she said. "That color is beautiful on you. I'm sure your lady will be delighted to see you looking so fine tonight."

The thought of Nora calmed her, and she felt more settled. "I look forward to seeing her," she admitted. Tonight, she would share her feelings with Nora and hope that they could be returned.

"Looking like that, you shall be the belle of the ball," Sally told her. "Lady Honora will not be able to tear her eyes away from your splendor. Shall I prepare anything for you two after?"

Jacquie hesitated. Although she would love for Nora to join her tonight, she wasn't certain of Nora's feelings. She shook her head. "Not tonight, Sally."

The ball was bright and bustling when Jacqueline and her mother arrived. She spied Nora right away and her spirits rose. She hurried over with unfashionable haste as her mother drifted over to greet her friends.

"I am so glad to see you," Jacquie said. She drank in every detail of Nora's face—her rosy cheeks, gray eyes, coral lips. If scandal was indeed going to catch up with her, she wanted to remember exactly what she was losing.

Nora smiled. "I am always happy to see you, Jacquie." She paused and looked concerned. "Are you all right?"

She hesitated. "The other day—in the park—I thought you gave me the cut direct when you were driving with Sinclair."

Nora blinked. "I would never have done that," she said. "I wanted to speak to you, but Sinclair insisted on driving on."

The words eased the pain in Jacquie's heart, but she still felt nervous. "Even though you didn't cut me, I am worried—has your aunt said anything about me to you?"

Before she could answer, the Earl of Sinclair approached them. "Enchanting Lady Honora," he declared. "And Miss Lockhart. May I secure your hands in a dance this evening?"

"You certainly may," Nora replied, smiling at him.

Jacqueline felt loathe to share her company with the earl, but arrangements were made that Nora would have the next dance, and then Jacqueline the one after. She managed a smile as the earl took Nora toward the dancing.

In all of her six seasons, a bevy of suitors would swarm around her almost as soon as she entered a room. Jacquie couldn't recall a time that she had not had most of the dances already penciled into her fan by this point in an evening. Tonight, only the earl approached, and she knew it was only because of his attraction to Nora.

She let her eyelids drop to half-mast in a calculated effort to appear bored instead of desperate, and accepted a glass of wine as something to do with her hands to pass the time. She sipped, barely tasting the wine as she stood alone.

Was this ruination, then? Had the rumors swirled more wildly and more widely than Phin had guessed? Did Nora know? No one was giving her the cut direct, but she caught more than a few wary unsmiling glances that she guessed to be its precursor.

Soon enough, Sinclair approached her for their dance, leading a smiling Nora. Jacqueline gazed at her. Nora was always beautiful, but never more so than when flushed with exertion. She thought of how lovely she was during exertions of a rather different nature.

She smiled at Nora as she took Sinclair's arm for her dance.

"You smile, Miss Lockhart? Does something amuse you?" he asked.

"Merely the pleasure of the evening, my lord," she said.

His grip on her arm tightened. "I've heard you are most free with your evening pleasures," he said, ice dripping from his voice.

Shock made her wordless, and all she could do was look up at him. She had never guessed to be confronted to her face with the rumors. A terrible thought struck her. "You?" she whispered. "Was it you who wrote those awful things in the betting books?"

He looked down at her. "I said nothing that was untrue, did I?" Sinclair said in mock concern. "Are you forgetting yourself, as you did that evening at Vauxhall? I saw you with Lady Honora on the dark walk, my dear. I am sure she was led astray by you in a girlish infatuation. She would never have been touched by such sordid goings-on otherwise."

It hadn't been Lydia, Jacqueline realized numbly. She had no one to blame but herself for not being as careful as she should have been.

"I care not about what you do in your spare time, nor with whom you entertain yourself. However, I do care about any rumors that my future countess may encounter."

They had been late to join the set, and the music sounded out its triumphant first notes. She curtsied, and he bowed.

"Your future countess?" she repeated, settling her hand on his arm as they wove through the first dance steps together.

His look was severe. "I had thought you more intelligent than this. Lady Honora Banfield will be my bride by the end of the season. The Duke and Duchess of Hawthorne approve of the match."

She pondered this as they danced in silence. Nora had seemed ready to accept his attentions. But had she really accepted his proposal? Or was her family still making all of the decisions on her behalf? Fury bubbled inside her as she thought of everyone trying to corral Nora into the path that they desired for her.

Surely Nora could not see herself married to such a stuck-up presumptuous man? Surely what they had together was worth more than whatever the earl could offer her?

And yet, the Earl of Sinclair had a fortune and a snug estate in Yorkshire. He could offer Nora children, and security, and a life of comfort. What could Jacquie give her instead?

As they swooped around another pair of dancers, she murmured, "I'm sure Lady Honora is most gratified by your honorable intentions."

"She will be, if her reputation isn't smeared by her association with you tonight. There can be no marriage if there is a hint of scandal attached to her good name."

"Then it seems you asked me to dance in order to insult me," she said. "I must say I am less than impressed by your manners. Perhaps I am uninterested in marriage because so many men of the *ton* are proud of boorish behavior."

Sinclair laughed and returned her to the edge of the ballroom, quite at the opposite side of the room to Nora. "Dear me, I seem to have miscalculated," he said. "Do forgive me for not escorting you back to your friend."

Jacqueline fumed.

She deftly wove her way around acquaintances and friends and former suitors, finally reaching Nora's side. But all of the anger inside her bubbled up and threatened to spill over.

"You seemed cozy with the Earl of Sinclair during your dance," Jacqueline said, unable to keep the anger from her voice, hoping that

Nora couldn't hear the thud of her heartbeat or the sound of her hopes and dreams bursting.

Nora looked at her in surprise. "I suppose most dancing couples look cozy," she said. "It's a very close activity."

"Well, I would assume something important must have transpired during your dance, as he is planning to ask you to marry him," she replied.

"We didn't discuss anything of the sort," Nora said, blinking at her. "He didn't mention anything of that nature."

"But this has been your goal all along." Jacqueline stared at the swirling couples on the dance floor, as they swept by full of laughter and bright conversation. Her chest felt heavy, weighing down her heart. How false it all seemed. How full of pretense. How had she ever been one of those happy couples, twirling and laughing while other people's hearts were breaking?

"It's the goal of most women who come to London," Nora said. "You know my aunt wishes me to marry."

"And what do *you* want, Nora?" Jacqueline cried. "What about *your* wishes? Your desires? Is what we have just a pastime? Are you planning to marry the earl and forget all about us?"

Nora looked at her. "Is there an 'us'? We never talked about this being a…a long-term affair."

The words sucked the air from around Jacqueline. Ice crept along her veins instead of blood. "But I love you," she said fiercely.

Shock spread over Nora's face. "A ballroom is not the place to talk about this," she whispered. "Please, let us meet tomorrow and talk about everything."

"If you are unable to say the words back right now, then what is there to discuss? Do you love me?"

"Please, Jacqueline." Nora's voice was calm. Too calm. "Tomorrow, let's meet in Hyde Park. We can talk for hours and be in private."

"Are you going to marry the earl?" she asked heatedly.

"He has not asked me. But if I should be so lucky, then—well, then I will accept." Nora grasped her hand and gazed into her eyes. "Jacquie, you told me you would not want to continue to be my lover after my marriage. But—could you reconsider? I am sure we would come to London often enough." Nora paused, her eyes shining with emotion. "What we have…it does not need to end with the season."

"So you don't love me, then," Jacquie said. "I don't want to be sneaking around in secret any longer while you marry another! I want to be with you, and you alone. We could find a way, Nora. Do you have any emotions at all? Or are you just a shell of a woman, doing anything your aunt tells you to do?"

Anger finally flashed across Nora's face. "Don't say things that you can't take back," she warned her.

But rage was now heating her blood to a fever pitch. "You won't admit to love, but you will defend the actions of your aunt, who would wed you off to the highest bidder for your dowry? I understand. I wish you happiness for your upcoming nuptials."

She pushed away from Nora, needing to flee before she did something regrettable. What she wanted to do was kiss Nora senseless and remind her of the passion that flared between them. But that would lay all rumors about Jacqueline to rest by making them indisputable fact.

At the edge of the ballroom was Lydia.

In that moment, the Countess of Straund had never looked more beautiful to her. Her hair was in an elaborate upsweep, stuck full with pearls and satin ribbons. Jacqueline's fingers itched to pull it down, to rake her fingers in that glorious curling mane of hair and pull those tender lips toward her own.

She ached desperately to be loved, to soothe the deep hurt that burned in her heart. What did it matter to her if she was never invited to another ball? The attendees were never anything more than a shallow group of judgmental people. Had she ever been one of them? If she had, then she wanted no more to do with them. And if Nora thought that she belonged with the earl in these exalted circles, then she wanted nothing to do with her either.

Lydia was an easy solution. Hadn't she admitted to her that she wished for their relationship to be rekindled? Perhaps this was the universe's way of telling her that they were meant to be, that she should forget all about Nora. After all, it had not been Lydia who had spread rumors about her.

Somehow the thought of sharing Lydia's bed while she married a nobleman was far less awful to her compared to the horror that she felt when she thought of Nora in a man's arms on her wedding night. Anger spurred her on and she strode up to the countess. "Lydia," she said steadily.

"Well, Jacqueline. Have you recovered your senses at last and come back to me?"

She leaned close. The scent of her lily perfume filled her nose with cloying fragrance, filled her head with memories, and filled her heart with warmth. "Let's leave together," she said. "Come back to my townhouse."

"Just like old times," Lydia sighed. She placed her hand in the crook of Jacqueline's elbow and smiled deeply, meaningfully.

Jacqueline scanned the room for a glimpse of Nora, who was staring at them from across the room, a stricken look on her face. Good, she thought, so full of spite that she thought she might burst. She turned on her heel to leave the ballroom, arm in arm with Lydia. She ignored the flurry of gossip that hummed in their wake.

Gossip had always followed her in the past. What was it to her if this time the gossip hit a little closer to the truth than usual? She was done with London society. There were plenty of engagements that she could attend with Lydia, or Phin, which were not so stringent in their hypocritical morality.

She didn't bother saying good-bye to her mother. Someone would be only too happy to fill her in, she thought, heart aching. All that mattered to her right now was trying to forget the pain of lost love.

Desire ran through her body as she settled beside Lydia in her carriage. It would be so easy to love her. So easy to run her lips all over that familiar body, to press herself against those curves. All she wanted was a night to forget about Nora, to drive the memories away. To create something new to think about.

New memories, new thoughts to crowd her head. Old lovers made the best bandages for wounds of the heart. Heaven only knew how often she had crawled back into Beatrice's bed time and time again, to erase the pain of the moment and replace it with the comfortable rhythm of their bodies moving together in the night.

She was never wanted for herself, was never enough for anyone. Lydia leaned in and kissed her. The nerve endings on her body fired up in response, leaving a restless ache between her legs.

But even as her desire increased for her former lover, her heart banged out a protest with every beat. Memories of Nora's sober gray eyes, her shiny blond hair, and her full pink lips crowded her mind. Her light rose petal scent teased at her nose through Lydia's heavy perfume. Her skin tingled with the memory of Nora's soft hands running over her hips, pulling her closer, loving her deeply.

She loved Nora. No matter how hard she kissed Lydia in return, it was no match for the feelings in her heart for Nora. All at once, her anger deflated and she was left with a fragile shell of remorse.

She pulled away. "I'm sorry," she whispered, tears threatening to fall down her face. "I can't do this."

Lydia frowned, but there was an expression of unexpected compassion on her face. "We had a good thing once, Jacquie," she said. "Let me love you again, and you'll see how good it can be between us. We understand each other now, we know the rules. The rumors don't matter to me. I'll be married soon to Montfort, and my name will be safe enough. He doesn't care a fig about me." She shrugged. "I suppose this is what happens when one marries for money, without affection."

Jacquie felt a rush of sympathy. "Lydia—"

"Neither of us will be hurt, Jacquie. I know that you will have your other affairs with other women. But we can always come back to this." She pressed one of Jacqueline's hands to her breast.

But Jacqueline shook her head. "I thought I could, Lydia. I'm sorry. I love another."

"And what's so different about her, Jacqueline?" she asked in exasperation. "Does she have two muffs or something?"

Jacquie sank back in the cushioned seat. "She understands me," she said. "She looks at me like I'm the only person in the room and makes me feel like I can do anything when I am with her. I love her, Lydia. Really and truly love her."

"Then what is stopping you from being with her?"

"I just can't imagine sharing her with anyone else. And she has made it clear that she's in London on the husband hunt. I've even helped her to be courted, if you can believe it. Her most ardent suitor told me tonight that a proposal is imminent."

Lydia shook her head. "Then why are you spending her last nights as an unwedded woman with *me*, instead of with *her*?"

"I don't think she loves me," she said. "And I don't know if I can be with her if she doesn't love me like I love her. If we could just be together, the two of us for the rest of our days, then I would be happy. But it would destroy me to be in her arms, loving her, right up until the moment that she looks at that man in Saint Paul's Cathedral and tells him that she is his forever."

Lydia sighed again. "You need to be having this conversation with her," she said. "Let's take you home and you can take tonight to think about what you will do to win her back." She smiled. "Good luck."

❖

Nora's heart shattered as she watched Jacqueline and Lydia walk out of the ballroom together. What did it mean? Obviously Jacqueline was giving up on her. She wouldn't have walked out with another woman if she was interested in what Nora had to say about their relationship. Tears threatened to spill from her eyes as she realized that Jacquie had always encouraged her to speak her mind, but was refusing to listen to her now when it was most important.

In truth, she didn't know what she felt. She knew she felt more alive when she was with Jacqueline than she had ever felt in her whole life. But…love? Did she *love* Jacquie? And if she did love her, then what would that mean for her own future? Neither of them had an independent income.

Her plan in coming to London had been to secure a nobleman's hand in marriage, and it seemed that her wish was coming true. Loving Jacqueline was just a distraction.

Nora drew in a deep breath and fought the panic that threatened to seep through her veins by trying to focus on the facts. Jacqueline was angry with her. She had left the ball with her former lover. Had their own liaison all been an elaborate scheme for Jacqueline to win back the woman she had professed to love before she even met Nora?

She felt sick at the thought of being used as a pawn in a larger game, but she could think of no other ending to their affair. She couldn't bear the thought of sharing Jacqueline with the countess. If she had chosen the countess over her, then their relationship was over regardless of what proposal might be forthcoming from a gentleman.

The Earl of Sinclair came back over to her with a glass of wine in his hand. "I thought to bring you some refreshment," he announced, and pressed the glass into her cold hand.

She accepted it without comment and took a bracing sip, hoping to fortify her nerves on the heavily watered beverage. How disappointing that he thought the same thing as her aunt, which was that she couldn't possibly have a glass of proper wine. She thought of the days when Papa had chosen the wines for dinner from the extensive wine cellar that he had built at Rosedale. How he would disdain the swill at this ball!

But oh, how Papa would have approved of the man before her, so thoughtful in bringing her a drink when he saw her without one from across the room. She sighed, defeat overwhelming her. There seemed to be no choice in the matter.

Jacqueline had abandoned her. The man who she thought she wanted stood before her, expectation plain as day on his face that he had something of some delicacy to ask her.

The wine settled uncomfortably in her belly. She searched the ballroom for her aunt. Had he told Aunt Mildred of his intentions?

"Lady Honora, I have a question to ask you."

Her heart thumped in her chest. This was it. This would be the start of stories that she would tell their children someday. She would have to admit that she felt like she would cast up her accounts at any moment, from nerves and fear. She would need to leave out the part where she felt horrified at the thought of meeting the earl in the marriage bed for their wedding night. And she would also omit revealing that her only thoughts in the moment were of her passion for another woman.

"Please, ask away," she murmured faintly.

"My cousin, the Duchess of Hawthorne, is having a house party this weekend in the country at Hawthorne Towers. There are a few friends and relatives attending the party at the estate. I thought perhaps

I could ask her to invite you and your aunt, as you are related to the duke and surely you are wishing to be reacquainted with His Grace?" Oh. It wasn't a proposal. She thought she would feel relief, but instead she was annoyed. If only he would ask her to marry him *now*, while she had the twin fires of anger and desperation over Jacquie coursing through her. She was so angry that she knew she would say yes if he asked her now.

If she saw Jacquie again before the proposal, she would not have the fortitude to accept him as a husband. If she saw Jacquie again, she was terrified that she would throw her future away and leap into her arms toward the unknown.

It would be for the best if she could be certain to avoid Jacquie altogether before the proposal so she wouldn't fall prey to temptation. The wisest option would be to leave London behind her for the house party. With any luck, she wouldn't have to return to the city and all of its memories at all. Despair raced through her at the thought of never seeing Jacquie or Gina again.

Sinclair must be preparing to ask for her hand in a more scenic setting, she realized, with his family around so that they could have an engagement celebration straightaway. Most likely he wanted to ask the duke for her hand, as he was her nearest male relative.

She gritted her teeth and steeled her spine as she focused on the best outcome for her future. "I should be delighted to attend the house party, my lord. I am certain that my aunt will be looking forward to seeing the duke again. We called upon him recently and Aunt Mildred was thrilled to recount his childhood misdeeds."

Sinclair beamed down at her. "Excellent. We shall all have a smashing time in the country together, Lady Honora. I look forward to seeing you there."

She smiled and gripped the wine stem so tightly that she feared it would shatter, just like her heart.

Chapter Twenty-four

Jacquie pulled her ear bobs off and flung them on the dresser while Sally unlaced her dress and her stays. She splashed cold water on her face and scrubbed away all traces of the cosmetics that had been applied earlier with such care.

"Did you see your lady, miss?" Sally asked.

Jacquie pulled a light wrapper over her naked body and hugged herself. "She was there," she said, unwilling to discuss the events of the evening. Understanding as always, Sally gave her a sympathetic smile and slipped out of the bedroom.

In the silence of her room, Jacquie stood alone. It had been a long, long night. One of the worst of her life. But she was exhausted not just from tonight, but from the culmination of all her fears and failures. The memories of six London seasons tumbled around her mind. Coming out into society as a young woman with Bea, gadding about with Phin in the corners of ballrooms, shopping and dancing and flirting. Loving and laughing. Tears and joys.

She blew out the candles, turned down the covers, and slid inside the soft bed. Her years as a young woman in London might be littered with regrets, but at least she had tried to have relationships. Unlike Lady Honora, who might have been content not to have their affair at all, to marry whomever her aunt desired. Imagine living out a life by the strict rules of a relative! It was no life for her.

The door to her room slammed open.

Her eyes flew open at the sudden brightness. To her great surprise, she saw her parents in the room, lighting the candles on her mantel.

"Mama? Papa?" She sat up in bed, blinking in the sudden light.

"How could you do this to our family!" her mother wailed.

Dread coiled around her heart and squeezed the air from her chest.

"Jacqueline, my dear. We love you. You are our daughter. But you must understand the scandal that you are bringing to us!"

Papa scowled at her. "You are unweddable, Jacqueline."

Jacquie shifted. "I—I am sorry to bring trouble to you both."

"Trouble? This is more than trouble." Her father was grim. "You were supposed to be our path to nobility. The Lockhart name was to become great through you. Failing that, you were to at least be respectable and wed a fortune, if you couldn't wed a name. But now you can no longer even do that. You had a love affair with a *woman*, Jacqueline?" The confusion was plain on his face.

Her mother sat on the bed and smoothed her curls as if she were a little girl again. "My dear, you have been in London for a long time. You are no green girl. You *know* better—the city might offer a lot, but you aren't supposed to take any of it! We have been too lax with you. This is our fault."

Her father shook his head. "I take no responsibility for this. You are disowned."

Panic fluttered in her heart. "What do you mean, Papa?"

His face contorted in agony. "I mean that you are no longer our daughter. We are divorcing ourselves from this terrible scandal. You will leave our household. If you cannot contribute to our family, then we cannot support you to do God only knows what with your friends."

Her mother gasped, but it was too late. Her father turned on his heel and strode out of the room.

"Mama," Jacquie whispered, feeling the blood drain from her face.

Her mother stood uncertainly. "You heard him," she said. "He is angry, my dear. It is best if you do as he says for now. I will try to work on him and win him over and maybe you can come back in a few days." She smiled. "You will always be my daughter, you know that."

Jacqueline threw her arms around her mother and hugged her tightly. "I love you," she cried. "I am so sorry for the scandal." She

sobbed in a way that she had not for years, not even over heartbreak.
"I hoped to make you proud."

Her mother held her. "It will work out," she said firmly. "I shall
send you to the family in Manchester and all of this will be forgotten.
This all shall pass."

Or it would not, Jacquie thought. Either way, she realized that
she had enough of the family and their expectations. Her father's
words were stuck like barbs in her heart. She had known that her
parents had expected her to wed highly, but the way he had spoken, as
if she had no value besides what she could give to them... She didn't
reply to her mother, but her mind was racing.

Her mother exited the room, and Jacqueline collapsed on the
bed. Sleep eluded her until the crack of dawn, and she caught a fitful
hour or two before she dressed herself in simple day gown and rang
for Sally.

Her mother might be convinced that her father would relent and
welcome her back into the family, but she knew that she could never
return. It might have taken her six seasons, but at long last, she knew
herself. She no longer needed to hide within the frenetic social whirl
where she didn't need to think, didn't need to feel. And gossip could
no longer hurt her, if she decided to accept her own truths.

Jacquie was done living as a carefree girl, and was ready to
embrace her independent womanhood, even if it was by herself. She
didn't want to hide in Manchester with her uncle and his children.
Hadn't George—Lady Georgina—said that he would help her if she
ever needed it?

Jacqueline looked around the bedchamber, feeling more hopeful
than she had in a long time. "Sally, we must pack my bags," she
announced. "My parents found out about my love affairs and are
asking me to leave the house."

Sally's eyes were bright as she folded Jacqueline's gowns into
the valise. "This is ever so romantic," she gushed. "I can only imagine
my Thomas loving me so much to follow me wherever I went."

"I am not following Lady Honora," she said with dignity, and
Sally's face showed her dismayed surprise.

"But, miss, you love her! And, begging your pardon, but where
shall you go? How shall you live?"

Jacqueline sat at her escritoire, pen in hand. She wanted to write a note to her parents to tell them where she was going but quailed at the task. She didn't want them to worry about her safety, but on the other hand, didn't want them to come after her even if her father did have a change of heart.

They had wanted so much for her. How could she confirm to them that she was forever throwing away all of their dreams and hopes for herself and for the family? How could she explain to them that the love in her heart was for another woman, and that living together as lovers would mean giving up their chance at living in good society?

Did she dare it? She tapped the pen against the sheaf of paper, hardly believing that she had it in her to oppose her family. After a long moment, she wrote that she would be safe but did not disclose where.

Feeling faint, she put the pen down and rose to her feet, taking the valise from Sally. "Come with me?" she asked.

Sally gasped. "Miss, of course I will come with you! It's not even a question. Wherever you go, I shall go with you."

Jacqueline flushed and felt tears brimming. "You are a darling," she whispered. "But I must warn you. It's safer for you to stay here in my parents' employ. I am not sure—well, I am not sure any longer what my future holds for me, or if I would be able to pay you what you are earning now."

"La and taradiddle, miss," Sally said firmly. "My Thomas has a strong back and a willing heart and is always telling me how tired he is of London life. I am sure we can make a living outside of these walls, and we would move with you wherever you choose to go. Take me as your maid and him as your footman and we shall all be right as rain, come what may."

Jacqueline pulled her close for a hug. "You are a true treasure, Sally."

Chapter Twenty-five

Jacqueline ran her fingers up and down the pianoforte in Gina's music room. She played, as usual, without much attention to the sheet music in front of her, but she needed to channel her restless energy somewhere.

Gina slid onto the piano bench beside her. "Perhaps you should take a break from the piano, my dear," she suggested, a smile curving her lips upward. "Are you finished unpacking your belongings? Is the blue suite comfortable for you?"

She scowled down at the ivory keys. "Very comfortable," she said shortly.

"If you would like to talk about what is troubling you, I am here to listen."

She turned on the bench to look at her. "What is there to say? How can you help me more than you already have? I cannot thank you enough for taking me in, with my servants." She swallowed her pride. "I have nothing now, Gina."

She smiled at her. "You have me," she said. "We are like a family. You, me. Phin. All of the others who dare to live outside of society's strictures."

"It is less of a daring decision for me, and more of a forced circumstance," she said.

"I've known a lot of people since I have lived in London, and when I lived in Paris. In the end, it doesn't matter how you get here. Once you are here, you are part of our community." She gave her a chaste kiss on the cheek. "Am I correct in assuming that you are pining for Lady Honora?" she asked.

Jacqueline closed the lid to the pianoforte with a precise snap. "You are correct." She hesitated. "You know, it is strange to talk to you now when I feel like I told all of this to George, and not—well, not to *you*," she said frankly.

Gina smiled. "You will get used to it. Everyone does, once they know. And even if you hadn't told me yourself, Hawthorne would have found out your story, and he tells me everything." She shrugged. "London holds no secrets. Paris didn't, either."

The elderly butler drew open the door to the music room. "Sir Phineas Snow," he announced.

Phin bounded into the room. "I arrived as soon as I saw your note, Gina." He lifted a small bag emblazoned with Gunter's emblem. "I have brought reinforcements. Flavored ices are just the thing to help heal a broken heart."

"I hope you don't mind that I sent word to Phin," Gina said. "But I thought you needed your friends around you right now."

Jacquie smiled. "Thank you," she whispered.

Phin drew out little metal cups of ice from the bag. "I purchased whatever they had," he admitted as he arranged half a dozen cups on the little table in front of the elegant sofa.

A tear slipped down her face.

"Darling, I'm sorry," Phin said, patting her shoulder.

"We went to Gunter's together," she murmured, lost in memory. "Nora had her first ice with me by her side."

"Let's get rid of them," he said contritely and slipped his arm around her for a hug. "Gina, could you ring the bell pull?"

"Under no circumstances," Gina said, and selected a cup. Tasting it, she made a sound of pleasure. "Lemon and mint," she sighed. "Lovely." She took another spoonful. "There is no point avoiding things associated with pain, Jacqueline. You need to face them and keep living. Make new memories." She thrust a cup at Jacquie. "Try the strawberry."

Gina might look like a woodland elf, Jacquie thought, but she sounded more like a military general. She accepted the cup and stuck a spoonful in her mouth. It might as well have been ashes for all she could taste of it, but she gamely took another bite and saw Phin smile at her.

She kicked her slippers off, curled into a corner of the sofa, and pulled her knees to her chest as she nibbled the treat. It felt cool on her throat, which was sore and scratchy from a night of sobbing.

"Why don't you go to her?" Gina asked gently.

"She doesn't want me. She made it clear. She has chosen the earl and a loveless marriage."

Gina patted her knee. "But you could go talk to her. You could ask her to listen, to hear you out."

Phin cleared his throat. "I don't think she is in London. The earl was planning to invite her to Hawthorne Towers on behalf of the duchess, and propose to her there. She should already be in the country by now."

Jacqueline stared at him. "However do you know?"

"I was with Hawthorne last night and he mentioned it. He is about to leave for the country today to join the party."

"The duke really does know everything," Gina said, nodding.

"You knew the earl was going to propose, Phin?" Unwarranted rage clouded her vision. "And you said nothing to me?"

He backed away, palms up. "I found out yesterday, Jacquie. Probably at the same time you did. And I have no control over the earl's actions, or Nora's reactions." He continued, "Beatrice is also going to be in attendance at the party as well, if you wish to know everything I discussed with Hawthorne."

"And however did Beatrice manage an invitation to a duke's country house?"

"She still has her cap set on the earl. I think her cousin Wilfrid managed to arrange it for her."

Jacqueline snorted. "Well, we all know she won't be successful. Poor Bea would have been better off staying in London with me." It hurt that Beatrice wasn't there beside her, soothing her after heartbreak like she always did. But she had her own need to marry as soon as possible, and she admitted to herself with her newfound understanding of herself that it was selfish to expect Beatrice to drop everything to comfort her.

Phin rose from the sofa. "Alas, this is all the news that I bring to share with you. I shall return to the duke and send you word if I hear anything else that may be of interest to your situation."

Jacquie leapt to her feet and hugged him. "Thank you for everything, Phin," she said, pressing her cheek against the wool lapel of his suit. Tears welled in her eyes. "Thank you for standing by me. And for bringing me ices."

He kissed the top of her head. "I am here for you, always. No matter what may come, I shall be on your side."

He gave her a jaunty salute and left the drawing room.

Jacqueline sat back down and scraped her spoon against the bottom of the cup. "When Nora returns from the country, she will be an engaged woman. By the season's end, she will be wedded to the earl and she will retire to the country where I shall never see her again."

She tossed the empty cup to the table, lay her head back against the pillowed sofa, and closed her eyes.

"Then you need to follow her and stop the engagement," Gina said.

"What are you proposing? That we loosen the wheels of her carriage and prevent her from leaving London?" Jacquie asked. "Even if we did—what point would there be to following her? What can I possibly offer her? If she marries the earl, she is set for a life of luxury. If she chooses to be with me...well. I want to be able to give her more than just stolen kisses in a ballroom or trysts in the bedroom of my parents' house." She scowled. "Or the guest bedroom of your house, Gina."

She looked thoughtful. "If you could have anything, what would it be?"

Jacquie swallowed hard and thought about the life she dreamed of having. "We would have our own home," she said. "We would wake up every morning together, and live our lives as if we were married to each other. I would move to the country that she loves so much, if she wanted it. But how can I offer it? I have no fortune of my own, no property. I have no family who would be willing to support me." She shook her head. "It's impossible."

Gina took her hand. "If there is anything I have learned in this life, it's that nothing is impossible," she said. "The first time I left the house in trousers, I shook like a leaf and couldn't believe that I could have the courage to do such a thing. But the moment another man tipped his hat to me as if I belonged, I felt as if I could fly. As if I could do anything. It taught me that if you want something, you can have it if you're brave enough to try."

She stood and paced to the window. "This salon that I hold on Tuesdays is a chance for women to express themselves and to live as they want to. Some of them hold professions. Any of them would help you should you need it."

"How could I get to Hawthorne Towers? My parents would hardly countenance sending me in a carriage to announce myself uninvited. It's impossible."

"I will send you in my own carriage," she said. "In fact, let's go together." She beamed at her.

Jacquie stared, nonplussed. "How is it any better if we *both* show up uninvited?"

Gina waved a hand. "I've told you. The duke and I are old friends. I am sure he would invite me, or allow me to show up. I'll just write him a note before we leave to make sure he knows." She smiled mischievously. "I grew up in Paris, and he lived quite close by. I used to sneak out of my parents' house all the time to attend his parties."

Jacquie gasped. "However did your reputation survive? I have never heard a breath of scandal attached to your name, but if you were always in the presence of the scandalous duke—!"

"Are you forgetting about George?" she said, wiggling her eyebrows.

"Are you saying that you dressed as a boy and wandered around Paris in disguise? Gina, that's admirably daring."

"I wouldn't consider George to be a disguise. He's very much *me*. Perhaps more me than I am now, in my frock."

"So who would be accompanying me to the estate? Would you take me as George? Or as Gina?"

"I'm afraid I couldn't offer my escort to you as Gina," she said. "My reputation would be entirely ruined if I were to be seen with you at a social event right now while the scandal is still so fresh. When the talk dies down, after enough time has passed, you might live down the gossip of an affair with another woman. There would be many who wouldn't believe such a thing anyway. But you will never escape society's wrath by gadding about unchaperoned to the country with a man like George. *Everyone* would believe it and would not hesitate to think the worst of you. Are you sure you want to take this risk?"

Jacqueline paused. "I can no longer imagine my life without Nora," she admitted. "And there are already so many rumors swirling around my name this season…what is this but one more piece of gossip? I don't think I care anymore about what people say."

"This wouldn't be mere gossip. If you are to hop into George's carriage and be my escort to a house party that we're not invited to for a weekend together, it means ruination."

"I have no choice. I love Nora. Even if she might choose Sinclair over me—I want to give her that choice. I ran away from her at the ball, and I need to go talk to her. I should have at least listened to what she wanted to say."

Gina grinned at her. "Then by all means, let's arrange the details and be on our way."

"What about your reputation as George?" she asked.

Gina waved a hand. "It's very unfair, but George's reputation will be enhanced by such adventures," she said. "I look terribly young as a man, and it's helpful to have a few scandals under my belt. The ladies go wild for these sorts of things. And of course, I am always interested in driving the ladies wild."

Chapter Twenty-six

Hawthorne Towers was the grandest country home that Nora had ever seen. Every element of its construction had been designed to intimidate and impress. The hallways were vast tunnels, the windows were countless, the rooms were cavernous. Staff moved from room to room in well-rehearsed patterns, polishing, dusting, arranging, serving. When Nora and Aunt Mildred had arrived yesterday afternoon, the duchess told them that simply anything was available at the Towers. All they needed to do was ask, and it would be done.

But Nora couldn't imagine asking for anything. Every luxury was already arranged. From the roses on the mantel of her bedchamber, to the gorgeous paintings hanging in her adjoining sitting room, everything felt calculated to please.

She ran her fingers over a luxurious velvet chair in the bedchamber and looked out onto the manicured lawn. Every blade of grass was placed in accordance to ducal decree. Nothing was out of place.

Except her. She didn't belong in such exalted company. She was numb, cold, lost. Her heart was hollow and heavy all at once. She considered crawling into the bed, burrowing into the deep nest of pillows and pulling the covers high over her ears. Then she could allow a river of tears to wash over her face. The memory of giggling under the covers with Jacquie at her home in London flashed through her mind, and she swallowed hard. She had enough tears inside her for an entire ocean.

The thought of facing hordes of other houseguests and listening to them coo over the perfection of the cold, stilted atmosphere filled her with dread. She considered her options. She could plead illness. She could refuse to come downstairs and hope that there were enough other guests that her absence would be go unremarked. Or, and this was the option that most appealed to her, she could fling open the window, shimmy down the glossy ivy vines that crept over the sandstone walls, and run away. How far away could Wiltshire be from here?

But of course there was Aunt Mildred to consider. She would be horrified to think of Nora plotting her escape when the Earl of Sinclair was so close to proposing.

The thought of the earl made her stomach feel sour. She couldn't marry him. But the thought held no emotion, and she feared that perhaps she could feel nothing but despair or grief ever again. If that was the case, then it wouldn't be a bad bargain to have him as a husband.

Aunt Mildred swept into the room. "Good, I am happy to see that you are ready, Honora."

Nora might have felt inadequate in the great country estate polished to a high shine by generations of dukes, but her aunt felt a keen sense of belonging. "Ready for what, Aunt Mildred?" she replied, uncaring which activity that she would be brought to.

"The duchess has been so kind as to offer us a tour of the grounds," she said triumphantly. "I knew she had taken an exceptional liking to you. Her Grace will be showing us the house and the garden in person. Isn't that kind of her?"

"Yes, very kind," she said, and forced a smile onto her face.

"Let us dillydally no longer," Aunt Mildred instructed, and swept out again.

After a moment in which she cast a longing look once more at the bed and its comforting promise of temporary oblivion, Nora followed. She trailed behind her aunt through several long corridors and down a grand staircase to the impressive great hall.

"We are so sorry to keep you waiting, Your Grace," Aunt Mildred exclaimed and hurried down the stairs, casting a dour look behind her at Nora.

It took all of Nora's energy to walk, so she did not rush after her aunt.

"It is the easiest thing in the world to become lost in Hawthorne Towers. Sometimes it seems as if it is ever expanding around me." The duchess's laugh was as sharp as glass breaking, and Nora shuddered.

"Lady Honora, I am glad to welcome you to the Towers. It's almost as if we are family already, is it not?" Her smile was cool.

"Through the duke, we are related by marriage already, Your Grace."

"What my dear niece means to say, of course, is that we are looking forward to being doubly connected to the family," Aunt Mildred said.

"Of course," Nora echoed.

The duchess inclined her head. "I will be happy to see Sinclair settle down." Her eyes met Nora's, who shrank from their clear intensity. "But I am even happier that it is you that he will settle down with. I promise you, Lady Honora, you shall not regret this decision."

Aunt Mildred broke in. "Honora is perfectly cognizant of the deep honor the union would be."

Nora noticed the pinch in her aunt's mouth and the crinkled concern around her eyes. She was anxious for her to succeed. Nora could see it, and she wanted to reassure her that she would obey, but her mouth refused to speak the platitudes that previously had dropped with ease from her lips.

To her annoyance, Lord Sinclair appeared as if conjured by their expectations. "Lady Honora, it is a true pleasure to see you again," he greeted her warmly.

She managed to smile.

The duchess nodded in satisfaction at them both. "I am so pleased to have the opportunity to show you our estate."

Nora snapped her fan open. "Shall we start the tour?" she asked, wanting nothing more than to have it over with. The prospect of spending more time in the presence of both Sinclair and the duchess was exhausting.

Although the duchess was a charming conversationalist, Nora's attention wandered. They were shown through rooms graced by expensive and overpowering statuary, music rooms with gleaming instruments, a large terrace where Aunt Mildred reminisced where the duke proposed to the duchess at a family Christmas party, and finally, the gardens.

The estate of Hawthorne Towers boasted endless acres of land, all of which were laid out with meticulous care. Formal gardens stretched out before them, dotted with precise lines of trees and flower beds.

Nora gazed at a wild rose arbor, with its tightly budded pink roses and was reminded of the slippers that she had given to Jacqueline. Her throat felt tight as she remembered how beautiful they had looked on Jacquie's feet, and how prettily she had showed them off at the dressmaker's atelier, swirling her skirts around her dainty ankles.

She told herself to think of Rosedale Manor instead. At this time of year, her home was full of roses in riotous bloom. Breathing deeply, she forced herself to remember their sweet summer scent and the vases of pink and white roses that she liked to arrange on her bedside table every evening.

Clearing her mind of Jacqueline, she told herself to remember that if the earl proposed to her, she would have the necessary funds to maintain the manor in the state that it had been when her parents had lived. She could set it up again as one of the great homes in the neighborhood. Of course, the earl wouldn't have time to visit it very often, but surely she could persuade him to visit every year. Unbidden, Nora remembered the duchess telling her that the earl would be a rather distant sort of husband. Maybe she could even live for part of the year at her beloved Rosedale Manor. The thought eased the ache in her heart a little.

An elegant gazebo perched near a lake with calm, glassy waters. The duchess told them that it was used for picnics, one of which they would enjoy for luncheon today. Nora looked at the wooden structure, lost in thought.

The gazebo was a quiet little place, with delicately carved posts and frontispieces boasting the duke's emblems. It had been built for the duchess as a wedding gift. There was a thunderous pause after Aunt Mildred mentioned it, for of course the duke had not stayed in London long enough to see his young wife enjoy it.

After what seemed an eternity, they returned to the front entrance of the Towers. "Now you have seen everything," the duchess declared. "These halls hold no more secrets for you."

Nora thought longingly of escaping to her room.

But then Sinclair asked Aunt Mildred's permission to take her along the wilderness walk. "I shall keep her safe from outlaws and bandits," he promised with a wink. "Lady Honora will be safe in my care."

Her aunt and the duchess exchanged very satisfied smiles. The earl whisked Nora away without further ado.

The walk itself was a charming prospect. The path wound itself among tall trees, and there were regular clearings of wildflowers to admire. With another companion, it would have been a lovely way to spend a half hour. Nora's thoughts went to Jacquie, but imagining her laughing face and bright eyes and dancing form amid the trees sent a sharp pang through her heart.

They came to an outlook where they had a marvelous view of the house and gardens. There was a wrought iron bench that Nora rather wished could be allowed for solitary contemplation of the vista, but of course the earl had another thought in mind.

He gestured for her to sit, but he seemed too full of nervous energy to take a seat beside her. Instead, he paced in front of her.

"Lady Honora, it must come as no surprise to you how much I esteem you." Lord Sinclair spoke with earnest sincerity, warmth in his eyes.

Nora bit her lip. Was there any way to avoid the proposal that must be forthcoming? She scanned the horizon but found no answers there.

Hesitantly, she said, "You have been very kind—"

"How could I have been anything but attentive to your graceful form and beautiful face, my lady?" he asked, he sat beside her and slid an arm along the back of the bench.

"You know how I have been searching for a companion to help launch my sisters into society. I can see that your thoughtfulness and quiet demeanor will be just the thing to calm their exuberant spirits and show them the proper way to enter society. I knew as soon as the duchess mentioned your name to me that I had found the perfect partner at last. Her taste is exceptional."

Nora braced herself against the bench and clenched the carved metal with such force that she was sure she would have permanent grooves embedded in her palms. She could feel the warmth of his arm at her back, and though he wasn't quite touching her, his nearness was overwhelming.

Sinclair leapt to his feet in front of the bench, grasped one of her hands in his own, and took a deep breath. "Lady Honora. My dear, would you do me the great honor of being my wife?"

She exhaled. They were only words, Nora realized with dazed wonder. She looked up at the sky above them, at the leaves that lazily moved in the summer breeze. Her breathing slowed, and she relaxed her grip.

These were words that she had dreaded and feared, words that she had felt sure would trap and bind her to a life that she had come to realize that she would never want to live. Once she had heard them, she had always thought that it would be impossible to escape their power, and they would transform her life forever.

But the reality of the world around her was unchanged. And now the moment to fear the words had gone. Everything seemed so simple and clear that she almost laughed with pure joy.

How was it that she had never understood before that such a question could be asked and *rejected*?

"No," she replied, testing out the word and found that it made her heart feel weightless and free.

"No?" he said incredulously. He dropped her hand.

"No. I do not think we would suit," she said in some surprise at how easily the words were to say, hardly believing that her voice sounded so calm. She had found it so difficult to speak up before, but now wondered at herself that it had so intimidated her.

Aunt Mildred would be horrified if she could see the scene unfolding here in the clearing. But her aunt was not here, and it was not her aunt's life that she had to live. Although the decision was clear in her mind, a swirl of emotion pounded through her mind and her heart. Was she throwing away her future? Had she wasted this chance of a season, wasted the considerable amount of time and huge expense that her aunt had put into making her debut a success?

"Suit? Whatever do you mean? I am a man in need of a wife, and you are a woman in need of a husband. We are of the same rank. We both want a quiet country life and wish to build a family. How much better could we possibly suit?"

She smiled gently at him. "We do not love each other."

Nora knew without a shadow of a doubt that she would never think again of marrying without love. Whatever this would mean for her future, she knew that it was true for her. She was capable of a grand passion after all.

The truth inside her heart was that she loved Jacqueline Lockhart.

Raking his hand through his hair, Sinclair shook his head. "Can't we trust that love will come with time, Lady Honora? As we grow our family together, we will grow to love each other. A strong mutual regard and similar ideals will be an excellent foundation for love."

He faced her and looked serious. "I swear I would be a good husband to you."

She knew that this was the best marriage prospect that she would be likely to get. If she couldn't bear to think of marrying the wealthy and handsome Earl of Sinclair, she might as well give up and retire to country life. Alone. Without a husband, without a family. Without the funds she needed to maintain Rosedale Manor in the way that she had hoped.

She sighed. "But if I don't love you, I could not profess to make a good wife to you," she replied. "I am sorry, my lord. I wish I felt differently."

Nora sprang to her feet and strode off as fast as she could in her flimsy walking shoes, twisting up a handful of her long skirts to free her legs' movement. Thoughts tumbled through her mind like an avalanche. Her heart twisted at the thought of disappointing Aunt Mildred. There were very few family members left in her life, and it tore at her to think of creating distance between herself and her only aunt.

But through the maelstrom of whirling emotion, her mind kept racing back to the thought of Jacqueline. Her black hair shining against the white linen pillowcase. Her beautiful smile, lighting up a ballroom with her warmth. Her earnest words of encouragement and love and praise.

Her love for Jacqueline felt pure and real. And even though she might have lost her to the wiles of the Countess of Straund, she knew without a doubt that she could find that kind of love to fill her life. It just wouldn't be with a man, and certainly not with the earl.

Hurrying past the flower beds, she thought of her future for the first time in a long time with a sense of relief and happiness, freed from the heavy weight of expectation and the dread of a loveless, lonely union. Living in Rosedale Manor in genteel poverty was worth more to her than a husband in a lavish estate filled only with duty and regrets.

Chapter Twenty-seven

The carriage rattled up the long driveway to the elegant estate. Jacqueline cast a sidelong glance at George. Even though she knew that the person sprawled across from her on the opposite seat was also her friend Gina, she could not help marveling at the transformation.

Gina was neat and dainty, wore frilled gowns, smiled peacefully at others, and walked with a delicate air like a fairy. George was a slender lad who took up a surprising amount of space—all gangly legs and arms, with a mischievous energy that felt on the brink of brimming over. Where Gina burned with righteous fire, George looked ready to gorge himself on the zest of life.

George grinned at her. "You aren't having last minute regrets, are you?" he asked. "That is exactly the sort of lark that I like to be embroiled in. I haven't had this much fun since Paris."

Jacquie groaned. "I don't know what I was thinking," she confessed. "What if Nora has already accepted the earl? What if I am too late?"

He straightened the fashionable cravat tied at his throat. "Then you talk to her and have it all in the open anyway," he said. "And maybe it's not a bad plan, if you want the respectability of marriage to cover your own love affair. She could wed the earl, and I suppose you could marry me. I wouldn't keep you from Nora—we could have separate households. Very modern. Extremely fashionable."

Jacqueline patted his velvet trousered knee. "That is the sweetest offer you could possibly make me. You are the most chivalrous gentleman that I know, George."

"And don't you forget it," he replied. "George is ever ready to rescue a damsel in distress."

"For no reward?"

"*Au contraire*, the lasses are very keen on rewarding me. Most eager, actually. I have seen my fair share of pretty damsels go from distress to various stages of *undress* in the twinkling of an eye."

The carriage pulled up to Hawthorne Towers and rumbled to a stop. George looked at her soberly. "We can turn around if you need to," he said. "The choice is yours—if you continue, I'll be by your side to help you weather the storm. But if you want to forget all about this, I can take you home and you would be welcome to stay with me for as long as you wish."

Jacquie flung her arms around him and kissed his cheek. "I appreciate it, George," she said softly. "More than you could know. But I need to see Nora, to explain everything. I need to know if she loves me."

He nodded. "Then let's go hunt dragons."

George bounded out of the carriage with a clatter, and helped Jacquie down the steps. She straightened her skirts and brushed the hair from her face.

"You're ready?" George asked.

"As I shall ever be."

The front door of the magnificent edifice cracked open. Startled, Jacquie watched the duke himself lope out of the house to greet them, crossing the flight of stairs in seemingly no time at all.

He grinned. "Well, well, my dear George. I didn't expect to receive your letter saying that you were coming up for the weekend, but then why should I ever be surprised to see you turn up on my doorstep? Follow me everywhere I go, do you? I left Paris for London, and there you were. I left London for the country, and you're here again! More persistent than pestilence, my lad."

George grinned back. "Someone has got to keep their eye out for you, Your Grace," he said, and scraped an exaggerated bow. "Left to your own devices, you'd be lucky to escape the stocks."

The duke clasped him on the shoulder. "And what do we have here, my good man? Are you ready for the shackle of marriage vows?

I thought I would never see the day that you would settle down, but Miss Lockhart is a pretty one."

Jacqueline curtsied. "It is a pleasure to see you again, Your Grace."

He kissed her hand with a flourish. "It is always a pleasure to be reacquainted with beauty, and I am most curious to learn how you managed to capture poor Georgie's heart in such quick measure. You met only recently. First I saw you with Lady Honora, then with Miss Everson, and now Mr. Smith? A more accomplished young lass I have never met."

"You know perfectly well all of my secrets, and that George's heart is safe from me," she told him. "I am here for another lover."

Hawthorne's low laugh rumbled through the courtyard. "I will help you as much as I can, though I must warn you that my duchess has other ideas for Lady Honora than you might have. If you wish for my advice, I would steer you toward the young lad beside you. I've been wanting to see him settled for years."

George bowed again, but gave a rather vulgar hand gesture as he rose. "You may take your advice and shove it, Duke." He was grinning, and the duke gave him a playful jab in the shoulder.

Jacqueline smiled at them. "The heart knows what it wants," she said to Hawthorne with quiet dignity, and watched a genuine smile spread over his craggy face.

"That it does," he said thoughtfully. "Far be it for me to investigate the intricacies of another's union. Mine is fraught enough with twists and turns to fill a Gothic romance." Hawthorne led them up the stairs to the great entrance. "You know, we are a ducal household with a great many rooms, but my duchess is in the midst of throwing a house party. I am sad to say that there is but the one bedchamber available, and forgive me, but I do not quite know just how scandalous you would like to appear by sharing it."

Jacqueline's smile was genuine for the first time all day. "I believe some dear friends of mine are here. I would not mind sharing a room with Miss Everson—or Lady Honora."

"I daresay you wouldn't," he murmured. "Please do avail yourself of any comfort that you can find in the ducal abode."

"We would be pleased to," George said.

The butler was summoned and guided them to their chambers.

Beatrice shrieked when she saw Jacqueline enter her room and held her in a tight embrace. "It is so good to see you again," she said, resting her forehead against Jacquie's shoulder.

A soft hand stroked her hair and she felt that everything might be all right after all. Bea was family. She would support her.

She sat on the bed and drew Beatrice down to sit beside here. "You would not believe how many things there are to tell you," she said, and fell backward onto the bed. "I am here with—with Mr. George Smith."

Bea shrieked again. "Jacquie, what are you thinking! Mr. Smith is a jaunty dresser, but I don't think he has any money to speak of. What are you *doing*?"

Jacquie sat up. "Well—he's only escorting me," she confessed. "We have no understanding, of course. I have come to pay court to Lady Honora and convince her not to marry the Earl of Sinclair. I just cannot live with the thought of her wedding him, if there is any hope at all that she bears any love for me."

Beatrice sniffed. "I certainly wouldn't mind marrying Sinclair. That man has eyes that could melt a saint. I still don't know what either of you see in Lady Honora, but if you want her—I will do my utmost to help you."

Jacquie hugged her again. "Thank you, Bea. For everything. You are a true friend."

"Anything for you, Jacquie. It's always been you and me."

Chapter Twenty-eight

Nora walked back to the gazebo near the lake, in search of respite from her turbulent emotions. How could she face Aunt Mildred and tell her that she had turned down the earl's proposal, and that she wished to be done with London? She wasn't sure if her aunt would listen. After all, she hadn't listened to any of Nora's opinions thus far in London, so why would she expect an understanding ear now, when she had done something that seemed so ostensibly nonsensical?

She trailed her fingers over the carved and painted wood of the gazebo and leaned against one of the columns. If she could just tell Aunt Mildred that she wanted her season to be over and to leave London, if she could go back to the way that she had lived for so long in Wiltshire. But she knew that there was no going back, not really. She felt different. Stronger, more alive. Instead of hiding herself away in the manor, she felt ready to be part of the community back at home. Someday she would find love again, and she wouldn't let go. Not for anything.

There was a certain sad peace in her soul as she watched a pair of birds darting around the bushes. She was alone now, but someday she would be part of a pair.

In the distance, she saw a woman walking in the gardens. Her heart clutched for an instant as she thought of Jacqueline, before dismissing the notion. Jacquie wasn't here at the estate. It must be one of the other guests. There were plenty of them—many more people that she had thought would be here when the earl told her about the gathering.

Something intrigued her about the way that the woman moved. There was a familiarity in the way that she walked with a sway to her hips, the way that black hair swirled in the summer breeze. The rhythm of her walking was ingrained in her mind, in her soul.

It was impossible. But surely it was Jacqueline Lockhart. Her heart pounded in her chest, and happiness welled up from a place deep inside. Jacquie was *here*. It didn't make sense, but the truth was in front of her eyes.

Nora took a deep breath, and then picked up her skirts and ran toward her.

She saw the exact moment that Jacqueline noticed her. She could see that smile from a mile away, and she started running toward her as well.

They collided, laughing as they stumbled and nearly lost their balance as they joined together in a fierce and exuberant hug.

"You're here," Nora said, grinning through her tears. "You're here. With me."

Jacqueline kissed her deeply. "There is nowhere else I would rather be," she breathed. "I have been a fool." She gazed at her. "I should never have pressured you to give me an immediate answer like that, in the middle of a ball. I should have listened to you and made sure that you were comfortable, instead of pushing you. Please forgive me for my thoughtless words."

Nora hugged her fiercely. "I would forgive you anything," she said. "Forgive me for not staying in London and running away from what we found together."

They clasped hands and walked back to the gazebo, haltingly spilling their hearts to each other.

Nora cupped Jacquie's face, marveling at the smoothness of her cheek underneath her hand. She hadn't thought she would have the opportunity to touch her again, and her heart ached. Nora swept a lock of long black hair away from Jacqueline's face. "I tried not to think of you since I last saw you," she said. "The memories were too painful. Especially when I thought of the future that I was going toward. Now that you are here, I can't believe my good fortune to have you back in my arms." She drew her close and kissed her.

"I couldn't stay away," Jacquie said. She looked around. "But I don't want your reputation to be ruined, like mine is—we should go somewhere more private—"

Nora grasped Jacqueline's hands in her own and looked into those clear emerald eyes with passionate intensity. "I love you, Jacqueline Lockhart. I love you. I should have said it in London, but I was scared and didn't know my own mind. But I'm not afraid any longer. I don't care about reputations. I would only be too happy never to go to another London ball."

Jacquie gave her a radiant smile. "And I love you, Honora Banfield." Her face fell and she looked uncertain. "But what about the earl?"

"Sinclair proposed this morning," she said.

Jacquie drew herself back. "Oh," she said. "I'm too late." She gave a sad, helpless smile. "I love you, but if you have chosen the earl—I understand."

"I turned him down," she said, and was richly rewarded when Jacquie gave an unladylike shriek and threw herself at her, covering her face in kisses.

"Oh, I knew you could never marry him!" she cried out, joy beaming out of every pore. "Well done, Nora!"

Nora giggled. "He was very surprised at the turn of events."

Jacquie was wild with joy. She kissed Nora, weak with relief. She hadn't chosen the earl, she realized in fierce wonder. She has chosen her instead. She was worthy of love after all. Jacquie ran her hands over Nora's slender waist and rounded hips, and then up to her bosom.

Nora pressed against her impatiently, her knee sliding between Jacquie's legs. She gasped, but felt the same fervor building inside her. She pulled Nora's lace fichu from her bosom and flung it away, then tugged at the modest bodice of her dress. The fabric easily pulled away from her breasts. Too easily. In her eagerness and haste, she accidentally ripped the fragile muslin bodice.

Nora grinned at her. "My new wardrobe still doesn't meet with my lady's expectations, even though we purchased it together? What would it take to please you, I wonder?"

Jacquie giggled. "I did tell you once that in London, we prefer less clothing," she teased.

"Ah, but now we are in the country," Nora replied, her eyes shining. "Things are altogether different here. I suppose the birds and the bees won't mind if I am in a natural state."

Jacquie traced a path with her lips from Nora's mouth to her neck to her nipples, which had Nora gasping with pleasure. "Your natural beauty is all I wish to see."

They were so caught up in their passion that they didn't hear footsteps approaching along the dirt path, and didn't notice the shadow that blocked out the sunlight, until it was too late.

"The picnic luncheon!" Nora gasped, and her face went white as Jacqueline sprang away from her.

"Ladies!" A disapproving voice rang out like a shot.

Jacqueline swallowed as she watched the Duchess of Hawthorne stride up the wooden steps of the gazebo to grasp Nora's arm. "Lady Honora," she said, exasperation plain on her face. "Despite all warnings, still you comport yourself with no thought to your future! Without the protection of a man's name, this behavior is ruinous." She gestured at Jacquie. "Simply ask your friend. Miss Lockhart will not be welcomed to any event of any note, now that she has found herself embroiled in scandal."

"Maybe I don't want to be welcomed by the sort of people who would shun me," Jacquie snapped.

The duchess glared at her. "You do not think of others!" she cried vehemently. "You refuse to see the impact of your actions on others around you. Now gossip has swirled around the Countess of Straund since you insisted on making a show the other night by leaving with her. And soon it could touch Lady Honora. It could touch all of us who share these feelings." She turned to Nora, her face set. "Do not worry," she told her. "I can still fix this."

Nora looked at Jacquie. "But nothing is broken here, Your Grace."

Jacquie grinned. As Nora stood there in the bright sunlight, her torn bodice revealing her chemise, her hair mussed from a lover's touch, defiance in every line of her body, Jacquie had never loved her more.

Lady Mildred rushed up the steps, hurt in her eyes. "Honora Banfield," she gasped. "I cannot believe such a thing of you. And with you, Miss Lockhart!" But words failed her, and she could only shake her head in shock.

Nora gently touched her arm and eased her onto the narrow bench that was installed along the perimeter of the gazebo. "It is all right, Aunt Mildred," she said. "I have made my choice, and I am happy."

The crowd was starting to gather for the picnic. Jacquie could hear the excited bursts of conversation and laughter as a gaggle of young ladies and gentlemen were approaching. They were still too far away to notice the dramatics in the gazebo, but two people had separated from their midst and were fast approaching.

The Earl of Sinclair strode to the gazebo with military precision, and hurrying after him, skirts in hand as she tripped to keep up with him, was the eternally determined Beatrice.

Sinclair sized up the situation and quickened up the steps. "I knew Miss Lockhart was a poor influence on you, Lady Honora," he proclaimed. "I understand now. She is the reason why you turned down my proposal. You are making a youthful mistake, that is all. You can forget about these senseless indiscretions once you are wedded to me. My dear, she has no power over you anymore." He glared at Jacquie and placed himself between her and Nora.

Bea slipped past him and looked into Jacquie's eyes. "Are you all right?" she asked urgently. Jacquie nodded, but she wasn't sure what was about to happen. She was grateful for Beatrice's support.

The earl turned around just as the crowd reached the gazebo, and he placed an arm around Nora's shoulders. She tried to shake his hand away but he gripped her firmly.

Sinclair bowed his head to the group of people who were murmuring uneasily as they looked at the tableau before them. "I am sorry that you have seen us like this," he said, holding Nora against his side. "My fiancée and I have been caught in a most compromising position."

An excited confusion of voices relayed the news from lips to ears and a blur of faces turned toward them as Jacquie gaped in shock at the earl's blatant lie.

Nora wrenched herself away. "I am not engaged to this man," she said loudly, and the crowd stilled.

Beatrice squeezed Jacquie's hand. "Wish me luck, my dear," she whispered with a grin. Turning away, Bea tore the lace trim from her own dress in one fluid motion, then whirled around to expose her torn bodice with an ample portion of her chest gleaming in the sunshine. She flung a hand to her brow and pushed her way in front of Nora and Sinclair.

"Lady Honora nobly tried to take the blame for my misdeeds just now!" Beatrice cried out. "What a kind and loving friend—her first thought was to sacrifice her reputation to save my own, even as she now realizes that the time has come for me to confess."

The crowd was silenced. The earl fixed Bea with a deadly glare. But Beatrice ignored him and fluffed her skirts to maximum effect, sinking to the stairs of the gazebo, as practiced and as compelling as any actress on Drury Lane. She pitched her voice so that everyone could hear her as she continued with her dramatics. "I admit it, I was in the gazebo with the earl just now and we were quite overcome with passion. We have been lovers this past age, but oh—I cannot hide it any longer!"

She batted her eyelashes up at Sinclair, scarcely hiding her glee. Jacquie was impressed. She should never have doubted that Beatrice would find a way to wed the earl. Hadn't she always found a way to get what she wanted, in all their years of friendship?

The earl cleared his throat awkwardly, while at the same time piercing her with a murderous glare. "Miss Beatrice Everson," he said with gritted teeth, "do forgive me for…forgetting myself with you."

She beamed up at him. "My lord, I would forgive you for anything," she cooed.

"Will you do me the great honor of becoming my wife?" he asked her coldly.

Bea leapt from the stairs and into his arms, and he stumbled backward. "Of course, my dear Sinclair!" she cried. "I would like nothing better to be wedded to you. I always knew that our distance in rank and stature would not get in the way of our true love!"

The crowd was abuzz again with confusion and congratulations for the newly engaged couple.

The Duchess of Hawthorne clapped her hands. "This is indeed not what I expected," she said. "But *someone* must now be engaged after all of this dramatic taradiddle. Of course I wish you happy, Sinclair. Now let us pull up some champagne from the cellars and celebrate your good fortune in marrying Miss Everson."

"I am delighted at the idea of gaining you as a cousin, Your Grace," Beatrice said without a trace of guilt, her smile as bright as the sun.

The duchess stared at her. "Indeed. I am charmed," she said.

Jacqueline tugged at Nora's arm. "I think we can safely abscond," she whispered.

Away from the crowd, they hurried, rushing through the gardens and up the stairs and into the bedroom.

"I don't care what my aunt thinks," Nora said, sinking onto the bed and pulling Jacquie down beside her. "When I lost your love, I was devastated. Life lost its color for me. I won't give you up now that we are together again. I refuse to marry a man in order to hide our love away."

"I know I don't have much to offer you," Jacquie said. "But if it comes to it, I can work. There must be something I could do—Gina said she would help me. I think I could find a way for us to survive."

"All I want is your love. I want to be with you, just as you are. Come with me to Wiltshire," Nora said. "I own Rosedale Manor outright as my inheritance. It would mean the world to me if we could live there together, married in heart if not by law. The estate is sufficient, though it is by no means a wealthy existence," she said. "It is not what you are used to in the city. It will not be luxurious. But the people there are kind. I think they would be most pleased if I returned home to live there with you as my companion. They would be far happier with a Banfield there in the house all year instead of me visiting it with my husband once in a great while."

Jacqueline grinned. "I would like nothing more," she said. She paused. "But I do wonder if maybe you would also consider having another Banfield in residence? Your aunt loves you so much, Nora," she said. "I know how important family is to you. If you give her time to understand, and to accept—I think Lady Mildred might like to live with us."

Nora smiled. Aunt Mildred had been there for her since the death of her parents, time and time again. She had spent so much time trying to make her a success in London. And she had liked Jacquie up until her ruination. Surely she would find it in herself to accept them. "Yes," she said. "I think that is a marvelous plan, my love. You are so kind to think of her."

Jacquie kissed her gently in reply.

"I thought we could host some events for the ladies in the county," Nora said. "Like the afternoons that Gina holds here in town. When I was younger, if I had known of any options for a woman besides marriage, I could have had different expectations of myself."

"That is a marvelous idea," Jacquie said, warming to the notion immediately. "Living together in and of itself would be an example to other women who wish the same thing. But helping to educate women of all statuses about their choices would be a worthy goal. And of course we would welcome anyone else who loves as we do."

"Rosedale is no London," Nora said. "The entertainments are not what they are in town."

She shook her head. "I can arrange entertainment enough if we need it," Jacquie said. "Perhaps we could arrange a night of dancing a month? And maybe I could invite an acrobat or two from Vauxhall, on occasion?"

Nora nodded. "The neighborhood would be delighted," she assured her.

"The only one I want to delight is you," she breathed.

Their lips met again in unhurried splendor, now that they had a lifetime of moments spread before them like a banquet of love and desire.

THE END

About the Author

Jane Walsh is a queer historical romance novelist who loves everything Regency. She is delighted to have the opportunity to put her studies in history and costume design to good use by writing love stories. She owes a great debt of gratitude to the local coffee shop for fueling her novel writing endeavors. Jane's happily ever after is centered on her wife and their cat and their cozy home together in Canada.

Books Available from Bold Strokes Books

Aurora by Emma L McGeown. After a traumatic accident, Elena Ricci is stricken with amnesia leaving her with no recollection of the last eight years, including her wife and son. (978-1-63555-824-1)

Avenging Avery by Sheri Lewis Wohl. Revenge against a vengeful vampire unites Isa Meyer and Jeni Denton, but it's love that heals them. (978-1-63555-622-3)

Bulletproof by Maggie Cummings. For Dylan Prescott and Briana Logan, the complicated NYC criminal justice system doesn't leave room for love, but where the heart is concerned, no one is bulletproof. (978-1-63555-771-8)

Her Lady to Love by Jane Walsh. A shy wallflower joins forces with the most popular woman in Regency London on a quest to catch a husband, only to discover a wild passion for each other that far eclipses their interest for the Marriage Mart. (978-1-63555-809-8)

No Regrets by Joy Argento. For Jodi and Beth, the possibility of losing their future will force them to decide what is really important. (978-1-63555-751-0)

The Holiday Treatment by Elle Spencer. Who doesn't want a gay Christmas movie? Holly Hudson asks herself that question and discovers that happy endings aren't only for the movies. (978-1-63555-660-5)

Too Good to be True by Leigh Hays. Can the promise of love survive the realities of life for Madison and Jen, or is it too good to be true? (978-1-63555-715-2)

Treacherous Seas by Radclyffe. When the choice comes down to the lives of her officers against the promise she made to her wife, Reese Conlon puts everything she cares about on the line. (978-1-63555-778-7)

Two to Tangle by Melissa Brayden. Ryan Jacks has been a player all her life, but the new chef at Tangle Valley Vineyard changes everything. If only she wasn't off the menu. (978-1-63555-747-3)

When Sparks Fly by Annie McDonald. Will the devastating incident that first brought Dr. Daniella Waveny and hockey coach Luca McCaffrey together on frozen ice now force them apart, or will their secrets and fears thaw enough for them to create sparks? (978-1-63555-782-4)

Best Practice by Carsen Taite. When attorney Grace Maldonado agrees to mentor her best friend's little sister, she's prepared to confront Perry's rebellious nature, but she isn't prepared to fall in love. Legal Affairs: one law firm, three best friends, three chances to fall in love. (978-1-63555-361-1)

Home by Kris Bryant. Natalie and Sarah discover that anything is possible when love takes the long way home. (978-1-63555-853-1)

Keeper by Sydney Quinne. With a new charge under her reluctant wing—feisty, highly intelligent math wizard Isabelle Templeton—Keeper Andy Bouchard has to prevent a murder or die trying. (978-1-63555-852-4)

One More Chance by Ali Vali. Harry Basantes planned a future with Desi Thompson until the day Desi disappeared without a word, only to walk back into her life sixteen years later. (978-1-63555-536-3)

Renegade's War by Gun Brooke. Freedom fighter Aurelia DeCallum regrets saving the woman called Blue. She fears it will jeopardize her mission, and secretly, Blue might end up breaking Aurelia's heart. (978-1-63555-484-7)

The Other Women by Erin Zak. What happens in Vegas should stay in Vegas, but what do you do when the love you find in Vegas changes your life forever? (978-1-63555-741-1)

The Sea Within by Missouri Vaun. Time is running out for Dr. Elle Graham to convince Captain Jackson Drake that the only thing that can save future Earth resides in the past, and rescue her broken heart in the process. (978-1-63555-568-4)

To Sleep With Reindeer by Justine Saracen. In Norway under Nazi occupation, Maarit, an Indigenous woman; and Kirsten, a Norwegian resister, join forces to stop the development of an atomic weapon. (978-1-63555-735-0)

Twice Shy by Aurora Rey. Having an ex with benefits isn't all it's cracked up to be. Will Amanda Russo learn that lesson in time to take a chance on love with Quinn Sullivan? (978-1-63555-737-4)

Z-Town by Eden Darry. Forced to work together to stay alive, Meg and Lane must find the centuries-old treasure before the zombies find them first. (978-1-63555-743-5)

Bet Against Me by Fiona Riley. In the high stakes luxury real estate market, everything has a price, and as rival Realtors Trina Lee and Kendall Yates find out, that means their hearts and souls, too. (978-1-63555-729-9)

Broken Reign by Sam Ledel. Together on an epic journey in search of a mysterious cure, a princess and a village outcast must overcome life-threatening challenges and their own prejudice if they want to survive. (978-1-63555-739-8)

Just One Taste by CJ Birch. For Lauren, it only took one taste to start trusting in love again. (978-1-63555-772-5)

Lady of Stone by Barbara Ann Wright. Sparks fly as a magical emergency forces a noble embarrassed by her ability to submit to a low-born teacher who resents everything about her. (978-1-63555-607-0)

Last Resort by Angie Williams. Katie and Rhys are about to find out what happens when you meet the girl of your dreams but you aren't looking for a happily ever after. (978-1-63555-774-9)

Longing for You by Jenny Frame. When Debrek housekeeper Katie Brekman is attacked amid a burgeoning vampire-witch war, Alexis Villiers must go against everything her clan believes in to save her. (978-1-63555-658-2)

Money Creek by Anne Laughlin. Clare Lehane is a troubled lawyer from Chicago who tries to make her way in a rural town full of secrets and deceptions. (978-1-63555-795-4)

Passion's Sweet Surrender by Ronica Black. Cam and Blake are unable to deny their passion for each other, but surrendering to love is a whole different matter. (978-1-63555-703-9)

The Holiday Detour by Jane Kolven. It will take everything going wrong to make Dana and Charlie see how right they are for each other. (978-1-63555-720-6)

Too Hot to Ride by Andrews & Austin. World famous cutting horse champion and industry legend Jane Barrow is knockdown sexy in the way she moves, talks, and rides, and Rae Starr is determined not to get involved with this womanizing gambler. (978-1-63555-776-3)

A Love that Leads to Home by Ronica Black. For Carla Sims and Janice Carpenter, home isn't about location, it's where your heart is. (978-1-63555-675-9)

Blades of Bluegrass by D. Jackson Leigh. A US Army occupational therapist must rehab a bitter veteran who is a ticking political time bomb the military is desperate to disarm. (978-1-63555-637-7)

Guarding Hearts by Jaycie Morrison. As treachery and temptation threaten the women of the Women's Army Corps, who will risk it all for love? (978-1-63555-806-7)

Hopeless Romantic by Georgia Beers. Can a jaded wedding planner and an optimistic divorce attorney possibly find a future together? (978-1-63555-650-6)

Hopes and Dreams by PJ Trebelhorn. Movie theater manager Riley Warren is forced to face her high school crush and tormentor, wealthy socialite Victoria Thayer, at their twentieth reunion. (978-1-63555-670-4)

In the Cards by Kimberly Cooper Griffin. Daria and Phaedra are about to discover that love finds a way, especially when powers outside their control are at play. (978-1-63555-717-6)

Moon Fever by Ileandra Young. SPEAR agent Danika Karson must clear her werewolf friend of multiple false charges while teaching her vampire girlfriend to resist the blood mania brought on by a full moon. (978-1-63555-603-2)

Quake City by St John Karp. Can Andre find his best friend Amy before the night devolves into a nightmare of broken hearts, malevolent drag queens, and spontaneous human combustion? Or has it always happened this way, every night, at Aunty Bob's Quake City Club? (978-1-63555-723-7)

Serenity by Jesse J. Thoma. For Kit Marsden, there are many things in life she cannot change. Serenity is in the acceptance. (978-1-63555-713-8)

Sylver and Gold by Michelle Larkin. Working feverishly to find a killer before he strikes again, Boston Homicide Detective Reid Sylver and rookie cop London Gold are blindsided by their chemistry and developing attraction. (978-1-63555-611-7)

Trade Secrets by Kathleen Knowles. In Silicon Valley, love and business are a volatile mix for clinical lab scientist Tony Leung and venture capitalist Sheila Graham. (978-1-63555-642-1)

Death Overdue by David S. Pederson. Did Heath turn to murder in an alcohol induced haze to solve the problem of his blackmailer, or was it someone else who brought about a death overdue? (978-1-63555-711-4)

Entangled by Melissa Brayden. Becca Crawford is the perfect person to head up the Jade Hotel, if only the captivating owner of the local vineyard would get on board with her plan and stop badmouthing the hotel to everyone in town. (978-1-63555-709-1)

First Do No Harm by Emily Smith. Pierce and Cassidy are about to discover that when it comes to love, sometimes you have to risk it all to have it all. (978-1-63555-699-5)

Kiss Me Every Day by Dena Blake. For Wynn Evans, wishing for a do-over with Carly Jamison was a long shot, actually getting one was a game changer. (978-1-63555-551-6)

Olivia by Genevieve McCluer. In this lesbian Shakespeare adaptation with vampires, Olivia is a centuries old vampire who must fight a strange figure from her past if she wants a chance at happiness. (978-1-63555-701-5)

One Woman's Treasure by Jean Copeland. Daphne's search for discarded antiques and treasures leads to an embarrassing misunderstanding, and ultimately, the opportunity for the romance of a lifetime with Nina. (978-1-63555-652-0)

Silver Ravens by Jane Fletcher. Lori has lost her girlfriend, her home, and her job. Things don't improve when she's kidnapped and taken to fairyland. (978-1-63555-631-5)

Still Not Over You by Jenny Frame, Carsen Taite, Ali Vali. Old flames die hard in these tales of a second chance at love with the ex you're still not over. Stories by award winning authors Jenny Frame, Carsen Taite, and Ali Vali. (978-1-63555-516-5)

Storm Lines by Jessica L. Webb. Devon is a psychologist who likes rules. Marley is a cop who doesn't. They don't always agree, but both fight to protect a girl immersed in a street drug ring. (978-1-63555-626-1)

The Politics of Love by Jen Jensen. Is it possible to love across the political divide in a hostile world? Conservative Shelley Whitmore and liberal Rand Thomas are about to find out. (978-1-63555-693-3)